MW00389118

Heartly Law?

By Wil 3

Published 2020 by Shorehouse Books
Printed in the United States of America

Book Cover by Tony Brandstetter and Mark Brandstetter
Photography by Tony Brandstetter
Artwork by Mark Brandstetter

ISBN-13: 978-0-9600085-6-8

"The darkest places in Hell are reserved for those who maintain their neutrality in times of moral crisis" – Dante Alighieri

"Cancel my subscription to the Resurrection; Send my credentials to the House of Detention" – Mr. Mojo Risin'

Acknowledgments

Wil 3 would like to thank Bret Ioli for friendship beyond editing, T. Scott Frank for mentorship beyond education and Donna Cavanagh for believing in the Wil 3 Project.

A special thanks to Garry Nelson for being a tremendous sounding board and technical adviser. Your written work is long overdue. And another special thanks to W. Allen Readie, gone, but not forgotten. I still hear your encouraging words, probably now more than ever.

Of course, my thanks and love to all my family and friends who have supported me in the past and during this project.

This book is dedicated to Rider Francis, my favorite hip-hop drummer, ball player and most importantly, humanitarian.

Preamble

"Blessed are they who didn't see, yet still believe" were the last words anyone heard Nico utter as he moved his index finger through the .38 caliber hole in his shirt just above his heart. Nico examined the enormous, slightly dented church key that saved his life, or at least stopped the bullet from ripping into his chest. He held it for just a moment before he dropped it to the ground. Ordinarily, the sound of a large brass key clanging off the marble floor in the stone church would have sounded like a rim shot from a drummer in a marching band, but in this instance, nobody heard it. Or noticed it. Or really cared at all at that moment. Except for those few souls on the altar, no one else even saw when Nico slowly pulled himself to his feet after taking one in the chest at damn near point blank range.

Father O'Toole may not have killed Nico, but when his gun erupted in pure violence and anger, it killed all the hopes of all parishioners and non-parishioners alike within the church's walls who believed that they had a front-row seat to witness something special that was about to happen, even if they weren't sure just what it would be. The muzzle blast and the lightning crack from the pistol, amplified by the numerous microphones on the altar, shattered several stained-glass windows closest to the altar and momentarily robbed attendees of their hearing. Fear never sounded so visceral nor looked so raw. Parents yelled for their children to flee, but the temporarily deaf kids could do little more than simply grab someone close to them and cry. Fear froze them in place like so many of the stone statues of saints that adorned the altar. Sadly, this paralysis was cured quickly by the frantic collision of bodies attempting to navigate around the statues to escape outside. After the initial shockwave had ceased, the sound of rolling thunder filled the stone church. Doors slammed open and nearly ripped from their hinges.

Church pews were upended with frail, elderly bodies pinned underneath.

At that moment, no one saw Nico on the altar. No one saw a beloved priest who single-handedly breathed life back into St. Mary's Parish, or even the most honored and respected Vatican Council. They saw a madman shooting a gun in a church packed two floors deep with people who were terrified beyond anything they had ever experienced. The splendid church grandeur alongside the chaos and destruction was a bizarre juxtaposition that normal comprehension could not grasp.

Even the sight of Dylan Ray, the religious nut-job who tried to assassinate Father O'Toole a year earlier in that very same location, paled in comparison to the sight of the victim-turned-predator dressed in an Army officer's uniform and pulling a trigger on the one who many believed to be the Second Coming. It was Dali-ist surrealism on steroids.

Those fortunate enough to escape the pandemonium simply kept running. Not to their cars or in any particular direction. They just ran. Others fell to the ground after escaping and wept whole-heartedly at what they had just witnessed, even though they didn't know the full extent of it all just yet.

When Nico finally rose to his feet, Detective Martin backed away, which is the exact opposite of what a law enforcement officer trained to assist people should have done. Father O'Toole and Detective Kelly did the same, but when Father O'Toole saw Nico put his finger through the bullet hole in his shirt, the priest fell fast to both knees. Detective Kelly, who had one hand cuff on O'Toole and the other firmly in his grasp, was pulled down with him. Father O'Toole stopped when his knees hit the ground, but Detective Kelly stopped when his face slammed off Father O'Toole's head, knocking both men out and rendering them mutually motionless on the altar floor. Detective Martin and the Vatican Council rushed to give aid to the fallen detective and the elderly priest.

And in that one particular moment, no more than a couple seconds in duration, Nico left. Or vanished. Or ascended. No one knew for sure, because nobody saw him leave or disappear or whatever he actually did. He was simply gone. The hundreds of screaming crying churchgoers didn't notice. And a trained law enforcement officer who'd basically stalked Nico for the past several weeks didn't notice. And the Vatican Council, who spoke Italian to Nico and had traveled a great distance just to witness him first-hand, didn't notice either. When the smoke cleared, as Father O'Toole and Detective Kelly sat on the ground rubbing their heads, all parties finally realized that Nico was no longer with them, at least not physically. Detective Martin rushed to the back room behind the altar and yanked open closet doors. He pushed open the back door and ran outside to look up and down the street, but there was no sign of Nico. Not anywhere.

An extremely recognizable young man in his mid-twenties dressed in all black with priest vestments just left the scene of another church shooting, and nobody in the entire Strip District seemed to notice. Within minutes, the sound of police sirens and helicopters filled the air.

Chapter One

SWAT officers arrived first on the scene and once again found that an "Active Shooter" situation was not at hand.

"Martin, you sonofabitch, how'd you beat us here?" said the SWAT Commander in charge not realizing that Detectives Martin and Kelly were in attendance prior to the shooting. "What's the deal this time?"

"We have the shooter in custody. He got smacked in the head pretty good. So did Kelly. Both are on the altar. We're just waiting for EMS, then I'll have someone take him in for processing."

"Who is it?"

"The priest."

"Getthefuckout! You serious? If that don't beat all."

Detective Martin continued to survey the situation but said nothing. Car tires squealed outside and sirens drew closer.

"Who did he shoot?"

"Rossi. He shot Nico Rossi. He was on the altar with him along with those members of the Vatican Council up there."

"Wait….what? He shot…well, where is he?"

"Don't know. Not here."

"What do you mean he's not here? How do you lose a shooting victim?" Detective Martin said nothing and continued to scan the church. "Okay, well then if there ain't a shooter, then you're in charge. Congrats."

"Yeah. Thanks. Just what I wanted. Just throw some tape up outside before you leave? I don't want people coming back into the church and contaminating the crime scene."

"Least I can do, buddy. Have fun with this one…again."

The paramedics arrived a minute or two after SWAT and effortlessly made their way to the altar of the now empty church. It had cleared quickly as though the lid had been removed from the top of the church and all the people inside were simply poured out in

5

one swoop. Being the eldest among the injured, Father O'Toole received medical attention first. He had a nice-sized goose egg on his head and wobbled when the paramedics tried to get him to his feet. He may have been concussed or perhaps dehydrated, seeing as how as he ran on nothing but coffee and booze for the past couple months. Perhaps it was exhaustion from the overwhelming workload. Perhaps it was the stress of a miracle which caused everyone from the corner grocer to the Pope to look to him for answers while the same miracle robbed him of both his parish and his legacy. Or maybe it was the simple realization that he just tried to kill a boy whom he had considered to be a son, in his own church no less, and that the remainder of his days, however long or short they may be, would be spent looking through the bars of a prison cell. For whatever reason, he wobbled. The paramedics handcuffed him to a gurney and wheeled him outside to a waiting ambulance. At the hospital he would receive fluids and semi-decent food nutritionally superior to anything he'd consumed in the past two months, and there he would wait for the wheels of the legal process to start turning.

Detective Kelly certainly took the worst of the head-on-head collision. The paramedics closed the gash on his face with a few butterflies and medical super glue, but he would need stitches. As the small pen light bounced from one eye to the next, no apparent signs of a concussion presented for him, but it was certainly possible that the adrenaline pumping though his system concealed any outward signs of traumatic head injury. Detective Martin hovered behind the paramedics as they treated Kelly. Martin talked to Kelly throughout the entire treatment. Sometimes he asked questions, sometimes made statements, but every word spoken was nervous and often shaky, which was extraordinarily unlike him. Martin's stoic, stone-faced demeanor was replaced by angst over seeing his partner injured and suffering, and he wanted to make somebody pay for causing that pain to the both of them. But who? And how? Kelly just sat on the altar and rubbed his neck but did not respond to his partner's questions or comments. The blank gaze from his occasional eye contact said more to Martin than the craftiest poet could ever communicate. Although a simple *WTF?* may have also captured the essence of the moment at that time.

Heartly Law?

The paramedics thought it best to take Kelly to the hospital for further treatment and more extensive observation from doctors. When they wheeled the gurney up to Kelly, he politely refused the accommodation. It was as if at that moment, he wanted to walk off the field for the last time under his own power. He showed his age as he trudged and shuffled out of the church and climbed, with assistance, into the back of an ambulance.

The crime scene investigators entered the church as Kelly limped out of it. They wielded their fancy cameras and digital tape measurers to begin the process of dissecting and documenting every inch of the altar.

"Yo, Martin, how'd I guess you would be in charge of this circus," said the lead crime scene investigator as he blazed a blinding flash from his camera into Detective Martin's face just to agitate him. "You turning into church po-lice or something? Being here is like De Ja Vu all over again." They marked the floor where people had stood and photographed the full priest vestments that seemed to be haphazardly discarded behind one of the over-sized altar chairs.

"Hey boss, come take a look at this," said one of the investigators to the lead CSI.

"What is it?"

"Not sure, but it might be the key to the whole case," said the junior investigator. Detective Martin did not react to CSI's ongoing attempt at levity. "Well, would you look at that…" said the investigator as he removed the mushroomed slug from the old brass key with a pair of forceps. "Bullets and keys generally shouldn't be together, right boss?"

And with that, all attempts at levity ceased. The investigators immediately realized that despite the fact that the gunman was in custody and that several people had witnessed the shooting, this case was not going to be open and shut. A large brass key with a bullet lodged in it ensured that more questions and fewer answers would be the only thing uncovered at this crime scene. For those investigators who participated in the first photography session about a year earlier, they already began to dread the late hours of analysis and confusion that were to follow in the back room of the police station. They continued to document the scene in silence.

Detective Martin was antsy and agitated. He wanted out. Unlike the first church shooting where he couldn't be dragged away, this time he wanted to be as far from the church as possible. He knew that nothing valuable would be found inside the church. Any relevant information would only come from Nico. Maybe some from the priest, but hospital regulations and other bureaucratic nonsense would prevent him or anyone else from interviewing O'Toole anytime soon. As Martin paced back and forth in the church, the high-ranking commanders and even the Chief arrived on the scene. Detective Martin asked to leave to pursue other leads outside the church. He did not have to say it, though it was clearly understood, that he was going after Nico, wherever he may be.

Chapter Two

Detective Martin chose to leave the church through the back door behind the altar because it was the most logical way that Nico would have exited, assuming that he did exit in a mundane traditional manner. Martin took his time and purposefully scanned the vicinity behind St. Mary's Church while the din of the activity at the front of the church dissipated. His eyes focused on the grounds behind the church and the old dilapidated alleyway that was deteriorating back into gravel. He walked away from the church and continued to just look…for something. For anything. Anything out of place. Anything out of the ordinary. Something that didn't belong or fit just right. He was looking…for a clue. It had been years since Detective Martin actually searched for clues, but that was what he found himself doing. Martin thought to himself: *"If Nico left the church, it had to be through the back door, otherwise everyone on the altar would have noticed. Or would they? Maybe it was possible for him to mix with the fleeing parishioners? But if that happened, he would have been mobbed by his followers, right? Maybe there was an accomplice? A get-away driver? Maybe I can find fresh tire tracks apart from the other cars? Yeah right. No chance of that, not on these crowded streets…"*

Detective Martin wandered to the end of the broken old alley where he found his clue. A seemingly abandoned old BMW motorcycle was tucked away in the corner of the alley. Martin thought that it was Nico's bike, but he wasn't exactly positive. He approached the bike and knocked several fallen leaves from the seat and gas tank in search of a VIN number, which he located and logged as the first item of a new investigation file on his iPad. Martin would call DMV later to confirm ownership of the bike, or at least confirm to whom it was currently registered.

Finding the old bike was both good and bad. It was good because it eliminated the way that Nico was able to get from the scene of the crime so quickly, but it was bad in that it made things more complicated, moreso than they already were. If Nico didn't leave on his motorcycle, then he had help — a waiting driver? The only way that a waiting driver made any sense was if this entire ordeal was planned from the beginning. Not just the most recent shooting, but rather from the very beginning, with the Dylan Ray shooting. Detective Martin got a lump in his throat as he considered the possibility that he and everyone else was completely punk'd. It was all an elaborate hoax.

That theory did make sense — it certainly complied with Occam's Razor. The hoax theory was the simplest and could explain with any combination of sleight of hand how bullets only travelled 10 feet in the first shooting or how the key in Nico's pocket miraculously stopped a bullet from hitting him in the chest. Detective Martin chuckled as he thought that the only thing that would have made this magic show any better would have been if Nico caught Father O'Toole's bullet in his teeth. Still, Dylan Ray was in jail and had been there for almost a year. Nobody is that dedicated to a prank, especially when there's no payoff. Nothing was gained by anyone less a few minutes of fame for Nico. Now Father O'Toole, like Dylan Ray, was facing attempted homicide charges. Considering O'Toole's current appearance, it was questionable if he would live to his trial.

A hoax was one explanation, but it only solved part of the equation while several variables remained unexplained. Detective Martin had to find Nico. His apartment seemed like a good starting point. Martin hurried to the front of the church where his squad car had been parked since early that morning. He turned on the siren and navigated among the crowd of pedestrians and police through the Strip District until he arrived at Nico's apartment in Bloomfield.

With no street side service taking place, Detective Martin could park right in front of the building. The low-rent apartment building returned to its normal run-down state with the makeshift altar, cross, and lighting now removed.

"That is odd," said Detective Martin to himself. "Did Rossi do this? When? He must have had help with the clean-up."

The front door was propped open with a wooden wedge that Detective Martin kicked out. He briskly made his way up the stairs to the second floor. A couple of sharp quick pounds with a closed fist followed by "Pittsburgh Police! Open up or I will kick this door down" produced an unexpected result.

A little old man in his mid to late 70s opened the door. "Now why would you do that? Pretty rude of you," snorted the old man.

"Who are you?" asked Detective Martin.

"Nobody really I guess. I just own the building."

"Where is Nico?"

"Who?"

"Rossi. Where is Nico Rossi," asked the impatient detective.

"Oh, Nicholas. I don't know. He hasn't been here for a couple weeks now."

"What!"

"He paid me his last month's rent then said keep the security deposit for cleaning the place and throwing out the furniture. I just got here. Really didn't have time to clean before today. Just seeing if I could do it myself or if I had to hire someone." Detective Martin pushed his way past the old landlord. "Sure. Come right in. Pick up a broom on your way through."

Detective Martin moved through the small apartment. Everything seemed as if Nico was still living in the apartment except that there was a weird-looking framed piece of art in the middle of the living room floor. All or at least most of his clothes were still there. A half-empty bottle of jug wine along with a half empty bottle of prescription sleeping pills rested on a rickety little table with mismatched chairs. Some uneaten frozen toaster waffles remained in the freezer, which was starting to ice over.

"How long has he been gone, did you say?"

"Who?"

"Rossi! Nicholas Rossi. The guy that lived here."

"Oh, him. I don't know. Maybe two, maybe three weeks at most."

"You said he paid you in advance, right? Gave you notice that he was leaving?"

"That's right. Thought that was nice of him. Most people usually skip out on the rent then leave in the middle of the night."

"Yeah, but look at this place. All his shit is still here. Looks like he left in a hurry. Did he say anything else to you? Like why he was moving or where he was going? Did he leave a forwarding address for any mail? Anything like that?"

"Hmm. No. I didn't really know him that well. I only met him to sign the lease. He was with a priest, so I figured he was okay. Never really saw him after that until he gave me that last check. We never really talked, I guess."

"What about the altar and the cross and all the lights? Did you take that stuff down or did someone else?"

"Lights where?"

"At the bottom of the steps to the entrance," snapped the Detective.

"Lights at the bottom of the steps would be good. It can get dark out front sometimes. Street light doesn't always work so good."

"Never mind," said the frustrated Detective. "Thank you for your help."

"Okay. Say buddy, if you know of somebody looking to rent, this place should be available in a week or so. Tell 'em to call me."

"Yeah. Sure."

Detective Martin shook his head and sighed as he stormed out the apartment. He drove back to the station to file criminal charges and lodge a warrant against Nico Rossi. Conspiracy and nothing more. He knew that the district attorney would make him withdraw the charges since it's not often that a shooting victim is charged with conspiracy in his own shooting. Martin hoped it might buy him a little time and maybe Nico might run a stop sign or something, then he'd get picked up on the warrant. At least that way he would be brought in and Detective Martin would have the opportunity to speak to him.

Chapter Three

"Good morning! And how is my favorite patient doing today?" asked the perky young nurse as she wheeled a cart of breakfast into Father O'Toole's room.

"Oh, you know. Things are good. I'm still handcuffed to my bed and only released to pee. I'm sure I'll be charged with attempted murder any day now, probably excommunicated shortly after that, and fairly certain I'll be going to Hell when all is said and done, but hey, why complain?"

"Pish posh. C'mon now, father, don't be such a Gloomy Gus. These things happen when you try to shoot people."

"I suppose you're right and I should look on the bright side. The bishop isn't breathing down my neck, the incessant phone ringing has stopped. And with any luck at all, I'll die before my trial."

"That's the spirit, keep looking on the bright side. And guess what? I have even better news for you," said the nurse as she approached the bed with a hot plate of something resembling pancakes and bacon. "I've been given permission to let you out of the handcuffs while you eat your breakfast, as long as you promise not to run away. You're not going to run away now, are you, father?"

O'Toole wanted to shoot her a menacing look that said "Little girl, don't mess with me," but the only look he could muster said "I am too old and too tired to play anymore. Please leave me be." The young nurse got the message and realized that she needed to tone it down a bit.

"Tell you what, father," said the nurse in a more serious tone as she looked over her shoulder for anyone who might be listening in. "I will be the only one checking in on you for the next 12 hours unless you really need something. We can leave the cuffs off, just keep your door shut." And with that, she uncuffed his wrist and fluffed his pillows. "Anything else you need before I leave?"

"No, dear, I will be fine. Thank you," said Father O'Toole. He watched the nurse wheel the awkward food cart out of his room and shut the door behind her.

He thought for a moment about turning on the television and perusing through the eight channels available to him, but then he thought better of it. He had long ago sworn off the nonsensical programming that television had to offer. Instead he just nibbled at the pancake-like substance and sipped his instant coffee, which under the circumstances, didn't even come close to hitting the spot.

What he said to the nurse did have an element of truth — at least the bishop wasn't breathing down his neck anymore. All the overwhelming feelings of anxiety caused by the bishop's constant scrutiny and the unbearable amount of work to handle both "the miracle" and the arrival of Vatican Council had completely evacuated from his mind and caused his body to be more at ease. Though it could hardly be described as pleasant let alone enjoyable, the ability to close his eyes and nap for a few moments without being awoken by the piercing blare of a ringing telephone was refreshing. But clearly the priest was sullen, as would be expected of anyone in his predicament — this time his Irish did not factor into that particular mindset. The realization that he would most certainly die in jail as a non-priest caused him anguish. Although oddly enough, that was not his most central thought; he was more consumed with the actual shooting, and in particular, why? He knew the reason for why he did it, but should it have come to that? Was he driven to it? Was he crazy like Dylan Ray? Was he so blinded by rage and anger from losing his parish and his legacy that at a moment of weakness, the decision to kill Nico actually made sense to him? He was positive that the answer to all those questions was unquestionably no. So, the better question, he thought to himself – was he tricked? Did he misread the sign? Father O'Toole used self-inspection and reflection to search for answers to this question as the other aspects of his life, for good or ill, were placed on the back burner. He even considered prayer. Praying was something that he hadn't done by himself in more than two months. Now with his right hand free from the hospital bed, O'Toole considered prayer an option, especially since he could now properly bless himself.

Heartly Law?

A slight knock followed by the door starting to open drew Father O'Toole's eyes away from his breakfast and his mind away from self-inspection. "Did I catch you at a bad time?"

"Brian! I was hoping you would pay me a visit. I thought maybe you didn't want to associate with me anymore, what with all the criminal charges and what not," said Father O'Toole with the first hint of something resembling happiness in his voice in what seemed liked months.

"Nonsense, Father," said Brian Conrad, a director at Mercy Hospital. "It's just, well, your arrival, under these circumstances, has caused a lot of administrative work not normally associated with patient care to be dropped on my plate. And being a director, I have to answer to a lot of people, you know, law enforcement, the Diocese, the DA. I'm not complaining, I'm just, I'm sorry. Just been busier than expected, that's all."

"I have no idea what you mean."

"So here I am. And I am glad to see you. How are you feeling? How has your stay been so far?"

"You're the doctor, you tell me. How should I feel? Your coffee stinks here, by the way."

"I know, it's pretty bad." Brian walked closer to the bed and pulled up a chair. He sat down next to Father O'Toole. "You've been here for three days now, and, to be blunt, you are not the victim here. The injuries you sustained should not even warrant an overnight of observation."

"I see."

"The District Attorney's Office wants to get this show on the road. They want to arraign you. They want you in jail, awaiting trial."

"That is what they do."

"But until I sign off on it, you are staying here. They know that, and it really pisses them off big time. I got into it just this morning with the actual DA, the big boss. First time I ever spoke with him. He told me – ME – to get off my ass and release you so that the police can cuff you and bring you in for an arraignment." Father O'Toole said nothing. He sank a little in his bed and sipped his instant coffee. "I wasn't going to be bullied by him," said Brian as he rose to his feet. "I told him, 'Quit being such a jagoff! You know how these things work. You may be the top-cop, but you're not a doc. And in my medical opinion, Father O'Toole is not physically ready to be transported. He still needs to undergo a full psychological assessment. You want to disagree with me? I'll be very accommodating. Send one of your doctors and I will ensure full access to the patient for examination. Then if your doctor arrives at a different conclusion than me and my doctors, file whatever the hell it is that you people file in court, and you can fight with our lawyers over there.'"

"Wow, Brian. When did you get so tough?"

"Not tough. Just frustrated. Getting too old for this job I think. I'm the director in charge of patient care, and every week it's less and less about patients and medicine and more and more about insurance or regulation or some other bullshit. I guess he just caught me on a bad day."

"Things change. People change, though it seems to happen much faster these days. The good times never last, or at least they seem to pass much quicker than they used to. Look at me now sounding my age. What does this all mean?"

"It means I can buy you some time, keep you out of jail for a couple more weeks, but that's about it. I'm serious about that psych eval. We need to know what's going on up there. Did you snap out, or are there other neurological problems starting to present?"

"I feel fine. Better actually since getting here. But you are the doctor, you do what you need to do."

"There is one more thing," said Brian as he took his seat again. "The Diocese called me. I figured they were calling to see if they could speak to you, but they really weren't interested in that. They wanted me to convey a message to you. They will not be funding a private lawyer for you, nor will the Diocese lawyers be representing you. They wanted me to let you know that so that you could get a public defender or pay for your own private attorney."

"Rather disappointing, now isn't it," said Father O'Toole. "Apparently, I picked the wrong crime to commit, didn't I?"

"In any event, I contacted the Allegheny County Public Defender's Office, and they said that someone would be down in the next couple days to speak with you. You are free to hire a private attorney if you want to."

"That won't be necessary. I know a few of the attorneys in that office from going down to the jail. They're good. They'll do a fine job."

"If you need money for an attorney, I can give you some. A private attorney who's not as busy as a public defender may be better for you in light of the fact that you shot Nico Rossi in front of maybe a few hundred people."

"But I didn't shoot Nico," said Father O'Toole.

"What?"

"I did not shoot Nico," said Father O'Toole.

After pausing a for a moment, Brian slowly got up from his chair and headed for the door. "I'm going to order that psych eval sooner rather than later, okay? I'll be back to check on you when I can, as will your treating doctor. Call me on my cell if you need anything."

"Thank you, Brian," said Father O'Toole. He watched Brian leave the room and pull the door shut behind him.

At least Father O'Toole was brought to Mercy Hospital, which was the first real break he caught in a while. Mercy Hospital was the first and only catholic hospital in Pittsburgh, but more importantly, it was a hospital where Father O'Toole had been ministering to the sick and dying for more than 40 years. He had developed many longstanding personal relationships with several doctors, nurses, and administrators over the years. One in particular was Franklin Conrad, who was the Director the hospital when Father O'Toole first started his ministry there 40-some years ago. His son Brian was just a little boy at that time. No matter what parish Father O'Toole was moved to during his career, even after the hospital went corporate like every other hospital in Pittsburgh, he always found time to minister at Mercy. He developed a close relationship with the Conrad family outside the hospital. He married Brian and his wife and baptized all three of their children. He also gave Franklin Conrad his Last Rites and held his hand while holding Brian's at the same time. Both men sobbed quietly watching Franklin pass away quietly in his sleep. Father O'Toole knew that Brian couldn't save him or fix his situation, but at least for the moment he was more at ease knowing that he hadn't lost his support. O'Toole knew that his support most likely started and stopped with Brian Conrad.

Chapter Four

It was not the slight creak of the door opening that woke Father O'Toole from his late-afternoon pre-dinner nap, but rather the smell of freshly brewed gourmet coffee that lofted down the hallway slightly ahead of the footsteps. Having spent so many years in the Strip District, Father O'Toole became spoiled by so many close places that offered a perfect cup of coffee to go with a well-made sandwich. Ari Meyer entered the room with his briefcase and two fresh cups in a cardboard carrier.

"Stay in bed, don't get up on my accord," said Ari.

"I wasn't going to, but then how could I drink one of those?" replied Father O'Toole as he shuffled to sit up straight in the bed. "Who are you now?"

"I'm just the lucky cat who gets to represent you in court, at least for now. Ari Meyer, public defender," he said as he set down his briefcase and stretched out his hand. Father O'Toole discarded the rosary beads he was holding when he fell asleep and reached across his bed to shake Ari's hand.

"This is for you. I was told you would appreciate a good cup of coffee."

"Who told you that?"

"Brian Conrad, the admin. I have to go through him to see you here. Hope you like it."

"I would like it better if I had something to mix with it."

"Oh, sorry, next time. I don't put milk or sugar in my coffee and I didn't think to grab any."

"I don't want milk or sugar. But I would like whatever you are keeping in your jacket pocket, or maybe in your briefcase. Just a splash?" said Father O'Toole as he held his two fingers sideways.

"I don't know what you are talking about Mr...Mr...Mr. O'Toole," said Ari as he started to flip through a manila case file.

"Father O'Toole. I haven't been stripped just yet. And what kind of attorney doesn't carry a flask, huh sonny?"

"Attorney Meyer, not sonny. And I think you must be mistaken."

"I don't think so, but that's okay," said Father O'Toole with a slight chuckle. "Thank you anyway for the delicious coffee. How can I help you today?"

"That's refreshing–a client who actually wants to help me. Go figure. Actually, I'm here to help you. Like I said, I'm your attorney. I'm from the Public Defender's Office and as for now, I will be representing you."

"What do you mean 'for now?'"

"Mind if I sit down? Here is where we stand. And by we, I actually mean you. Pretty much you exclusively at this point. You have been in this hospital for five days now and nothing is really wrong with you, from what I've deduced, medically speaking. A little dehydration, some fatigue. The DA, God love 'em, is ready to charge you. You probably can't stay here too much longer, but that's not in my control. You will be charged and eventually arraigned. Bond will be set. Don't know how much money that will be, but attempted murder is usually pricey. But based upon your age, your zero-prior record, service to the community, to your country and all that happy liberal crap less skilled attorneys like to ramble on about, maybe it will be something affordable. Don't know but I will argue it."

"I see," said Father O'Toole. He was a bit taken back by the tone of the conversation.

"When that's finished and you're back to being all good once again, you'll have to fill out more forms and do a proper intake. The public defender is need-based, and you really need an attorney right now, but the need is based on your finances. If you make too much money, we can't defend you and you'll have to hire someone. If you're within the financial guidelines, then we're here to help. Not sure if I'll still be your attorney or if you'll have someone else. I'm just here for the initial phase, and we'll see where it goes from there."

Father O'Toole said little and simply listened as he sipped his La Prima coffee.

"Okay, then I just have a few questions. Nothing too tough at this point, it's just, your file is pretty slim seeing as how you haven't actually been arrested yet. Where do you live?"

"At St. Mary's rectory. Smallman Street right behind the church. For now at least."

"What do you mean 'for now?'"

"Living there is just for priests at that Parish. I guess technically I'm still a priest, I haven't been fired yet as far as I know. But who knows? Maybe I'll go there and all the locks will be changed."

"That would totally suck."

"I suppose it would."

"Do you have any family in the area? I take it you're not married, but do you have brothers or sisters or any family that could take you in if you do get fired and presumably evicted from your current residence? Assuming you can bond out?"

"None to speak of," Father O'Toole said somberly. He picked up the rosary beads from his bed.

"This is going to be tough," said Ari as he set down the file folder and picked up a notepad. "Let's talk about the shooting that occurred in the church a few days ago. I read the initial police report by the illustrious Detective Benjamin Martin, and it is surprisingly short, especially by his standards and considering it was a shooting in a church and what not."

"You're familiar with him?"

"He's a complete prick. No love lost between us. I'm sure he would say much worse about me. But I'll give the man his due. He is thorough and his reports are usually detailed and precise. This one is brief and rambling. I'm sure he'll supplement it at some point, but right now, not a lot to go on. The gist of it basically says that you shot the altar boy Nicholas Rossi from about 15 feet away while wearing what appeared to be an Army uniform of some kind and somehow, he survived."

"If that's what it says."

"I'm pretty sure that's what the report says. Really doesn't say anything else. Do you disagree with his assessment? Did something else happen?

"If that's what the Detective said happened, then I guess that's what he saw."

"I see," said Ari with a look of confusion. "Let's start from the very beginning. You must understand that I'm your attorney, and since I am your attorney, you have the absolute right to lawyer/client privileged communication. That means whatever you tell me is just between you and me. It's not advisable that you talk about your case to anyone else, but that is your right to do so. But as far as what you tell me, I take that information to my grave. If you want me to give you the best opportunity for a defense, you must be honest with me. The worst thing that can happen is if you lie to me or if you choose not to tell me about something and I get sucker punched by it at trial."

"I understand."

"Good. Now that we have an understanding, let me ask you a few more questions. The altar boy, that is a boy or a girl who is there during the church service to help out the priest in some way, right?"

"It's called a Mass in the Catholic church, and it's usually a boy or a girl, but Nico is about 26 or 27, not exactly sure. We don't have a school associated with our church, so younger boys or girls to serve on the altar aren't as available at my church."

"Ok, now we are getting somewhere. So, Nico, as you called him, is in his mid to upper-twenties and he was the altar server at that Mass. Was this the first time he helped you, or has he worked with you before?"

"He was my regular help for about two years or so."

"You knew him pretty well?"

"Known him for most of his life. He was almost like a son to me."

"Like a son? But you shot him?"

"I did not shoot Nico," said Father O'Toole.

Ari felt very much confused and tried a different route of questioning. "Were you dressed in an Army uniform of some kind, complete with a sidearm?"

"That is correct."

"Sorry, I'm not a churchgoer, forgive my ignorance. Do you normally wear an Army uniform to church?"

Heartly Law?

"Nope. First time."

"So, for whatever reason you decided to dress that way for church, for Mass that day, in the Army uniform. The gun just went off? By mistake? And you didn't mean to shoot him?"

"There was not an accidental discharge. But I did not shoot Nico."

"Do you not remember shooting Nico? Did you black out? Did you suffer a stroke maybe? Are you having memory issues?"

"Of course not. It happened five days ago. I remember it all very clearly."

"You're not giving me a lot to work with here. If you think the way to defend this case is simply to deny that you shot Nico, it may be difficult to rebut the eyewitness accounts of two trained police officers of distinction, not to mention all the other witnesses."

"Don't you know who Nico is?" asked Father O'Toole, who by now seemed more perplexed than his attorney.

"He is the victim in this case. The one that you – the one that the police claim you shot while he was on the altar."

"I'm glad you understand that part. Do you know about the shooting that he and I were involved in about a year ago in the same church? Do you know how it's been said that he stopped bullets from hitting me with just his hands, and that he's been performing miracles all through the city? It's been all over the news for months on end."

"The miracle man, I remember hearing about it on the news. But to be frank, I really don't pay much attention to Catholic church stuff, even when it's on the news."

"Me neither. But claims of miracles and stopping bullets mid-air? Goes somewhat beyond the Catholic Church now, doesn't it?"

"I just don't pay attention to that stuff. It's all nonsense, if you ask me. What the hell do I care if there are miracles in the Catholic church? Not my concern. I don't know, maybe it's because I'm Jewish. Does it bother you that I am Jewish?"

"Not at all. My boss was a Jewish carpenter."

"I saw that bumper sticker once. Catchy. Maybe I'm getting ahead of myself. It's not my job to defend you, at least not yet. If it becomes my job, we can dig deeper another time. Generally speaking, I enjoy the benefit of a theory of the case. Even if the theory is outrageous, at least it gives me something to work with. It puts the evidence into perspective and allows me to advocate for my client. In this case, we have no theory. We have absolutely nothing. Saying you didn't do it is not a theory in light of a couple hundred people who would most likely say otherwise."

"You got a tough job ahead of you," said Father O'Toole as he sipped his coffee.

"You're not going to be a good source of information if you stick to that story. For me to get more information, we need to get this case moving. We need discovery, more police reports, witness statements, the whole deal. How do you feel about video arraignment, if its possible?"

"What is it?"

"It's actually pre-arraignment. You will appear before a judge and will be told what crimes are being charged against you and bond will be set. If it is possible, and it's a long shot, I would like to try to do that via video conference while you're still in the hospital. Maybe the judge will feel sorry for you in some way and keep the bond low. Then before you're discharged from the hospital, you can post the bond so that you can go home instead of going to jail."

"I'm not opposed. You proceed how you feel is best. I'm sure you will do a good job."

"No promises, but I'll see what I can arrange. I don't have many friends in the DA's office, and most likely they'll have to agree to this unorthodox procedure."

Ari picked up his folder and notepad, which did not have one single note on it. He placed them into his briefcase and got up from the chair. "What about Nico? Where is he?" asked the attorney.

"What?"

"Nico. The alleged victim. The miracle man. Where is he?"

"I have no idea. He hasn't stopped in to see me if that's what you're asking. I guess he's at his apartment or on a street corner giving sermons somewhere. I don't know," said the confused priest.

"He isn't there. He isn't anywhere according to what I've heard. And you don't know where he is? A guy who was involved with you in not one but two church shootings, someone you thought of as a son, but you don't know where he is right now? But you did shoot him, so maybe he's laying low."

"I did not shoot Nico," said Father O'Toole in a calm tone.

"I keep forgetting that little detail. I'll be back to see you when I hear anything about the bond hearing. Here's my card, feel free to call me if you happen to remember anything somewhat important," said Ari as he turned and headed for the door.

"Attorney Meyer, can I ask you a few quick questions?"

Ari stopped just short of the door and turned around. "What's on your mind?"

"You said you wanted me to be honest with you?"

"I did say that."

"And you are serious about defending me?"

"I am. I will advocate on your behalf with the same zeal that every one of my clients receives from me. You will be no different in that regard."

"Then why do you not believe me when I tell you that I did not shoot Nico?"

Ari paused for a moment and looked down to the ground. He opened his briefcase, pulled out the manila folder, and flipped through the brief police report one more time. He eventually lifted his head and said, "I think you have a better chance of convincing me that this guy knocked bullets out of the air and healed people just by touching them. I think I you would have an easier time convincing me that stone statues can cry blood, or that stigmata actually exists, than you can at convincing me that you didn't shoot this guy. You just remember that only two things are certain at this point. At the end of this case, I will have tried my best to defend you, with or without your help. And at the end of this case, I will be leaving the courthouse without wearing handcuffs."

"I'll keep that in mind. Thank you again for the coffee, it was a very kind gesture. But next time…" said Father O'Toole as he held two sideways fingers in the air.

Ari turned and walked out of the room. This interview was the first of its kind for him. He sat down on a bench in a quiet section of the hospital lobby. He pulled the flask out of his pocket, took a swig, and made a call on his cell phone.

Wil 3

"Hey, doc, it's Ari... c'mon, you're being unfair. I call you all the time when I don't need anything ...you're right, I'm not calling just to talk, I need something....Assessment and then probably mitigation for a client...Right up your alley, he's a priest, a Catholic priest...No, not that kind of case."

Chapter Five

Ari Meyer was a charming and brilliant 15-year veteran of the Allegheny County Public Defender's Office. Juries loved him and the police could not stand him. He was witty and good-looking, and he loved to smile. He wore expensive suits of fine material that were well above his pay grade and would cause any corporate attorney to feel envious. More than anything, he loved trying cases, especially the hopeless ones, for the pure challenge and reward of being able to look across the courtroom and know that he was better and more talented than that day's assistant district attorney de jure.

Ari's lack of pedigree created an enormous chip on his shoulder. He was born into a nice suburban home with a father and a mother. His father worked as an executive at WABCO and his mother was a stay-at-home mom. Shortly after the birth of the family's second child, Ari's mother "went completely nuts" according to his father and simply left. She took Ari's little sister with her. Ari never saw either of them again. He was five years old. There was no custody fight, no child support, no weekend visits that alternated with each parent. It was simply him and his father. After a couple years with no contact from his mother, Ari's father filed for divorce. It took some time since the whereabouts of Ari's mother were unknown and the courts were hesitant to grant a divorce lacking service of the divorce papers. Eventually it was granted through the mail, and nobody ever stepped into a courtroom.

Ari's father could not keep it together after the divorce. He lost his job at WABCO after losing a long battle inside his head, which resulted in a complete mental and emotional breakdown. After his unemployment ran out, he collected Social Security Disability payments. The 90 percent reduction in income meant that he could no longer afford the house in the suburbs, so he and Ari relocated to Turtle Creek, Pennsylvania, to live in old run-down government-owned housing built by George Westinghouse for his employees.

Ari grew up and went to school in a rough area and became a tough, street smart street kid who more affluent people, which was just about anyone, would simply call a hood rat. Ari's father attempted to supplement his SSD by working as a bartender under the table in morally corrupt dive bars throughout the Mon Valley. On days when his father worked, Ari would join him at the bar, where he learned how to shoot pool and ate Slim Jims and orange Tic Tacs until his father closed down the bar for the night. By the time Ari was 13 years old, he was a better pool player than most of the adults who had been playing pool longer than Ari was alive. This skill would prove to be a valuable asset as Ari grew older.

On one hot and particularly dull summer night when no one but he and his father were in whatever dive bar they were working that night, breaking news came across the television screen that made Ari put down his pool cue and Slim Jim. A local news helicopter in California was broadcasting live and nationwide a slow-motion police chase involving a white Ford Bronco followed by several slowly moving police cars with berries lit. The oddity of the situation fascinated Ari. Even though he was still at quite the tender age, Ari had witnessed numerous crimes including drug deals, drug deals gone bad, beatings people took from shylocks, and even high-speed police chases that were not uncommon in the Valley. But until that evening, he had never witnessed the slow-motion police pursuit of a sports legend and movie star.

When cameras were allowed into the courtroom and live broadcasts of the "Trial of the Century" were shown daily, Ari was completely hooked. Watching re-caps on the nightly news was not enough. Ari wanted to see every second, which was impossible because the trial and broadcast occurred at the same time he was in school. So that night, Ari walked a couple miles to a local pool hall. At the end of the night, he left with $30 in his pocket. It was the first time he made and won bets at the pool table, but the money would not last. The next day Ari visited the local "used VCR dealer" and purchased a brand-new VCR that, as luck would have it, just fell off the truck. He had enough money left over to purchase a few blank VHS tapes, and that afternoon he set up his VCR to record the trial from his television that had pirated cable courtesy of the cheater box his father purchased a year ago from a bar patron.

Ari was mesmerized, but his fascination wasn't in the superstar defendant who fell from grace or the salacious and gruesome details of the murder. Nor was it in the other characters in the trial who seemed as though they were taken directly from a Hollywood script, including the trial judge who appeared to have no control of the courtroom and at times looked so inept that he was the brunt of jokes on late-night television shows. Ari was absolutely captivated by the defense attorneys and how they exercised complete control over everything that happened during the trial. If the prosecutors were agitated it was because the defense attorneys wanted them to be. If the judge appeared to have no control over the courtroom it was because the defense attorneys wanted that appearance. When the verdict of not guilty was rendered, Ari was more impressed than surprised. He learned a valuable lesson that he would carry with him throughout his career – no matter how overwhelming the evidence may appear, the 12 dumbest people in the courtroom can still be influenced simply not to believe their eyes and defy logic. The not guilty verdict may have ended the Trial of the Century, but for Ari, it started him down the path to his true calling.

After high school, Ari enrolled in Allegheny County Community College. He would catch a bus to class in the morning and study in the afternoon through dinner. In the evening, he would grab his McDermott and head to a bar or pool hall to make money at his full-time job. Ari graduated from Allegheny County Community College at the top of his class and applied to the local law schools. It was rare that an applicant from a community college was accepted into an ABA accredited law school, but Ari's grades combined with his outrageously high LSAT score not only got him accepted but also earned him a partial scholarship. Not bad for a Valley hood rat. After he received his acceptance letter, he caught a bus into the city and made his way to the registrar's office where he paid the tuition for the entire first year in cash – mostly in 10's and 20's. He told the registrar that he did not need a receipt, as he was in the habit of saying. The registrar nonetheless gave him one, which was their habit.

Chapter Six

The day after meeting with Father O'Toole, Ari made his way to the District Attorney's Office and proposed a bond hearing for O'Toole via teleconference from the hospital. He was laughed out of the office. Ari was used to that response anytime he proposed a defense-friendly plea agreement or something similar, but he never understood why it always happened. Most of the time when his guilty plea proposal was rejected, Ari would go to trial and achieve a better outcome for the defendant than what he offered as a plea. In many instances, Ari won acquittals for defendants who had no business even going to trial, yet the District Attorney continued its path of winning a small battle by being spiteful only to lose the war at the end of trial. "Whatever," said Ari as he removed himself from the DA's office. Ari would ride this one out and see what happens just like everyone else.

The District Attorney continued to berate Brian Conrad with daily demands that he provide a timeframe when Father O'Toole would be discharged. Brian remained steadfast with a stock response that he will be discharged when his doctors feel that he can be medically cleared and not before then. He also reminded the DA that O'Toole still needed a full psychological assessment as well.

The DA was in an uncomfortable position. He wasn't used to being told "no" by anyone. He realized that he could force the issue by having Father O'Toole examined by doctors favorable to the DA's office and follow that up with an appearance in Motions Court, but that route didn't seem advisable with the continued media scrutiny of this case. Any actions taken that were peripheral to the case at hand would become newsworthy in and of themselves, which would only provide more opportunities for Ari Meyer to seize upon them and twist the reality with the smoke and mirror tactics for which he was known. The DA wanted to limit those opportunities, so not throwing fuel on the fire seemed like the right play for now.

Three days later, the assistant district attorney assigned to the case called Ari and said that a bond hearing via teleconference was acceptable if Ari would agree to waive the preliminary hearing and allow Thomas O'Toole to be arraigned by mail. Ari gave the standard answer of "let me see what my client says, and I'll get back to you." Two days later, after a brief phone call with Father O'Toole, Ari called the assistant district attorney and agreed to those terms.

Brian Conrad was more than helpful to both the DA and Ari in setting up Father O'Toole's hospital room for a teleconference. As much as he wanted to protect O'Toole, Conrad realized that his ability to do so was quickly coming to an end. He allowed the District Attorney's Office to borrow some of the hospital's teleconferencing equipment so that a seamless connection could be made with the judge's courtroom. A week later, Ari appeared with Father O'Toole in the hospital room. O'Toole was dressed in hospital garb, again handcuffed to the bed and lying down per Ari's directive. Brian Conrad personally operated the video equipment. Ari sat in a bedside chair so that both he and O'Toole could be in the video feed. Ari wanted to ensure that the judge had a good look at his client. The assistant district attorney appeared in the courtroom along with the judge.

The red light on the video camera lit up to indicate that they were broadcasting. The extra-large video screen illuminated to show both the assistant district attorney and the judge from inside the courtroom.

"Now is the time and place set for the bond hearing of Thomas O'Toole. Counsel, please identify yourself for the record," said the judge.

"Lindsay Kennedy for the Commonwealth."

"May it please the Court, Ms. Kennedy, Ari Meyer, Allegheny County Public Defender's Office, on behalf of the defendant, Father Thomas O'Toole."

"Very well," said the judge, "Ms. Kennedy, you may proceed."

"Thank you, your Honor. The defendant is being charged with attempted murder of one Nicholas Rossi, that is R-O-S-S-I. The defendant is also being charged with one count of aggravated assault against Nicholas Rossi, one count of unlawful discharge of a firearm, one count of carrying a concealed firearm without a permit as well as multiple counts of risking a catastrophe and multiple counts of reckless endangerment of another person at the above information. In essence, the defendant attempted to shoot and presumably kill the victim, Nicholas Rossi, when he opened fire upon the victim, striking him on or about the chest, in a church full of people, including several who were in the immediate proximity to the victim at the time of the shooting. Included in the immediate proximity to the victim were several members of the Vatican Council who had traveled from Rome on behalf of the Pope to attend the church service."

Ari looked at Father O'Toole and winked. "Mass," he said quietly under his breath.

"At this time, the Commonwealth would ask that bond is set at $500,000. Thank you, your Honor."

"Mr. Meyer, your response?" said the judge.

"Allegedly, your Honor. It is alleged that the defendant committed the acts the Commonwealth is accusing him of doing. I don't appreciate the conclusions the Commonwealth is already making."

"Attorney Meyer, I am certain I do not need to tell you that this is not the time or the place to start arguing your case. How do you respond to the Commonwealth's request that bond is set at $500,000?" the stern judge said.

"I have a better suggestion, your Honor. When he is healthy enough to be discharged from the hospital bed he has been lying in for a couple weeks now, why don't you order him to the second floor of the rectory where he lives and order that a child safety gate is placed at the top of the steps. He will never be able to hurdle that kind of obstacle. He would be stuck there until he is needed."

"Attorney Meyer, do you think this is some kind of joke?" scolded the judge.

"Yes, your Honor, I do think that. Absolutely it is a joke. A request for a bond at half a million is the best joke I've heard all day, though it is early. But since I'm the only one laughing it appears that I must be the only one to find humor in the unfortunate misgivings of the Commonwealth, as usual. I'm sure that I do not need to remind the court, but apparently opposing counsel needs to learn, that the purpose of bond is to ensure that the defendant will appear for court proceedings. It is not used to punish a defendant. Furthermore, my client has been working as a priest for more than 50 years. As such, he could never afford to bond out at $500,000, not even $500,000 at ten percent. So, naturally that means when he is healthy enough to leave the hospital, he will go straight to the Allegheny County Jail. Well, that is just wonderful. Do you see him lying here, your Honor? Are your cameras getting this — my client is 80-plus years old. He is weak and his health is failing. You know how he would be treated in jail. I would say that any time spent in jail would make it certain that he will not appear at trial. But maybe that's what the Commonwealth wants? Maybe they would rather he die in jail as an ALLEGED criminal than go to trial."

"That is a completely unfair and outrageous statement, your Honor. The defendant is charged with attempted murder. He shot a gun at another person in a church full of people. These are serious charges."

"Agreed, your Honor. The charges are serious. Maybe I would be more sympathetic to the Commonwealth if we heard from the victim. What did the victim say? Does he want to press charges with the same zeal as the District Attorney?"

"Counsel, do you want to respond to that?" asked the judge to the assistant district attorney. She nervously stumbled and flipped through her file.

"Uh, your Honor, I apologize, I was just handed this file this morning. I can't see, I can't find anything here related to the victim in this file, other than his name. Must not have been included in the file I was given."

"Not included in the file! Are you serious? Not even I can believe things are that disorganized at the DA's office. Okay, let me get this straight – the Commonwealth wants you to believe that this old frail human being, who is hanging on to his life by a thread, committed these atrocious acts that put potentially numerous lives at risk, including the actual shooting of another person on or about the chest, as the Commonwealth so eloquently put it, and is such a threat to our peace-loving society that they feel only a half million dollar bond can protect us – yet there is nothing from the victim? I would suggest that the absence of a statement from the victim can only mean that nobody has spoken to the victim. Yeah, crime of the century here and in two weeks' time, nobody has interviewed the alleged victim," said Ari in a manner both condescending and outrageously confident.

"Your Honor, unlike opposing counsel, I will not speculate as to why certain items are not in this file. Regardless, the seriousness of these charges warrants a high bond. There is nothing unusual about that. If the defendant cannot post bond, then I am sure arrangements at the jail can be made to account for his safety," said the flustered assistant district attorney.

"Oh, I'm sure the Warden will love that! I was unaware that the jail provided 24-hour security. What are they going to do? Put him in isolation? That will be just great, nothing bad will come from that. I have a better idea, your Honor. Why don't we bring this argument back into terms of reality and let us not get distracted by the red herring cleverly disguised as 'serious charges.' My client is not a flight risk. He does not even have a passport. He has no family to live with and nowhere to go. He has nothing but a rectory at this point. I would ask this Honorable Court to release my client, when he is medically cleared, on his own recognizance."

"An ROR. bond for attempted murder? You are right, your Honor, I think counsel does think this is a joke."

"Still waiting for your punchline, Ms. Kennedy."

"Alright, enough from the both of you. You especially, Meyer. You're giving me a headache," said the frustrated judge. He paused for a moment and reviewed a few notes in front of him. "Ms. Kennedy, I will grant the Commonwealth's request for bond to be set at $500,000." Ari was speechless and held still as the judge paused for an extended time. "But it will be unsecured. When the defendant is cleared to be released from the hospital, he may go back to the rectory, but only under supervised electronic home monitoring. Attorney Meyer, let me be very clear with you — when you get my order, I expect you, *you* sir, to meet with adult probation to make sure that home monitoring is in place the minute he walks into his house. If I find out that this defendant is at home without an ankle bracelet, in no uncertain terms, Attorney Meyer, will I not hesitate to bring you before me on contempt of my order. Am I clear, Attorney Meyer?"

"Crystal clear, your Honor. And fair enough."

"Right. In the case of <u>Commonwealth v. Thomas O'Toole</u>, it is hereby Ordered that an unsecured bond of $500,000 is set for the defendant. Furthermore, the defendant may only be released from the hospital, pending his medical clearance, if the Allegheny County Probation Office has equipped the defendant with Electronic Home Monitoring. If said monitoring is in place, the defendant may live at his rectory residence. Violation of the terms and conditions of Electronic Home Monitoring will result in immediate removal from the program and will subject the defendant to said $500,000 bond. Failure to appear at any scheduled court appearance will also be cause for the immediate removal of Electronic Home Monitoring and will subject the defendant to said $500,000 bond. So ordered."

"But your Honor," piped ADA Kennedy.

"No buts. Nothing further from anyone" said the judge as he slammed his gavel against the bench. Ari turned to Brian Conrad with the "cut" sign, and Brian immediately killed the video feed.

"Well, how about that?" said Ari proudly.

"Frail? Barely hanging onto life? Who do you think you're talking about," said Father O'Toole.

"No, not who I am talking about. Who I am talking *to*. I wasn't talking to you. I was talking to a judge who was considering sending you to jail unless you could post a half mill bond. And don't let it bother you, completely subjective opinion on my part."

Father O'Toole said nothing. He simply stared at Ari with a bitter scowl on his face.

"Thank you, way to go counselor, 'atta boy.' Any of them will do, Father O'Toole."

Father O'Toole let loose a huge sigh in part relief, part exasperation. He did not like the process, but he knew the result was better than could be expected. "You're right. Thank you, counselor. You did an excellent job."

"See, doesn't it make you feel better to get that off your chest?" said Ari.

"Yes, nice job, Attorney Meyer," said Brian Conrad as he stepped from behind the camera. "A bit unorthodox, but nice job," he said as he shook Ari's hand.

Heartly Law?

"Unorthodox? Yeah, well, let me tell you, there is nothing regular or normal about this case. Not in the least. You're in for a fight, Father, that's for sure. And there is no playbook for this one. They don't teach this stuff in law school. Not exactly trial ad material here."

Wil 3

Chapter Seven

The next day Ari was summoned to the office of Vince Mastro, the official Public Defender in charge of the entire office. The assistant public defenders reported to a supervisor, and the supervisors reported to Vince Mastro, except for Ari. Vince assumed the unofficial role of Ari's supervisor because he often assigned Ari special tasks that he trusted only Ari to handle. Ari respected Vince, and as much as was possible, enjoyed him at times, often referring to him as *capo di tutti capi*. Vince was responsible for hiring Ari and was his supervisor when he was a young assistant public defender. Ari never forgot that or took it for granted, but over the past couple years, tension had built between the two of them, mostly because Vince wanted to move Ari into a supervisor's role, and Ari would have none of that. Becoming a supervisor might put a few more dollars in Ari's pocket and would lessen the hours of his work week, but it would also take him out of court, unless he was there only to supervise another assistant public defender.

"Vincenzo, how are you, paisan? Big win yesterday morning, huh?" said Ari with a huge grin.

"Heard all about it. That poor little ADA. She didn't know what hit her now did she?"

"Poor girl thought she was going to a routine bond hearing. That'll teach her."

"Sometimes you surprise even me. A ROR bond for attempted murder with a thousand witnesses. Man, you were good."

"Thank ya', thank ya."

"I would love to hear all about it, but I'll just have to wait for the transcript. I got a lot on my plate today, no time for war stories," said Vince as he hustled around his office to gather files and papers and stuff them into his oversized canvas work bag. "Type

39

up a quick memo on where you are in this case and get it to me by tomorrow at the latest."

"Um, okay. Why?" asked Ari.

"Because I asked you to, that's why."

"Alright, but why?" asked Ari again in a somewhat childish tone.

Vince stopped moving about and looked at Ari. "A directive from me isn't enough for you anymore? Who's your supervisor? I'm going to have to speak to him about reigning you in, about your failure to follow directives from the top. Oh wait, I'm your supervisor, I forgot," said Vince in an attempt to lighten the situation ahead of the firestorm he knew was brewing. Ari didn't say a word. He just focused on Vince, who took a seat behind his desk. "Look, Ari, I decided that this case is going to be given to a younger attorney. I think this will be a good case for someone to cut their teeth on."

"Are you freakin' serious? You got to be kidding me? Do you know anything about this case? It's horrible, for both sides, maybe more so for us. The media scrutiny will be like no other this county has ever seen. It'll be our own Bill Cosby cluster fuck of a trial, that's what it will be. C'mon man! You give this case to anyone but me, anyone with less experience, and it'll be a disaster!"

"Most likely a conviction after a two-day trial. It'll take longer to pick a jury than it will to try this case."

"So, you don't even want to try! What kind of shit is that?"

"Calm down, cump."

"I will not calm down. I don't understand. You just said you were impressed with the fact that I got him an ROR bond on attempted murder. I got a hot hand right now, let's ride it out."

"You took a young, inexperienced ADA to school, but you know she isn't going to try this case. It'll be assigned to a lifer over there in the DA's office who's good. You can't think that you'll be able to do the same thing again. It'll probably go to the whatever clown is next in line to be a judge."

"Is that supposed to intimidate me? I'm a lifer, 15 years here. I go up against their best five or six times a year, each of them. How many verdicts did I steal from them over the years? I'm the best chance of winning this case and you know it." Vince didn't say a word. "I'm not going to guarantee a win like Broadway Joe, but their case has holes in it. I'm sure that they think it is a rock-solid case, but I assure you it's not. For starters, they have no victim. Nobody knows where he is, and nobody's even spoken to him. I can exploit that. I can take that little hole and make it gaping wide right through their whole entire case. Nobody can do that but me. It's at least worth looking into, and maybe that'll lead to a favorable guilty plea? Maybe I get a plea and he stays out of jail and won't die there. Who else but me will give him that chance?"

"Bullshit, Ari. Those arguments won't work on me, you should know better. You know they don't need a victim to go forward and get a guilty verdict. And when have you ever tried a case when there was not one but two trained police officers who actually witnessed the shooting live and in person? We aren't talking about drug dealers and confidential informants with rap sheets a mile long as witnesses. We're talking about two highly damn respected detectives. You can talk all you want about a lack of victim. The testimony from those two cops will sink you. And if not from them, the hundreds of other witnesses should pretty much end it."

Ari paused for a moment and gathered his thoughts. "Is this payback for me not wanting to be a supervisor? We've had this discussion, I can't do it. I need to be in court trying my own cases in my way until I can't do it anymore. That's just the way I am."

"I, me, mine. I got him ROR, I got a hot hand, I'm the best chance you got. Do you hear yourself talk, or do you ignore yourself the same way you ignore everyone else? This case is not about you, Ari. This case is about us, the Public Defender's Office, not Ari Meyer. This case provides an opportunity to get a young PD the painful experience of taking a week to pick a jury. It gives them the opportunity to have microphones stuck in their face and to try a case in the public's eye. And when they lose, no big deal. No way to win in the face of overwhelming evidence. But I am pissed off at you. I'm pissed that you're a wealth of knowledge that I, me, mine won't impart on anyone else. I'm pissed that you continue to be so selfish."

Vince Mastro got up from behind his desk and pulled a seat over to where Ari sat. "There's a bigger picture here. It's my job to make sure these young guys get some training and experience. And it's a tough job, not that you would understand or care. As soon as we get someone trained well enough to try the tough cases without somebody holding their hand, they jump ship and go to work at some law firm, you being the exception to that rule."

"I'm the exception to a lot of rules."

"Agreed. Look, this isn't the end of the world. It's one case. And since you brought it up, why don't you revisit the idea of being a supervisor? I tell you what," said Vince. He stopped moving about the office and looked directly at Ari. "I'll give you a list of four or five PDs who I think could try this case, and I'll let you pick which one. I promise you that you can be that person's supervisor. What do you think? You can teach them your style."

Ari got up slowly from his chair and shuffled toward the door of Vince's office with his head low. "What do I think? Do you know what the most important case in the courthouse is, Vince? It's the case that you're responsible for. And the most important client is the guy or girl sitting next to you at counsel table. Know who taught me that, Vince? You did, 15 years ago. And now you're taking my most important case away from me for what? To train somebody? Doesn't sound like training. Sounds like somebody without a heart who's giving up without a fight. Sounds like a priest turning into the sacrificial lamb, not a training exercise. When did this office shift from fighting tooth and nail for every inch of ground to just trying the ones where we might have a chance? Not sure when that paradigm shift happened, I must have been too busy winning jury verdicts. Yes, I said it again. I was winning juries. Sorry if you think that makes me selfish. If working my ass off for every single client in every single circumstance to make sure the Commonwealth proves every single element of every single crime without exception, just like the Constitution mandates, or if working so hard and winning so many juries results in defendants knowing that they have a real fighter behind them and not a "Public Pretender," or if forcing cops to work overtime to prepare for cases when they know I'll be representing a defendant, or if pissing off private attorneys whose clients say they would rather be represented by me instead of some poser in a silk suit, if all that make me selfish, then I guess you're right. I must be selfish."

"Get out of my office."

Heartly Law?

"Gladly. But you know what? I think I'm going to take the rest of the day off. Maybe even tomorrow, we'll see. I have about 7,000 hours of PTO accrued over the past 15 years. Sorry to be so selfish, I guess I shouldn't have taken so much time away from work."

Ari gently closed the door behind him and headed to his car. When he got to this car, he popped the trunk and made sure his McDermott was there. No better place to think and perhaps earn a couple extra bucks than over a nine-foot piece of slate.

Chapter Eight

BANG BANG BANG. Ari's fist slammed off the ancient metal door more appropriate for a bank vault than a pool hall from the 1920s. The metal slide creaked and squeaked open slowly. Then it slammed shut. The door dragged open to reveal a tiny old man who looked like an even older version of Mickey from the *Rocky* movies. He might have been five feet five at one point in his life, but now he was closer to four-eleven. He hunched over when he walked and braced himself with a rusty nine-iron. "Son of a bitch, you're early" said Sal, the presumptive owner.

"So?" said Ari.

"No work today, son of a bitch you?"

"I took the day off."

"Whoopty fuckin' do. Must be nice, asshole. I haven't had a day off in 60 god damn years, son of a bitch."

"You should have gone to law school instead of running a pool hall" said Ari, unfazed by the old man's belligerence. "You got a game for me anytime soon?"

The old man's demeanor immediately changed. "Oh yeah, yeah baby I do, if you're going to be around tonight? Some hotshot piece of shit is coming in from Harmarville. Thinks he's hot shit because he was on TV last year. Straight up game. No funny stuff, straight up. No shaggin' balls to get bigger bets. Straight up."

"So I can use my cue and not your piece of shit house sticks?" said Ari with a slight snicker, knowing that his comment would drive the old man crazy.

"Son of a bitch, there ain't a bad stick in this place and you know that!"

"Relax, I'm just bustin' balls."

"Two hundred a game. I'll stake ya'. We split or I pay, got it? Plus, my finder's fee for lining this up."

"Just get him in here. You won't have to pay. You never do."

"Cocky son of a bitch. You better practice."

"I'm here ain't I? Why else would I be here, crazy old bastard."

"You practice then and quit bullshittin' around. Use the cloth on the break and keep the stick below your waist. If I see that stick come up or hear balls bouncing, I will throw you the fuck out of this place. Hit balls easy or leave. Go up the street to the bowling alley if you want to play like a jackass."

"I know the rules, Sal. I've only been coming here for 20-some years now. Rules haven't changed." Ari made his way to his table, and the two guys already playing there picked up and immediately moved to another table without being asked and without a complaint.

It would require tremendous artistic liberty combined with an absolute reckless abandonment of common English to describe Ari's hangout as a pool hall. It was a solid brick building that was built sometime in the late 1800s and was located in between where the Spang Steel & Iron Works and the Vesuvius Rolling Mill used to be in a particularly rundown part of Sharpsburg, which was a particularly run-down mill community just outside Pittsburgh city limits. Perhaps it was once part of either of those mill works when they were up and running, and for some reason it wasn't razed when they were. Perhaps it was always a pool hall. Nobody knew for sure. Nobody really cared. One thing for certain is that the pool tables dated back to the 1920s, so it had to be a pool hall for at least that long.

Outside on the half-glass block beside the entrance door was an old piece of cardboard with handwriting on it that read "Sally Billiards." It was sandwiched between the glass and the rusted metal mesh that covered the window. Maybe that is why everyone called the old man who ran the place Sal. Nobody knew for sure if that was his real name. Nobody really cared. That's just what people called him. Besides looking like a much older version of Burgess Meredith and walking with a nine-iron for a cane, Sal always had a cigarette in his mouth. Lucky Strike. No one ever saw him light a cigarette and nobody ever saw him inhale it either. But one was always there, sitting in a groove on his lip, as it bounced up and down while he swore at people. He constantly swore at people. He didn't know anyone's name. He didn't care to. If he liked you, he called you son of a bitch. If he didn't like you, well, the profanity was endless.

It was 10:00a.m. and Sally Billiards was full of people. It seemed to be that way — 24 hours a day. No one ever saw Sal leave or saw him open the place up. He was just there, always. No matter what time of the day or night it was, Sal would be there and people would be playing pool. And they were all scoundrels, every one of them. Ex-cons, current cons, car thieves, pimps, drug dealers, and gangsters of every conceivable variety. Ari fit right in. Yet despite the awkward, somewhat anti-social clientele, the place was straight. It wasn't a shooting gallery or a place for homeless to gather. It was a place to play pool and make or lose big money. No funny business was tolerated. When disagreements occurred, which happened regularly, they were taken outside to the riverbank and away from Sally Billiards. The place was well known in the underground billiards circuit, and it was widely known by professionals as well, but few dared to go there for fear of ending up down by the river.

Sally Billiards also lacked amenities, such as light or heat or a clean floor. There was an old Ben Franklin coal stove in the middle of the floor that looked as though it may be connected to something resembling duct work that almost vented out of the ceiling. It was right beside the main table, Ari's table, the big money table. During cold weather months, the big money table was the only spot in the building that was warm enough to shoot stick without wearing a jacket. People who played at other tables would have to wear their coat until it was their turn to shoot, then they would remove it just long enough to take their shots. Next to the stove was an old cigarette machine with metal pull handles where one could buy Lucky Strikes for two dollars in quarters. No one ever saw Sal fill the machine, but it was always full of Luckys. There was also a refrigerator from the 1950s where Sal allowed people to put beer during the summer months. Soon it would be cold enough to keep your beer on the floor near your table.

Despite the lack of amenities, the pool tables were immaculate. Every one of them was remarkably pristine. Not one scratch on any of the woodwork. Every bumper was true and exact from the big money table to the last table in the corner. Not one mark on any of the felt. Sal made everyone break by putting the cue ball

Wil 3

on a small secondary piece of white-ish felt that the shooter would quickly remove after striking the cue, but still the tables appeared as if they were just installed yesterday. Every table was level with blemish-free solid marble. Even the house cues were amazingly perfect in every way, like a smooth piece of blown glass that slid through your hand like flowing silk. Any outsider or first-timer to Sally Billiards who grabbed a house cue and rolled it on the table to make sure they had a straight stick would immediately be thrown out under the threat of a nine-iron to the face from Burgess Meredith, followed of course by a litany of profanity that would make a Hells Angel blush.

This was Ari's church. Here, he was at peace. Cell phones signals did not penetrate the old bomb shell building, so he would never be bothered as long as he was inside. Ari was a better pool player than he was an attorney. He made more money at that table than he did working his job as a public defender. Ari did most of his pre-trial preparations at this table. It is where he prepared his arguments. Sometimes he would be doing just that while sharking other people at the same time. Ari's head was clear when he was standing over the slate. Despite his claim to Sal that he was there to practice, he was actually there to think. He didn't need practice. He needed a plan. He was contemplating a career move for the first time in 15 years. Something that significant wouldn't get accomplished in a law library, a coffee shop, or a public park, for God's sake. He racked a 9-ball, put the cue ball on the white piece of felt, grabbed a house cue for the break, and stared at the table as the stick glided back and forth over his bridge hand.

48

Chapter Nine

Ari left Sally Billiards with such a large wad of $50 bills in his pocket that it looked like he had a gun. He jumped into his car and headed to a local greasy spoon, the only place he knew he could get a bite to eat at 4:30a.m. Although he was not a smoker, he reeked of cigarette smoke and extinct industrial labor, but he knew the clientele in the diner wouldn't notice. When he was done eating, Ari peeled off one of the $50's and gave it to the waitress. He left without getting any change, hoping that in some way his generosity would help the young waitress who was working a terrible job with even worse hours. It was probably, hopefully, her second job.

Ari popped the trunk on his 1987 White-on-White Monte Carlo SS. He took off his shirt and pants and threw them into his trunk to minimize the smell he was bringing into his car. He stood in the empty parking lot in his boxer shorts and under shirt just before sunrise and he noticed his license plate: "1MNDRMTM".

"Huh," he said to himself, "Maybe Vince has a point."

Ari fired up his muscle car and sped home for a hot shower with pumice soap and multiple shampoos.

Ari made it into the office in plenty of time. Going from work to Sally Billiards and back to work while foregoing a night of sleep was not unusual. As long as he only did it a couple times a month, it never really bothered him or impeded his job performance.

This day, however, he sat still and motionless at his desk as his tie hung loose over his shoulders instead of in a Windsor knot. His calmness and lack of precision in dress led some of his co-workers to ask if he was sick. He just nodded politely, signaled he was fine with a thumbs-up, and remained untalkative, all in stark contrast to his normal demeanor. Ari picked up his phone to call his secretary and noticed the beeping of a message in his voicemail.

"Hi Ari, this is Doctor Flynn. Just following up with you on your need for an expert witness and mitigator. Despite my better judgment, I will help you out. Just so happens that I'm a little bit slow right now on the court side of my practice, so I could probably be available as long as my work remains the same on the therapy side. I'll need more information. Call me back when you have time to talk. Thanks."

Ari immediately called his secretary, Sarah Parker. "Good morning, doll, how are you today?"

"What, are you so busy you can't walk down the hall to see me?"

"Never too busy to see you, love. I'm just in the middle of a thousand things right now and wanted to call before I forgot about it. You know my mind is like a sieve these days."

"Oh, I doubt that. What can I do for you?"

"Please fill out the forms to request the appointment of Dr. Flynn for the O'Toole case. Just get them filed as soon as possible and sign my name, please and thank you."

"Wow. Too busy to sign your own name. Or do you just not love me anymore?"

"Now how could I ever stop loving you, momma? Tell you what, it's been too long since we had lunch. How about you make lunch reservations at Capital Grill for this Friday at 12:30 and I'll meet you there?"

"Oooh, Capital Grill, fancy. Not sure I deserve that, but okay. Does this lunch come with drinks?"

"You deserve much more than a nice lunch, momma. And what do you think? It's Friday, it's lunch with me, drinks are included."

"Yes!"

"Just make sure your husband is okay with it. I don't want him gunning for me if he thinks that getting you sauced at lunch is going to lead to funny business. I don't want him thinking I'm making moves on his best girl."

"Honey, I have been married to that man for almost 40 years now. If he thought that a torrid romance with a man half my age was in my future, he would probably be supportive and proud of it. Ha!"

"So you're saying I have a chance? This day just got better."

"Oh ,you are adorable, honey. I'll make reservations, and I'll get the Dr. Flynn appointment forms filed by lunch. Anything else?"

Heartly Law?

Ari paused for a moment as he felt a slight tightness in his throat. "Ari, you still there? Is there anything else you need me to do?"

"No, thank you, Sarah. That's all for now. Thanks, thank you for all you do. Bye." Ari slowly hung up the phone and swiveled his chair away from his desk. He resumed his previous state, somewhere between meditation and bewilderment, and struggled with what lied ahead of him. After a few minutes of no activity, Ari got up from his chair, grabbed a half-consumed bottle of Maker's Mark, and left his office to see Father O'Toole at the hospital. He stopped at La Prima and bought two large cups of gourmet coffee.

Chapter Ten

"Knock, knock, knock," said Ari as he opened the door to Father O'Toole's hospital room. He found O'Toole sitting up in his bed mindlessly flipping through the limited channels on his hospital room television. "My, don't you look rested." Ari exaggerated a look over both of his shoulders as if to see if anyone was near. "Here you go. Thought you might enjoy a special blend today," he said as he handed Father O'Toole a slightly spiked coffee.

"Oh, God love ya' sonny. Thank you. You look troubled today. Maybe concerned?" said Father O'Toole as he gulped his coffee.

"Don't know yet. The day just started." Ari pulled up a chair and sat down beside the priest. Ari sipped a slightly more spiked cup of coffee.

"We need to talk. Ha! I think that's the first time I've ever said that to another man." O'Toole got the reference and chuckled a bit.

"Okay, sonny, what's on your mind?"

"Your impending criminal trial, for one. But before your trial, we need to talk about some type of defense. And before that, we need expert witnesses."

"What kind of expert witnesses?" asked Father O'Toole. He understood what kind were needed, but wanted confirmation.

"Psychological experts."

"Oh, you think I'm nuts, huh? Deranged. Looney bin."

"Doesn't matter what I think, it's what the jury will believe. Maybe you are, how would I know? All I know is that you shot this Nico kid."

"I did not shoot Nico."

"See? We really need an expert. The Commonwealth is *alleging* that you shot Nico Rossi and that it happened before several hundred witnesses in church. Two of those witnesses are well-respected cops, and I suppose there is a presumption that the other witnesses would be somewhat truthful, seeing as how they were in church at the time of the shooting."

"Well I am not nuts."

"Maybe so, maybe not. You're not the first person to tell me that. Maybe you aren't fully nuts, you know? Maybe you just had a temporary breakdown. We'll see what the expert says."

"Tell me, counselor, does a person who is nuts take the time to find an old Army uniform, holster a sidearm, then put vestments over it so that they wouldn't be noticed?"

"Why are you making things even more difficult?"

"I just want you to know the facts. All the facts."

"The fact is that you shot somebody in front of hundreds of witnesses, and but for a miracle, for the grace of God, out of pure luck, or whatever else, he survived because a church key stopped the bullet. That is attempted murder. Even if that isn't proven, it is still aggravated assault. If convicted on either of those charges, you will die in jail. Aren't you the least bit concerned by those facts?"

"It is all in God's hands now. It always has been. I am content with that."

"You are content with that! So, you don't want to fight? You want to enter a guilty plea? See if the judge can be persuaded to keep you out of jail in exchange for your plea of guilt?"

"Not sure. What would I be pleading guilty to?"

"Depends on what we can negotiate. Best case scenario, agg. assault. Worst case would be attempted murder. I wouldn't be all that concerned with the charge. I would be more focused on an agreed-upon sentence. If it is probation or house arrest or some other long shot like that, I would take it regardless of what charge is pled."

O'Toole paused for a moment as he sipped his coffee. "Attempted murder? Really?"

Ari was getting frustrated and spoke too quickly before he was again cut off. "Yes, attempted murder. You shot Nico Rossi in the chest from 20 feet."

"I didn't shoot Nico. Not pleading guilty to that."

Ari set his coffee down intentionally. He stood up and started to slowly pace across the small hospital room. "Okay, let's go a little bit slower here. This lack of perception or lack of reality is starting to bother me a bit."

"Your lack of reality or mine?" asked Father O'Toole.

"You bring up a good point. I see this situation and I feel that you are either not comprehending it or you are in complete denial. But perhaps you're right. Maybe it is me who doesn't quite get it. Maybe it is me who just doesn't grasp reality. Maybe it is me who should be in the looney bin? Fair enough. Then help me. If I may summarize thus far," said Ari as he stopped pacing and intentionally cleared his throat. "The Commonwealth is alleging, *alleging, mind you*, that you shot Nico Rossi. This allegation is going to be based upon several hundred eyewitnesses who were at the Mass at the time of the shooting. Now mind you, I have not read any statements from the witnesses. They won't be turned over until we get to discovery. But I have assumed, based on the initial report from Detective Martin, that all witnesses will be saying something along those lines. But, more to my point, the allegation that you tried to shoot and kill Nico Rossi is further supported by a literal smoking gun that was removed from your hand a few seconds after you allegedly pulled the trigger. It is presumed that said firearm was the weapon that delivered one single shot to the chest area of Nico Rossi. However, Allegheny County Crime Lab has not completed a ballistic report. That, too, is something I won't be able to view until discovery. But maybe you're right. Maybe I'm connecting dots here a bit too haphazardly and possibly prematurely. What I have been able to deduce and assume, based upon my reading of Martin's initial report, is that you shot a gun, the gun in question was pulled from your hand by Detective Kelly, and the church was packed full of people who will be called to testify against you at trial based upon what they saw while they were in the church. At this point, those facts seem to be rather certain."

Father O'Toole listened carefully as he sipped his coffee. He looked as if he was fighting to hold his smile back. Ari noticed Father O'Toole's strange countenance, and in Ari's mind it confirmed Father O'Toole's lack of perception or absence of a reality regarding case. There was no way that anyone who was mentally sound would be smiling during a discussion of a church shooting, attempted murder, and a hopeless legal defense. The coffee, even with the special creamer, just wasn't that good.

"Ok, so now we come to the x's and o's of a defense. Any defense attorney who is halfway decent will tell you that eyewitness testimony is generally the worst kind of testimony. Prosecution or defense, eyewitnesses can be made to look really bad on the witness stand. But in this case, it may be asking a bit much to try to discredit a couple hundred eyewitnesses, two of whom are homicide cops, not to mention the other holy rollers who were there in the church that day, allegedly in close proximity to the victim as well as the alleged shooter, which is you, in case you've forgotten. Now, not to toot my own horn, but I think I am a marginally competent defense attorney. And being a marginally competent defense attorney, I have suggested entering a guilty plea to any charge or charges that result in a sentence of probation or house arrest, thereby preventing your death inside jail. Along with this course of action I have also suggested that you undergo an evaluation by a psychiatrist or psychologist who can determine the viability of your mental state and also serve as expert at trial or provide mitigation at sentencing, if need be. You, on the other hand, remain steadfast in your belief that you did not shoot Nico or presumably anyone else for that matter, that you will not plead guilty, and that mentally speaking, you are sharp as a tack, while also suggesting in a nuanced manner, by the way, that it is perhaps me who is the person struggling with a conceptual grasp of reality. Now, would you say that my summation is fair and accurate thus far?"

Father O'Toole could no longer keep the smile from his face. Perhaps the special coffee was working its magic. "Well, son, I must say, you certainly have a brilliant ability to make a convoluted situation simple to understand, that's for sure. You're like anti-Irish. We turn simple situations into unnecessary chaos on a regular basis. I get it, you got a tough job ahead of you. I thank God you're so talented."

"Is that what you're doing here? Are you intentionally making what I view as a rather simple issue unnecessarily complicated? For what purpose?"

Heartly Law?

"No son, I am not doing that. I am simply listening to what you have said and am responding. I leave the legal stuff and strategy to you."

"I see. In any event, I am putting the cart before the horse. We can go round and round about which of the two of us is more crazy or less sane, but there is a strong probability that it won't matter. At least to me, anyways. Like I said, we got to talk."

"I see you're troubled, and by more than just how I view this unfortunate situation. You may think I'm crazy, but I think on some level you're enjoying this discussion, and you certainly enjoy hearing yourself speak. I was initially reluctant about using you as my attorney because I didn't want this situation to turn into a complete circus. But after prayer and reflection I am certain that you are best suited to defend me. Then again what choice do I have really?"

"That's what we need to talk about. My boss, the head of the PDs, is going to take your case away from me. He's going to assign it to a younger attorney so he or she can get some experience. He doesn't think you have a snowball's chance in Hell to win, so it becomes a good learning opportunity."

Father O'Toole said nothing. He took another long sip of his coffee. "Makes sense to some degree, justice be damned. Is there any way you can find a way to keep my case with you?"

"I tried. I argued and pleaded with him, but his mind is made up. Best I can do is pick your next attorney and be a supervisor. But I won't be in court. At this point, the only way for me to keep you as a client is to quit working at the Public Defender's Office and start a private practice, of which you would be my first and only client."

"There it is. That is what's troubling you. It's not my case or even the apparent gap between how we view the actual events. You are faced with quitting your job if you want to represent me. And you've been there a while right? Pretty much the only place you ever worked as a lawyer. You do have quite a difficult choice to make. Quit the only job you've ever known and venture out on your own with a difficult case, or keep the security of your job, your weekly paycheck, your health insurance, and wonder 'just what if' as I die in a jail cell. I don't envy your position right now. If I could trade with you, I certainly would."

"No thank you. And I'm not wondering 'just what if' right now. Here is the reality: If you continue to be represented by the PD, it will not be by me, and you will die in jail. I'm not saying your results will be any different if I do end up representing you, I am not promising any outcome. But I am promising that I am the only chance you have at not dying in jail. No other PD has the clout I do, no other PD has stolen 'slam dunk' verdicts like I have. My record speaks to that. The only thing I can really offer you is a chance. It may be a relatively small chance, but I'm certain it's far more than the zero chance you'll have with a lesser attorney."

Father O'Toole finished his coffee and set the empty cup on the tray beside him. Ari sat back down on a chair closer to the door, folded his hands, and waited for a response. After a few moments, the silence became awkward. "Look, Mr. O'Toole, I know this is a lot to drop on you, and I am in an awkward position, professionally speaking. If you want to hire me, I'll need $10,000, all paid up front. And do yourself a favor, pick up the phone and call some other attorneys, call the good ones you see on TV every other night. See what they tell you. I know all of them charge well above 10 grand for attempted murder, but maybe one will cut you a break. Maybe some of them are churchgoers and they'll consider the press coverage as good advertisement. Who knows? But I need an answer by the end of the week so that I can make a move one way or the other.

Father O'Toole said nothing. He simply picked up the remote control and turned on the television.

"Okay, Mr. O'Toole, you think about it. But you have until Friday. Call me on my cell phone to let me know your decision. IF, and I know that's a big IF, you choose to hire me, we cannot play this chess game between us. We need to get on the same page ASAP."

Ari stood up and walked to the door. As he closed it behind him, Father O'Toole piped up. "Counselor, do you actually play chess, or was that just a lazy metaphor on your part?"

"I play. I used to play all the time. Not so much anymore."

Heartly Law?

"Then you understand that to play chess well, a player has to keep their strategy secret.

"I understand the concept."

"So, I've told you everything. I've told you what I saw and what happened, and I even shared my feelings with you. That's not very chess-like, now is it? Why do you think I'm playing chess with you?"

"Call me by Friday. Or don't."

Frustrated. Bitter. Confused. Ari didn't know exactly how he felt, but he also realized, with or without O'Toole as his client, he could no longer work in the Office of the Public Defender. He called the office, took the rest of the day off sick, and headed home.

When he arrived at his house, he turned on his laptop to draft a letter of resignation. He stared at the screen for 30 minutes without typing before he crawled into bed to go to sleep.

Chapter Eleven

"Detective Martin, sir? I did what you asked. I called everywhere. Every place within a 50-mile radius of here that rents cars. I called all the moving van rentals. Even called Lowe's and Home Depot to see if any work trucks were rented by the hour. But sir, there is absolutely no record of Nicholas Rossi renting a vehicle of any kind," said a young uniformed police officer.

Detective Martin closed the laptop on his desk and swiveled his chair around to face the young officer.

"Okay, son. Nothin' there, huh?"

"No, sir, not as far as I can tell."

"I'm sorry, what is your name?"

"It's Flynn, sir. Marcus Flynn."

"Alright, Flynn, tell me, what does that mean to you?" asked the senior detective.

"What does it mean? I don't know. Maybe he had a friend help him move?" Officer Flynn haphazardly flipped through a short stack of papers while he thought out loud. "According to… in here somewhere, I'm sure I read that he had a lot of people following his street ministry. It's here somewhere."

"Good thought. He did have — does have lots of followers. But what does that mean?" asked Detective Martin.

"I suppose any one of them could have helped him move out of his apartment. He might even be staying with one of them right now?"

"Put together a list. Every known associate, follower, friend, whatever the hell you want to call them, anyone with a known association to him. See who has a truck or moving van. See if anyone rents property, if anyone has an extra place, like if their mom or dad died and their parents' house is just vacant for the time being or if anyone has a summer home or camp up in Tionesta. See what you can come up with. And call storage unit places, too. Pods and facilities. He has to have some stuff somewhere."

"Okay, sir."

"Stay late. I'll make sure you get as much overtime as you need. Bring me the list when it's done. I'll be here," said Detective Martin. He knew that this assignment would overwhelm the rookie.

"I'll get it done, sir," replied officer Flynn as he removed himself from Detective Martin's desk.

Detective Martin knew it wouldn't take long to put together a list of Rossi associates, but it would take weeks, maybe months, to perform the detailed research he asked for. Martin did not want to be bothered by anyone until he could get his own mind around the situation. Or maybe he simply didn't want to deal with this case any longer. He reluctantly opened his laptop and placed it on his desk. He slouched in his chair and mindlessly gazed into the blank screen as if he was in a staring contest. Martin blinked and the laptop won. He closed the lid again and put the device in its canvas portfolio. Martin headed down to the crime lab and approached the lead CSI.

"Finally, nice of you to show up. I busted my ass to get ballistics done and called you last week to come get the results," said the crime scene scientist. Martin said nothing and continued his half bewildered, half exhausted, half desperate stare. "Judging by the look on your face, you weren't in a hurry to get them. I guess we both know why."

"What do you got?"

"The slug is .38 caliber and has the marking consistent with being fired from the Colt .38 Special service revolver recovered from the crime scene. The mushroom of the slug is consistent and is what you would expect to see if it was fired from about 10 to 12 yards away into a brass plate. And there were even trace amounts of brass from that old key imbedded into the mushroom of the slug. Pretty cut and dry. The old priest snapped and shot the boy with his gun, and the bullet was stopped from ripping into his flesh by an old brass key in his shirt pocket. No sleight of hand. No illusion. No parlor trick or three card monte of any kind here."

"No magic, huh?"

Heartly Law?

"I didn't say that," said the scientist with a slight nervous chuckle. He handed a manila folder to Detective Martin with copies of the full ballistic analysis and report.

"Thanks, Doc. Sorry that it took me so…I mean, I know you and your crew were working hard to get the result quickly. Thanks again." Detective Martin turned and dragged himself out of the crime lab looking as if he'd just euthanized the family dog. The results were hardly unexpected and at least one aspect of the case – the most important aspect – was locked up. But Martin's curious demeanor suggested he was hoping the results would be different, somehow better.

Detective Martin moped all the way to his car. He thought for an instant that maybe he should go home, spend some time with his wife and family, but compulsion or maybe obsession made him drive to St. Mary's Church. Though it had been a couple weeks since the shooting, the yellow crime scene tape was still in place. Martin thought to himself that the crime scene tape no longer seemed like a barrier to keep people away, but rather served more as a yellow highlighter against the ancient gray drab stone of the church. Just as a college student would highlight important text in a book so that it stood apart from the dicta. But what was it highlighting? Detective Martin continued to ponder the concept of what was important and what was not. After a few minutes of silent deliberation, for the first time in his career, he decided to stop for a beer or two before going home to his family.

Chapter Twelve

Friday morning arrived to find Ari awake hours before the shrill siren of his alarm clock. He sipped coffee and tried to lose himself in the old records playing in his living room. When the sun snuck in from behind the drapery, Ari figured it was time to get moving.

Ari stared at himself as he brushed his teeth in the bathroom mirror. He noticed that he looked tired, and not just from a night of little sleep. A deeper emotional exhaustion had come over him, and the effects were manifesting in his appearance. Luckily, Ari had become a master at compartmentalizing his feelings. It was a necessary tool that every good attorney developed. Truly great attorneys excelled at it. It was a tool for both effectiveness and self-preservation. He wiped his face, ran his hand through his hair with a little gel, and jumped into his Monte Carlo. When the pitch of the engine settled, Ari pulled away and drove to the hospital to see Father O'Toole.

"Knock, knock, knock, rise and shine," said Ari in an attempt to feign zeal for the early morning.

"Good morning, son. My, you don't look good," said Father O'Toole who was too old at this point not to cite to the obvious.

"I still look better than you."

"That really isn't saying too much," said Father O'Toole as he rose from his chair to greet Ari.

"I hope this is a good time for you."

"It is, thank you. Morning prayers have been said, and what they call breakfast has mostly been eaten."

"In light of everything, you're still praying? I wasn't sure how that whole thing worked."

"Oh yes, I still pray. All day long. Not a whole lot of other options at this point. I'm confident that my Lord will not abandon me in my time of need."

"At least you got that goin' for ya'. Pardon my directness this morning, and apparently my appearance as well, but I have a lot going on. I need to know where you stand with my proposal to represent you as a private attorney. Have you come to a decision?" asked Ari who remained standing while Father O'Toole returned to his chair.

"After prayer and consideration, I have nearly made a decision."

"I see."

"I just have a few questions before I can render my verdict, so to speak."

"If you're wondering about the cost, I will need 10,000 up front. I may need more later. All depends on the costs involved. That may seem like a lot to you, but honestly, I don't know of any notable defense attorneys who would jump in on this mess for anything less than 50 to start," stated Ari with confidence even though he had no real idea what private attorneys actually charged. He pulled up a chair and sat down eye-level with Father O'Toole.

"That seems reasonable considering the time you will be spending." Father O'Toole paused and looked Ari in his eye in a way that Ari had never seen from him. The look from the old priest was calculating, as if he was sizing Ari up. The look unnerved Ari who was already on edge for a litany of reasons.

"I can pay that, but you'll have to wait until I get out of this hospital. I can get you the money shortly after I return to the rectory, assuming I can still live there."

"What do you mean, 'assuming you can still live there?' You heard the judge, you have to live there with the ankle bracelet."

"Yes, but the judge does not own the house. The diocese does. No one has told me that I can't live there anymore."

"Do you have any idea when this place is going to cut you loose?"

"I'll be here for at least one more week. At most, 10 days."

"That gives me some time. I'm a big proponent of not poking a stick at it, but I think in this case, we should be sure you'll have accommodations. We show up at the rectory and you can't get in, most likely you'll be taken straight to the jail.'

"You mean I couldn't live with you?"

"I've heard stories of priests...no, you can't. But I'll send a well-written letter to the diocese. No, I'll call them and talk to somebody to confirm you can still reside. If it looks bad, I'll demand their attorneys immediately call me, and I'll remind them of the judicial order."

"Good idea. Threaten more litigation, they won't like that. Lawsuits are bad for business."

"I don't think landlord/tenant litigation will make the papers. That'll be the plan, assuming you've retained me."

"As I said, two to three days after I get back, you'll have your money."

Ari looked at the priest with hesitation. He remained silent.

"Look, son, I promise, I will pay you. I haven't lied to you at all thus far. Why would I lie now?" said Father O'Toole with slight indignation.

"You haven't lied to me? Did you shoot Nicholas Rossi?" asked Ari in cross-examination fashion.

"I did not. See? Still not lying."

"You'll never know how much I want to believe that. Anyway, I'll contact the diocese and make all arrangements," said Ari as he stood and gathered himself to leave.

"And at that time, I'll sign the retainer agreement?"

"Oh, yeah, of course. At that time you can sign the retainer," said Ari who was tripped up by the question. It dawned on him that he has been practicing criminal defense for 15 years but had never once drafted a retainer agreement. What do they even look like, he thought? His hesitation did not go unnoticed by Father O'Toole, who sat up straight in his chair.

"And where is your office, should I need to see you for preparation or what not?" asked the wily priest who already knew that answer.

"I don't have one yet."

"No office?" said Father O'Toole with exaggerated surprise. "What about a secretary? Paralegal? Any runners?"

"None of that, not yet. I've always typed my own pleadings and letters because, quite frankly, I don't trust anyone else to do it. Since I don't have an office, no one will be calling me, so there's nothing for a secretary to do. And considering you're my only client,

I think I'm capable of managing my schedule on my own for the time being. Trial prep will be important, but I'll come to you. It'll be easier for me to visit you than going to court on a motion to get you a window every time I need to see you. So, I think that despite not having an office or staff, I will manage just fine."

Father O'Toole said nothing and but gave Ari a look like 'I can't believe what I am about to get into.' After pausing for a couple moments, Father O'Toole smiled. "Son, I'm not nervous. I think you'll do a great job. Maybe you're the answer to my prayers. Maybe not." With that uncomfortable exchange, Ari shook the priest's hand and headed back to his office at the Public Defenders while he still had one.

Chapter Thirteen

Even after the quick trip to the hospital, it was still early in the morning when Ari arrived at the courthouse, which had been unlocked for about half an hour. No one was there yet except the county sheriffs who worked the courthouse detail and the janitorial staff. The courtrooms were still dark as their doors remained shut and locked following the close of business the day before. The absence of light from the courtrooms made the hallways dim despite the best efforts of the outdated florescent lights which strained to illuminate the stairwells while their ballasts hummed and cried for attention. Even the most eternal of optimists would not view a typical morning in the courthouse as a bud waiting to spring open to the warm rays of light and justice. After minimal time spent in the courthouse, people soon realize why Lady Justice is blindfolded — she can no longer tolerate the color of heroine gray, the immutable color of the criminal justice system and its components. The gloomy cloud that Ari dragged with him to the courthouse did nothing to help that appearance.

Ari struggled with his situation in a way he had never struggled before. He wasn't thinking about Father O'Toole, or the impossible case he was about to undertake, or the fact that despite his genuine belief that there was no defense in this case, he still charged Father O'Toole $10,000. He tried to psych himself out by thinking that there must be something wrong with him. People resign from jobs all the time. He never doubted for an instant that he would always be able to make money — as a lawyer or otherwise — which should have given him confidence. So why was this resignation so difficult? Yeah, there must be something wrong with me, he thought.

As he trudged up four flights of stairs to the Public Defender's Office, the gravity of his task at hand became clear to him. "What a shitty place to have an epiphany," he muttered to himself in the empty hallway. He moped toward the end of the hallway where an office light shone through Vince's halfway open door. Ari knew that Vince would be there, even at that early hour. All the best attorneys get to their office early, and not because of work ethic or a desire to do great things compels them, but because the distraction of the hustle and bustle of coworkers isn't there yet. The din of people in the hallways hasn't started, and most importantly, the phones aren't ringing. It was the time that the best attorneys were most productive. For a second, Ari felt bad about intruding on Vince at this almost sacred hour and thought maybe he should table this move until lunch. But he had to get this out of the way, and it was good that no one else was around. He didn't know how Vince would react as he made the final push to the office. His feet felt heavy and clumsy, like he was walking in the mud while wading through the shallow part of the river's edge.

He wanted to turn around and forget the whole thing, but he knew that was his mind's last attempt to betray him, or maybe his mind's last attempt to comfort him in his time of need. Ari wasn't certain about anything at this point, so why should he have clarity as to his feelings? Pushing those thoughts aside, he strode into Vince's office and paused for a faint knock at the door before he let himself in. Vince did not get up from his desk. He heard Ari and knew he was there. After a moment, Vince turned away from his computer and looked up toward Ari. He tried his best to look pleasant.

"Good morning, Ari."

"Good morning, Vincent."

"Here, sit down," said Vince as he pointed to a folding chair with several files on it.

"I'm okay. I think, I mean…" Despite having practiced in his head ad nauseum, the eloquent defense attorney struggled with his words.

"Look, Vince, I don't want there to be hard feelings, you know?"

"Why would there be hard feelings?"

"I can't work here anymore. I can't work in this office. I can't work for you," blurted Ari in a vomitous spew that was more sad and pathetic than direct and blunt.

Heartly Law?

Vince said nothing. He just looked at Ari. "Why would there be hard feelings?"

"I worked here for almost 15 years. That's only slightly less than you have. You weren't running the show when I started."

"But I was your supervisor."

"You've been my only supervisor, the whole time I've been here. The PD pays me but I always sort of saw it that I worked for you. And I was always fine with that. Now I just said that I can't work here anymore, and that doesn't bother you? Even a little? It bothers me."

"You asked me, or rather told me, that you didn't want hard feelings. Now, when you leave, are you going to cause me or my office any problems?" asked Vince in a cold tone.

"Of course not. Why would you even ask me that?" said Ari, a bit taken back by Vince's stoic reaction.

"Listen, Ari," said Vince as Ari started to roll his eyes in typical fashion, but stopped himself when he realized what he was about to do. "I'm not going to lecture you. Any attempts of lecture in the past have failed miserably, so I'm just going to lay it out. You are a brilliant attorney. You try cases better than I ever could. You try them better than anyone I have ever seen. But trying cases is not what I do. I run an office. It's an office that is severely under-funded and full of about 40 extremely hard-working attorneys whose development is my responsibility. You have no idea how difficult it is doing everything I can to train great defense attorneys only to watch them leave year after year for big money in private firms, all the while battling the perception of the "Public Pretenders Office," just like you said. I know that's real; not deserved, but real. Is your absence going to be felt? Of course. You want me to cry about it? You want me to beg you to stay? I can't do that. I know your mind is made up, and whether I agree with you or not, I know nothing I can say will change your mind. I still have a responsibility to those who still work here and to those clients we represent ensuring that this office runs as smoothly as possible. That will remain my focus."

Ari stood at attention, stunned by the lack of any type of hurt feelings from someone whom he considered his mentor and friend.

Vincent continued, "You know what's worst about you not being here anymore? I always knew I could count on you. I always knew you wouldn't duck a case or pass the buck. That'll be tough to replace, but I'll find a way. As long as you're not causing me problems after you leave here, there'll be no hard feelings. I wish you the best of luck in whatever new endeavor you undertake."

"So that's it then?"

"I do need a resignation letter for your file. I'll forward it to county payroll and they'll contact you about COBRA benefits, your pension, and all that other shit you don't really care about."

"I'll get you a letter by the end of the day," said Ari in defeat.

Ari turned away as Vince returned to his computer. When he was halfway out the door, Vince spoke up.

"Ari. Come Monday morning, when I walk past your office and I know that you're not there, and I know that you're not coming back — then it'll hurt."

Ari exhaled deeply. "Thank you, Vince," said Ari as he headed out of the door en route to his "office," which was a cubicle at the other end of the hall.

When Ari got to his cubical, he sat in his chair one last time. He opened a desk drawer and took out a small tape recorder that was state of the art 15 years ago when he started. When the light turned red, he spoke into it quietly. When he finished, he ejected the tape and put it in his pocket. He left the recorder on the desk. He grabbed two Polaroid pictures that were thumb-tacked on the side of his cubical wall and put them in his jacket pocket. One picture was of a young man and lady who were both holding an infant. The other picture was of the same man when he was older. The man looked very sad though he was trying to force a smile. Ari got up from the chair and walked away. After three or four steps, he turned around and walked back to his desk. He grabbed every blue pen and highlighter as well as the stapler and he shoved them into his work bag. "One less thing to worry about now," said Ari, and with that, he started his trek down four floors to exit the courthouse.

Chapter Fourteen

Ari sat alone at a table for two in the Capital Grill, an elegant restaurant patronized by the upper crust of legal and business professionals who preferred Manhattans and small plates for lunch rather than Buffalo chicken salads with French fries on top. He arrived early for his lunch date with his secretary and wondered how he would break the news of his resignation to her. When the lives of the accused hung in the balance, he could effortlessly articulate such dramatic prose to judges and juries that it left them incapable of seeing anything other than his point of view. Yet now he struggled to tell his secretary that he just quit a job for which he was clearly overqualified, that paid next to nothing, and had become extremely aggravating due to office politics.

"I quit," he said to himself as he sucked the last drop of water from his glass and made a slight slurping sound. Ari needed a drink and signaled for the waiter. "Hello, my date will be here any minute. In the meantime, could you please bring me a Seven and Seven?"

"We do not carry Seagram's 7. Is Crown Royal acceptable?" sneered the condescending waiter.

"I suppose if you don't have the good stuff, I can tolerate Crown Royal." Ari always got a kick out of ordering well drinks in highfalutin places.

As Ari waited for his drink and for his secretary to arrive, he stared at the private lockers along the front wall where well-to-do patrons stored their own private supply of high-end wine. Their names were emboldened on brass plates on the front of each locker for all the restaurant patrons to see. Ari wasn't sure if this was the restaurant's attempt to validate the quality of their establishment by showing the world who dines here, or if it was it an attempt to quasi kiss asses of well-to-do patrons by saying, "you are so special and so important that we are not nearly qualified to suggest a wine pairing with your meal. Please allow us to store your perfect vintage and have it for you when you grace us with your presence." Ari recognized most of the names on the lockers. Some professional athletes, a couple local celebrities who were from Pittsburgh but no longer lived there, a few judges, and many lawyers. Ari wondered if this was the path to which private law practice would take him. Would he in time become a guy who stores his own wine at a five-star restaurant known for their wine selection? The arrogance of that concept far exceeded the times he brought a $50 bottle of wine to a local BYOB mom and pop Italian joint in Bloomfield in an attempt to impress a girl.

"Your Crown and 7-Up, sir," said the put-upon waiter as he placed the drink on the white tablecloth in front of Ari. The arrival of his drink snapped Ari away from what was clearly his most morbid thought of the day.

"Thank you, my good man." Ari gulped a mouthful and looked back up at the wine lockers. "Genius," he said to himself as he realized that the restaurateurs would make more money renting space to these people than they would actually spend on drinks in any given month. "Man, do I wish they had a pool table in a back room here. This place would be ripe for the picking."

Just then, Ari saw his secretary Sarah walk in the door. As the maître d' showed her to the table, Ari could see her eyes were wet and swollen. He took another drink and stood up to greet her. The two did not speak a word as they hugged in the middle of the restaurant.

Ari pulled away first. "How did you find out, Mrs. Parker?"

"I stepped into Vincent's office this morning and he didn't look right."

"Didn't look right?"

"If I didn't know better, I'd say he looked upset. Maybe even sad, different from his usual stressed out look. I asked him if everything was okay, and that was when he told me. He asked me if I knew anything. I told him I didn't and I was shocked. Then he kinda' looked embarrassed that he was the one to tell me. I went back to my desk and it just sort of hit me, all at once," said the secretary as she did her best to hold the tears back. "Oh, sweetheart. You little bastard, now you're going to ruin my mascara," she said with a faux chuckle.

"I'm sorry, love. I don't know what to say," said Ari as he finished his drink.

"I'm happy for you, I really am. You should have done this 10 years ago. You are so much better than this place."

"Don't say that. I am just a scrapper from the Valley who plays pool. For tax reasons, I need a job to show legit income."

"Alright tough guy, say what you want if it makes you feel better. In some ways, I feel like I watched you grow up."

Ari looked Sarah dead in the eye and said, "Feels like you helped raise me." Before his eyes filled up, he turned from his secretary back to the waiter and held up his empty glass. The waiter got the message.

Sarah exhaled deeply and cleared her throat in an attempt to regain composure. "Well, sir, just what plans have you now? Private practice in a big law firm? Something corporate? White collar criminals?"

"Thought I'd hang a shingle. Working there that long, I learned that I'm open to keep learning, if there are opportunities. But I just can't seem to take direction well. Not sure if I could work for someone who tells me what to do. You being the exception, of course."

The waiter delivered the second drink. "Would you like to hear about our lunch specials? The chef has prepared a delightful Virginia Spots glazed with–"

"In a minute. Please, just give us a couple more minutes, then we'll order," said Ari with a slight crack in his voice.

"I'll gives you a few minutes."

"Hang a shingle, huh? Old school. Makes sense for you. I can see it."

"Can you? Because I'm nervous as fuc – nervous as heck."

"Oh, sweetie, I don't think you have anything to be nervous about. You've made some great connections. Some people actually like you. Well, a few. But you know a lot of people and many of them always seem to need you, so I think you'll be just fine. Do you have any clients yet?"

"One so far," said Ari who seemed slightly embarrassed as he started on his second drink.

"There you go. You just started out and you already have a client. Can I ask who it is, or can I no longer know that since we don't work together?"

"I have no idea how those rules work. It's the priest, Father O'Toole. He's my first and only client."

Sarah sat up straight in her chair and was visibly taken aback. "Oh, Ari, are you sure? Do you really think that's the first case you should take on? The media coverage will be outrageous, and from what I've seen, it doesn't look like a very good case. Are you sure you want to start your new career with that one?"

"I had no choice. Vince was going to take that case away from me and give it to someone as a training exercise. Basically throwing the priest to the wolves with steaks in his pants. I couldn't let that happen."

"There you go again, acting like anything but another scrapper from the Valley. Is there anything I can do for you?"

"One thing," said Ari. He pulled the mini-cassette from his pocket and laid it on the table in front of her. "Can you please type up my dictation and give it to Vincent before the end of the day?"

"Certainly, love." Sarah grabbed the tape and put it in her blazer pocket. She reached across the table and took Ari's hand with both of hers. She squeezed tightly and gently caressed the back. Ari sat with his head down resting on this other hand.

"Well, just what do we have here, huh!?!" said a booming voice that drew the attention of every patron in the restaurant as well as the waiter, who froze in panic. "Some pencil neck little runt making a move on my best girl!!"

Ari looked up, grabbed his drink, chugged what remained in his glass in one gulp, and slammed it back down on the table. He got up and walked to the side of the table. He planted his back foot on the ground as a deliberate show of force, tightened his right hand into a fist, and puffed out his chest. "Yeah. So what? What are you going to do about it, old man?"

Heartly Law?

The burley giant, twice the size of Ari, walked to him and got in his face. "You think you're better than me, you little pinhooker?"

"Not better. Badder. And better looking, that's for sure, you old codger."

The perturbed giant stepped to Ari and in one fell swoop wrapped his tremendous arms around Ari's entire body and lifted him off the ground. He bounced him in his arm like a small child. The old man's facial scruff scratched Ari's clean-shaven baby face like 60-grit sandpaper. Ari turned his face away and looked down to see the Vietnam-Era tattoos on the old man's Popeye forearms bulging under the enormous muscle beneath them. "Oh, look at him, honey. Don't you think it's just adorable how this little boy thinks he's so tough. You're just as cute as the dickens," said the old man. He released his grip and set Ari back to the floor.

"Oh for the love of Pete! For as long as you two have known each other, can't you find a more socially acceptable way to greet one another?"

"How much fun would that be?" said Ari as he signaled for the waiter who was still shaking but now relieved that there would be no altercation.

"Mearl, what are you doing here?" asked Sarah.

"Pencil neck over here called and told me he had a hot date lined up for me and that I'd be an idiot to pass it up. I guess the kid was right."

"Sir, will this, ahh, gentleman, be joining you and the lady for lunch? Should I set another place?" asked the waiter.

"That won't be necessary. He's taking my place. He should be the one to get to dine with this beautiful woman. She's his best girl. Please, share with them the specials. The spots did sound delightful."

"Yes, very well, I will get two menus and be right back."

"What is the occasion?" asked Mearl.

"I didn't realize until a few minutes ago, but I just got a promotion," said Ari.

"Ari, that's great. You get a promotion, and I get to have lunch with my wife. Seems a bit odd, but okay. I'm glad I dressed for it."

Sarah smiled and rolled her eyes at the same time.

The waiter came back with two menus. "Here," said Ari. He pulled a wad of money out of his pocket. "For their lunch and my drinks. And this is for you," said Ari as he peeled off some bills and handed them to the waiter.

"Good Lord, that money stinks," said Sarah.

"I love the smell of Lucky Strikes on my currency. Smells like victory." Ari pulled the chair for Mearl who sat down. He moved around the table to Sarah and gave her one last hug. "Thank you darlin'," said Ari. Sarah was silent. Her eyes filled with tears. Mearl noticed that something wasn't quite right but remained quiet. "Enjoy lunch, Mearl. Always a pleasure," said Ari as he headed for the door. Before exiting, Ari turned back to the waiter. "14s are better than Crown. Just sayin'. I know what I'll store in my private locker." Ari turned and walked out of the restaurant with every eye upon him. He figured he'd better start getting accustomed to that feeling.

Chapter Fifteen

It was 9:30a.m. and Ari had been awake for about an hour, just lying there listening to the AM radio on his alarm clock, but he couldn't get out of bed. He had energy and motivation in spades, but lately his drive and desire had been sucked out of him as if from a cosmic Hoover. Maybe he was starting to fall into depression, or maybe 15 straight years of nonstop work had manifested the natural fatigue one would expect at the first opportunity when he slowed down.

Ari thought about O'Toole, his only client. When he received the call from the hospital, he made sure to be at the rectory to meet the probation officer. The GPS ankle bracelet was attached to the old priest in a very unceremonious fashion, and when the probation officer confirmed its working order, he left the residence. Business as usual and completely unremarkable. Ari had already explained the process of staying put to the priest and that if it was absolutely necessary for him to leave the rectory, Ari would have to arrange a window for him so that his absence from the rectory would not be noted as a violation. Ari informed O'Toole that he should expect a call from Dr. Abigail Flynn, the forensic psychiatrist who would interview him as part of his defense. It was the last time he had spoken to his client. Although it was almost three weeks ago, the conversation still echoed through his mind.

"I don't need to talk to any dammed psychiatrist!" said Father O'Toole in protest.

"You don't have a choice. Not your call. You are accused of attempted murder. If you can't see how there might be a psychological component to this case, then you're worse off than you think," said Ari. "If I failed to have you psychologically evaluated, I would be committing professional malpractice. And you haven't paid me enough to commit malpractice. I don't even have insurance yet."

"Fine, I'll talk to her. I have nothing else to do anyways."

"That's right. You have nothing else to do. Sit here, be peaceful, wait for her call, and answer her questions. And don't try to play any games. Don't try to give answers that you think are right. Be honest. Your answers will be put into a report by the doctor, and that report will be turned over to the DA. If you try to play games, their expert will notice, and you'll get picked apart at trial. Understand?"

"I will do as you say."

"Okay." And with that, Ari left the priest at the rectory and went back to his house. A few days later, a personal check for $10,000 came in the mail.

Ari rolled over in his bed and stared at the undeposited check sitting patiently on his nightstand. Thoughts meandered through his mind in slipstream consciousness. "Why don't I have the energy to cash a $10,000 check? Maybe it's all psychological. Maybe I'm just bored. Maybe I'm just hung up on something. Maybe O'Toole will call me today and fire me. That would be different, quitting one job then getting fired from my next, but then I could give him his money back and be done with it. Maybe I could stop lawyering all together. That is starting to sound good. Then what would I do? Pro billiards tour? That idea has potential. I already play some of those guys once or twice a year, and I do better than just alright. I took some money from some of them. With a little dedication, I might be able to make a living as a touring pro. Yeah, O'Toole needs to fire me so I don't have to open a business banking account or find an office somewhere. I need sponsorship money, something more than Sally can provide."

As Ari laid in bed and stared at his ceiling, his cell phone rang in his new home office and snapped him from his daydream. Ari knew he was spending too much time pondering things that had nothing to do with a defense strategy for attempted murder committed in front of hundreds of witnesses. Better answer the phone he thought as he limped from his bed.

"Good morning, Abigail. To what do I owe the pleasure of this call?"

"Cut the crap, Ari. And it's Doctor Flynn."

Heartly Law?

Ari sat in his chair behind his desk. "What's with the stern tone so early? What's the problem?"

"You're the problem. Is there something you want to tell me?"

"I think you're darling?"

"I said to cut the crap. I spent more than an hour filling out stupid forms to get approval as your court-appointed expert. That is time I could have used for people who really need me. And guess what I got back in the mail this morning? Every one of those stupid forms!"

"Wait, you get your mail this early in the morning?"

"It's 11:00 a.m., not exactly early," irked Dr. Flynn. "I got the forms back because they were all denied."

"How dare they! What did you do to deserve such treatment?"

"Apparently the Public Defender cannot approve my services, and thus not pay me, when A) You no longer work for the Public Defender, and B) The Office of the Public Defender is not representing Thomas O'Toole."

"Oh," said Ari after a slight pause. "Yeah, I guess they can't do that."

"I feel like you're wasting my time. I do not have time or money to spin my wheels, and I have people who need me."

"Okay, just cool it for a minute. I resigned from the PD's office a couple weeks ago, and it was rather sudden and unexpected. I know I should have told you, that's my bad. But it's been absolute chaos since my resignation. Getting an office up and running and all the logistics, my clients, you know how that all goes," said Ari as he twirled lazily around in his office chair while still wearing his pajamas. "But look, I am not wasting your time. Maybe just a small part of it. I'm still representing the priest, and I still want you to help me out. Can you still do it?"

"What, as a private expert?" said Dr. Flynn with a pause. "I guess I can. My fee for private work is higher than the fees I can charge the county."

"Oh, of course, Abby Cat."

"Don't Abby Cat me, Ari! If you think you can charm your way out of this —"

"No, no way. I doubt you'll find anyone who describes me as charming."

"I'm serious. This is your case, but it's my livelihood. I literally cannot afford to do a bad job."

"If I thought you would do a bad job, why would I ever ask for your professional assistance?"

"If the attorney I'm working for is unresponsive, doesn't communicate well with me, or is unprepared, then my report, and more so I, will be made to look foolish in court when I'm on the stand. And I can't have that. One bad review, one bad outcome, and attorneys won't use me. I might even lose my in with the PD's office if they think I'm damaged goods. And even if I keep my court-appointed work, I can't live off that alone. I need the private side even more than I need the court-appointments. Do you understand what I have at stake here? Do you? And it's not like this is a case that will fly under the radar. The whole state, probably the country, will be following this case. I can't afford to botch a case like this, especially if it's caused by you," said an exasperated Abigail Flynn.

Ari stopped spinning in his chair and cleared his throat before he responded. "Dr. Flynn, my apologies. You're right, I did not appreciate how this case can stress you out beyond the duly expected stress associated with your type of work and this service. But I can assure of a few things. First, I promise you that with your help, I will be well-prepared for trial. Second, I can absolutely assure you that no one will blame you for any bad outcome. And one other thing."

"What's that?"

"My guy is accused of shooting somebody else in full view of hundreds of people in a church. They have the gun, and I assume that ballistics will not be favorable. I'll find that out when I pick up the discovery. I don't even know what a favorable outcome would be at this point. If I can arrange something that keeps him from dying alone in a jail cell, that would be a huge win. But maybe even that is out of the question. I just don't know. That's why your work is so crucial. I know you'll give me something to work with, anything more than I have now, which is nothing. I know you can do it, Dr. Flynn. And just one more thing."

"You're really laying it on thick now."

Heartly Law?

"You could be Barry Scheck."

"From the O.J. case? I don't understand?"

"Follow me now. If I lose this case, no one will be shocked. A verdict of guilt handed down following the presentation of overwhelming evidence. Certainly no one will blame the expert witness for the defense. But if by the grace of…maybe if I could get a couple practicing Catholics in the jury box, maybe by smoke and mirrors – a miracle, perhaps? If by a miracle we can achieve any sort of improbable result for O'Toole, then you won't ever have to do another court-appointed case in your life. You'll be too busy doing private work. Every defense attorney in this state will be asking for you. If we get that outcome, whatever it might be, you will have established yourself of the next Barry Scheck. Just like he did in the O.J. trial. You have the world to gain and absolutely nothing to lose. Let that sink in," said Ari in a tone normally reserved for closing arguments to a jury.

"That is something to think about. But you're getting a bit ahead of yourself. I haven't even spoken to him yet."

"Then get to it. Sooner the better. You have his contact info. He's in the rectory, and he can't leave unless I get him a window. Do your forensic interview and when you're are done, call me and we can meet to discuss your findings. I'll pay your private-rate fee in full, so you're not taking a flyer on this one."

"I'll call him this morning and set something up."

"Dr. Flynn, I really believe in you. And now, duty calls. Phones are ringing off the hook. I will take these calls, then I shall work on O'Toole's case with the little information I have."

"Okay. And thank you, Ari, for your confidence."

"See you soon." After their conversation, Ari turned his cell phone completely off. He got up from his chair, exited his home office, and returned to his bed.

Chapter Sixteen

Fortunately for Ari, the investigation and subsequent prosecution of the church shooting was as stagnant as Ari's defense strategy. Detective Martin now strolled into the office around 9:00 a.m. The detective who regularly worked 12-hour days, nights and weekends, had reduced his schedule to nine to five. He stopped personally investigating everything. He assigned junior detectives and officers to do the real work while he quarterbacked everything from his desk. His lack of activity was noticed by the brass, as was the stress on his face and body. His clothing had become loose and baggy due to slight weight loss. As long as he was showing up and being slightly productive, his superiors would let him ride this wave out a bit to see if he could sort things in his head before they had to initiate the "you need to take some time off" talk.

Detective Martin had assigned Officer Marcus Flynn to be acting lead investigator on the Father O'Toole shooting, which was quite a promotion for a young officer who wasn't even a detective. Martin agonized over the disappearance of Nico Rossi immediately after taking a slug to the chest. Martin theorized that Nico Rossi's "parishioners" were in on the plan. It was the only explanation for how he could have escaped from the church unseen and why he's been able to remain undetected despite his notoriety and the massive police effort to locate him.

Officer Flynn would meet with Detective Martin at least twice a week to update him on the progress that he and his crew were making on new leads, of which there were none, and on statements made during interviews with Rossi's parishioners. The statements were all the same — nobody had seen Rossi since the shooting. All the parishioners appeared to be honest and forthcoming with the police, and some even expressed their desire for the police to find Rossi because they wanted him back.

At the end of every meeting, Martin told Flynn to continue to investigate and interview Rossi's parishioners. He told Flynn there was no way that everyone could keep to the same story, and at some point, somebody was going to slip up and give up the goods on Rossi's whereabouts.

After a few weeks of doing the same choreographed dance, Officer Flynn spoke up.

"Sir," said Officer Flynn, "with all due respect, and I'm really, very grateful for all the overtime. It's a huge help to me and my family. It's just, well…"

Detective Martin closed his laptop. "Son, save the politicking for the people outside this department. We don't have time to mince words in here. Be direct. Say what's on your mind."

"Well sir, I just don't get it. I mean, seriously with all respect, I just don't understand, but I want to, I really do." Detective Martin responded to the young officer with a menacing get-to-it glare. "We have more than three dozen eyewitness statements from people inside the church at the time of the shooting. We have the firearm, and the ballistics are a match. And you yourself witnessed this crime firsthand. That is more than enough evidence to hand over to the DA for prosecution of attempted murder, even if we don't have Rossi. Does it even matter if he's here or not? I mean, what is that going to change, sir?"

Detective Martin paused for a moment. He knew his young officer was correct, but he was taken aback by the fact that a young officer was calling him out before any of the brass did. This kid, he thought to himself, has balls and is going places. But he suppressed these feelings and opted for a more indignant response. "As the lead investigator in charge of this circus, I'm used to being held accountable to my supervisors. You know, following the chain of command. Am I to be held accountable to my subordinates as well? Is that what you're suggesting, Flynn?"

"Oh, no sir, not at all, I was just trying to –"

"Can it, junior. I'm in charge, and there's a reason for that. I have skill and knowledge that can only be gained by real-world experience. This case is not the run-of-the-mill attempted homicide. But you wouldn't realize that now, would you? You haven't been around long enough to know anything at all."

Heartly Law?

Officer Flynn knew his best option was to take the verbal assault and lick his wounds later.

"Now, Flynn, the only thing I'm concerned about is your directive. Are you clear on your directive?"

"Yes, sir. Continue to take statements from all known associates of Nicholas Rossi. Take statements from others who were in the church whether they are associates of Rossi or not. Look for new leads and evidence of a plan to hide Rossi. And report back to you in a timely manner to keep you informed, sir."

"Then, unless you have any further suggestions, you may leave now," said Detective Martin.

"Yes sir. Thank you, sir," said Officer Flynn as he turned and headed toward his desk, which was thankfully on the other side of the precinct right beside the evidence room.

Detective Martin stewed by himself at his desk. He knew that as a supervisor he was just presented with an absolutely teachable moment that he had squandered by acting like a complete dick. *"But what would I teach him, really,"* he thought to himself. *"I'm sure that there's a completely rational reason why two perfectly good bullets fired from a top of the line Sig only traveled 10 feet before dropping to the ground as if they were thrown underhand. We just haven't asked the right questions or run the right test. We just haven't explored the right area. But this second shooting with Rossi, I was there. I watched him fall to the ground after taking it in the chest. Even if the bullet was stopped by the key in his shirt pocket, he shouldn't get up. Cops wearing vests who get shot in the chest usually break a rib or two, and they're grown men with muscle, not some skinny punk pretending to be priest. He shouldn't have gotten up, let alone escaped in front of 500 or so people without anyone noticing. How the hell do I teach Flynn about anything when I don't understand it myself?"*

After a few more minutes of sitting in silence, Detective Martin thought it would be best to call Flynn back to his office to try to explain the situation. Not necessarily to apologize, but he recognized that Flynn was working hard and deserved a little insight. But just before he was about to get up, his secretary called his desk phone.

"Martin.....yeah...who, Kelly?...Well why didn't he just call me?... I've been at my desk all afternoon....no, I didn't miss any calls," said Detective Martin as glanced at his cell phone to see if any calls were in fact missed. "Yes, I can meet him. Where did he say? The church?... Maybe he has information, who knows? What time....now? Okay, can you sign me out of the logbook, please? Alright, you know where I'll be." Detective Martin left the precinct to meet with his old partner, Retired Detective Kelly, at St. Mary's Church in the Strip District, under unusual circumstances.

Twenty minutes after Detective Martin left the precinct, Officer Flynn noticed the noise level increase in the precinct, but in a good way. He saw an older gentleman dressed in street clothes with a light jacket make his way through the department. Many people shook his hand with smiles and seemed very happy to see him. Although Flynn did not know who he was, the gentleman made his way toward Flynn's desk.

"You must be Officer Flynn. Nice to meet ya' lad."

Flynn stepped away from his computer and got up from behind his desk to extend his hand. "I am Officer Flynn. How can I help you?" said the confused young man.

"Sit back down, relax. Oh, forgive me, my name is Francis. Francis Kelly."

"Detective Kelly! You used to be Detective Martin's partner, right? Man, I am glad to meet you. It's nice to put a name to a face. He talks about you all the time."

"It's Retired Detective Kelly now, but you can just call me Francis. And it's also nice for me to put a face to the name as well. Ben talks about you all the time."

"Oh. What's he said about me?" said Officer Flynn with an embarrassed tone, not wanting to know the answer to that question.

"What does he say? Ha! What doesn't he say! He thinks the world of you. Said you're one of the finest young officers he's seen since he's been here. And that is saying something, especially when you consider the officers that came through the ranks with him."

"That's surprising. He doesn't really say that to me. He's kind of tough on me."

"Don't let that bother you, son. That is just Ben being Ben. Two possible reasons for that. First, Ben just has this really old school mentality of tough love, but I promise you it's better for him to be tough on you than it is for him to ignore you. If he didn't ride you at times, that would tell me that he really isn't that impressed with you. He's just making sure you turn out good, that's all."

"I see. What's the other possibility?"

"He is a curmudgeon. Worse than I ever was, even though I'm twice his age."

"Ha! I'm not complaining. He's great to work for. I appreciate his tutelage."

"You better believe it, one of the best." Francis Kelly paused for a moment and looked Officer Flynn over in a grandfatherly way. "If you're fortunate as I am, and if you get to live as long as me, one day, you'll run into people who you know, but they won't know you. That's what we have here."

"Sorry, I don't follow. You know me or something?"

"Yes of course. Your sister, too. Smart as a whip, that girl. And cute as the dickens, if you don't mind me saying."

"I don't mind, I mean, she is my sister, so, I don't really think about her, like that."

"I understand," said Francis Kelly with a chuckle.

"Okay, so how do you know us, my sister and me?"

"I know your parents. I got to know them from the old neighborhood when I walked my beat, way before I was a detective. I remember when your sister was born. You too. So I guess I just always sort of kept an eye on the both of you, just seeing how things turned out. And I must say, you both did well. It's great to see you wearing that uniform. It makes me proud when fine young men of good character choose this life. And it is a life, not just a job. But I'm sure you figured that out by now.

"I'm starting to."

Officer Flynn's desk phone rang. "Good afternoon, Officer Flynn here…attorney who?... Shouldn't Detective Martin speak with her?... Oh, he is?… Then I guess I'll come see her. Thank you." Mr. Kelly, it seems I have a visitor, some attorney I don't know wants to speak to me, and Detective Martin isn't here at the moment, so I have to field this one. Please, wait here if you want, but I don't know how long this will take. Or, just keep walking around. It seems you're quite the rock star in these parts."

"Yes, quite. I know you're busy. Go take care of business, I know the way out of here. I'll say hello to a couple more old friends, then show myself out. Truly, it was great to meet you." The two said goodbye and shook hands one more time. "Officer Flynn, stay safe out there. And thank you for your service."

"Thank you, sir. It was a pleasure to meet you."

Officer Flynn headed to the front of the precinct to meet the mystery attorney, and Francis Kelly meandered toward the evidence room.

When Officer Flynn arrived at the front desk, he was shocked at the sight of a younger female attorney dressed more like a model than a litigator. Flynn knew she was an attorney from her briefcase, but that was hardly noticeable compared to her long blond hair, six-inch heels, and Chloe sunglasses. She wore an unusual silver peace sign which hung from the choker around her neck. This accessory would normally seem out of place, but for some reason it completely fit her image. She was a cross between a female-terminator-lawyer and a Victoria's Secret angel. Officer Flynn took a beat to compose himself before he approached her.

"Good afternoon, I'm Officer Flynn, how may I help you?" said Flynn as he attempted to appear professional and composed.

The attorney pulled her glasses down slightly and peered over them as she purposefully looked him up and down before pushing her glasses back into place.

"Maybe I can help you," she said in a somewhat condescending fashion.

"Okay, I'll play along. I don't need any girl scout cookies if that's what this is about," said Officer Flynn. He immediately realized his attempt at humor made him look foolish, but in her presence, he didn't know how else to respond. The attorney chuckled a bit.

"I'll be brief. I represent Mr. Nicholas Rossi. I'm not one to pay much attention to the grapevine, but rumor has it that someone from this fine department is trying to get in touch with him."

"Rossi? Really? Holy shi–, uh, yes, that's true. You want to speak to Detective Martin, but he's not here right now."

"Pity. So, you can't help me, officer?" said the attorney as she mocked a slight pout.

Heartly Law?

"Actually, I can. I'm part of the investigation."

"Investigation? Oh my, this sounds serious," said the attorney in a sultry voice as she stepped closer to Flynn.

"Yes, there's an investigation. Detective Martin, and I, me moreso, I want to talk to your client."

"About what, pray tell?"

"Oh, you know, usual stuff cops like to talk to people about. Getting shot in a church, by a priest, disappearing afterwards, usual cop stuff."

"You're funny. Cops aren't supposed to be funny."

"I wish it was funny. This is serious business. If you represent Rossi, we need to talk to him."

"I tell you what, you and the detective – no, you, give me a call later and we can arrange to meet."

"And you'll bring Rossi?"

"Maybe. If you're good."

"What's your name? You got a card?"

"Of course." As the attorney reached into the top pocket of her blazer to remove a business card, Officer Flynn's eyes were drawn to her chest, which was unfortunate, because she busted him for it.

"Uh-hem, here is my card, sweetheart."

Officer Flynn looked at the card and read he name: Jeannette Royale, Esquire.

Attorney Royale extended her hand for a shake. When Officer Flynn extended his, she grabbed it and placed her other hand on his forearm. "Nice to meet you, Officer Flynn. Call me at the end of the week." Without letting go of him she moved closer and whispered in his ear, "We can, get in touch, then." She released her grip, smiled, and exited the building.

Officer Flynn stood in shock. As he turned around to go back to his desk, he noticed the audience of men watching the whole scene play out. They, too, were in a state of shock, and most certainly were jealous.

Attorney Royale walked across the parking lot and got into her jet-black Mercedes Benz Coup with tinted windows. Francis Kelly sat in the passenger seat waiting for her.

"We good?" asked Attorney Royale.

"Easy Peazy," said Francis Kelly as he patted his jacket pocket.

As she started the car, Kelly looked down at her six-inch heels and asked, "I just want to know one thing. How the hell do you drive in those things?"

"Easy Peazy, Frankie." Attorney Royale eased off the clutch and pulled away from the station offering a view of her license plate, which read "IAMAZE."

At the same moment on the other side of town, Detective Martin arrived at St. Mary's Church. He pulled his car directly in front of the enormous church doors and waited for his old partner to arrive.

Chapter Seventeen

As Detective Martin waited, he stared at the crime scene tape still wrapped around the entire church like a fluorescent highlighter. If his cop's intuition was correct, then what was it highlighting? He checked his watch. He'd been sitting in front of the church for almost 30 minutes with no sign of his ex-partner. It wasn't like Kelly to be late. Martin thought back to the last time he saw his old partner. It was several months ago, in the hospital, the day after the shooting. Kelly was alert and improving from the head trauma, but the hospital wanted to keep him there for a couple days, just for precaution and observation. Martin remembered their last conversation:

"Look, Kell, I'm not going to pester you. Take your time, rest up. I'm sure there'll be plenty of work for you when you're up to returning. This shit is crazy, never seen anything like it," said Detective Martin.

"Thanks, but no thanks, Benny. I think I've had enough of this case. I think I've had enough of all of it," said Detective Kelly with fatigue in his voice.

"I don't think now is the time for you to make major life decisions. I mean, get healthy first. Relax. Take some sick time. Take workers comp if you want. Take all the time you need, but don't start talking about retirement while you're here in a hospital bed."

"I know, you're right, but I have been thinking, for awhile now. I'm really thinking that I don't want to play cops and robbers anymore. I think I'd like to do something different."

"Not to sound selfish, but what am I going to do without you? I mean, this case –"

"Benny, you are too much, sometimes. I think you give me too much credit. You'll do what you always do, and you will be excellent. Maybe a new partner will be good for you. Someone young, someone you can train up, the right way."

"I don't want to think about that now. I don't want you to think about it either. Get some rest. Call me when you're are up to it," said Detective Martin. He hugged his partner in the bed and walked out of his hospital room.

Detective Martin's mind drifted and reflected on their conversation. *"It's strange that neither of us have reached out. We aren't the closest of friends, but professionally speaking, I couldn't ask for a better partner. And we always checked in with each other during extended absence. Why hadn't he called me? Why didn't I call him? Professional courtesy alone should have obligated me to call him? And why did he say he wanted 'to do something different?' Could he just not say retirement? He could have retired a few years ago, he certainly had the time in. I bet he wishes he did retire a few years ago. It's just odd that he said he would like to do something different instead of just saying he wanted to retire. But I guess in light of this entire situation, Kelly's choice of words is rather low on the oddity depth chart."*

As Detective Martin's thoughts wandered, his internal dialogue became an external monologue in the car by himself. He thought back to the second shooting. He remembered sitting there in the church pew. The chaos, the fear, the pandemonium in the congregation after the single shot rang out like a thunderbolt on the inside of the church.

"No, they couldn't be in on it," said Martin out loud. "In both shootings, the people were frightened, terrified and screaming. I saw that the second time myself. If this shooting was staged, if the first shooting was staged, if this was all an elaborate hoax, if Rossi had help, then nobody would have been frightened. Not to the extent they showed. Nobody can fake terror like that. People were trampled, they got injured. Why would anyone go to that length for some sort of sick gag? What's to gain? What's the point? Occam's Razor tells us that the simplest solution is usually the correct one." Martin took his last sip of coffee and threw the paper cup on the floor of his car.

The first shooting attempt, on Father O'Toole by Dylan Ray, was motivated by Ray's fanatical rage over the direction O'Toole was taking the church. A bit extreme, but that's what fanatics do. And that is consistent with Ray's own admissions. The second shooting attempt, on Rossi by O'Toole, was motivated by the fact that Rossi was stealing the church away from O'Toole. Again, in a vacuum, that seems extreme. But if the starting point is the original shooting by a religious zealot, then a priest attempting to shoot someone stealing his most valued possession isn't really that far left of center."

Martin's attempt to force linear analysis upon inexplicable chaos continued. "If both premises are sound, i.e. fanatics are capable of extreme measures, then the most logical conclusion is that both Ray and O'Toole, both of whom are religious fanatics, acted independently, and the shootings were the manifestation of their maniacal rage. Alright. Test the conclusion, work it backwards, what can be eliminated to get closer to the razor? Ray was part of the original church protestors, but nothing indicates that any of them worked with Ray in his attempt to kill O'Toole. Eliminate all protestors. As for O'Toole, 40-plus interviews of witnesses, most of whom were closely tied to Rossi, and nothing suggests that any of them were working in conjunction with Rossi or O'Toole. Thus, also an independent act. Adding in the genuine fear and injuries sustained following the second shooting bolsters the legitimacy of the conclusion that O'Toole's actions were insane and independent. If nobody else was in on it, then eliminate all other people, Rossi associates or otherwise."

"Okay so what have we got? Two separate church shootings attempted by two different people with absolutely no assistance from anyone else. Both gunmen were religious fanatics, which explains why they tried to kill, presumably in the name of God, so we know why they did it. What we don't have is the how. How do we explain the failure of the bullets to hit O'Toole, and how do we explain the disappearance of Rossi when he was, in fact, actually shot? Okay, well, we just aren't there yet. Still more to learn, but we are getting closer."

Martin exhausted himself from his logic exercise. He put his head in his hand and rubbed his temples. "One thing for sure is that I need to talk to Flynn. And don't be a dick this time, Martin. Man up, apologize. I got to let him know that all these interviews are worthless. He needs to go in a different direction. What specific direction? Hell if I know. But maybe he will. He's young, but he's smart and doing a good job working this case. Maybe he'll have an idea. Maybe the thought of his ideas being genuinely considered will inspire him. Who knows? I sure as shit don't."

He lifted his head following the conclusion of his monologue and turned back to the church. His eyes were drawn to the crime scene tape and the lightbulb in his mind lit up. "IT'S HIGHLIGHTING THE FUCKING BUILDING!!"

Detective Martin got out of his car, sprinted to the side door of the church, and ducked under the crime scene tape. He used the key he was provided as lead investigator to open the side door of the church. He rushed through the threshold lobby of the Romanesque building to the timeworn wooden doors and heaved them open wide. He entered the church and stopped dead in his tracks. An enormous weight set upon his back and in his chest. It forced him to bend over and place his hands on his knees like an exhausted defensive back who just got beat deep to the endzone.

As he tried to regain his composure, the natural light from outside allowed him to scan the area without having to turn on lights. He was appalled by what he saw. Since St. Mary's remained an active crime scene, the church was closed and had remained exactly as it was following the last of the police investigations several months ago. Dust had covered the pews, several of which were still turned over and partially blocking the main aisle. Hymnals and personal prayer books were strewn about. Even a few rosary beads and some jewelry, violently dislodged in the ensuing panic, were scattered like a debris field among hats, coats, and children's toys. The inside of the church looked more like a tornado had touched down on a flea market than a revered place of worship.

Although Detective Martin had been to hundreds of far more gruesome crime scenes, with outlines of bodies and markers for spilled blood and shell casings, this crime scene caused him to feel more sadness than he'd ever experienced at any of the previous ones. He shuttered. He cast his eyes to the ceiling and stared at the incredible murals of angles flying through the heavens. Some were peaceful, others were not. Martin paused at the sight of St. Michael, the Archangel, who was actively engaged in battle with his angle warriors against the forces of Satan. Martin blessed himself as it appeared that St. Michael the Archangel was staring directly at him, as if to say, "I have done my job, why haven't you done yours?" Maybe that was the feeling in his chest and back, guilt over being responsible for investigating two church shootings that seemed to be rather cut and dry on the surface, yet still had far more questions than answers after so much effort had already gone in.

Martin kept the church lights off. He pulled out his flashlight and navigated his way through the aisle up to the altar in a slow and deliberate fashion so as not to disturb any contents of the debris field. The altar was less scathed than the rest of the church. There was one marker where Nico Rossi was shot and another where the key in Rossi's shirt pocket dropped to the floor. Detective Martin stood there and faced in the direction where Father O'Toole would have been standing when he shot. He dropped to the ground where Nico would have fallen face down and used his flashlight to look around.

"C'mon, you gotta be here somewhere," said the detective as he searched for a trap door leading to the boiler room in the basement of the church. Finding none, he rose to his feet and stood in about the same area as Rossi would have stood when he was shot.

"I get shot here. The shooter would be in front of me, so if there isn't a trap door at my feet, I would naturally back away from the threat in this direction," said the detective as he moved to the rear of the altar. He dropped to his knees and looked once more for the trap door. Still nothing.

When he rose to his feet the second time, he noticed that he was now close to the door that lead to the back room behind the altar where the priest and the altar servers would change into their garb. He opened the door and went into the back room, where he found the door leading outside. He remembered opening this door to look for Rossi as soon as he realized he was gone. He opened the outside door and peered around the corner to the alley. Rossi's old motorcycle was still parked there, covered with leaves and other debris. Martin came back inside and scoured the back room for 30 minutes in search of a trap door. He even used his flashlight to tap on the walls to see if any were "fake" and concealing a secret passage. Nothing. He returned to the altar and spent 20 minutes on hands and knees tapping and tugging and searching everywhere for a trap door entrance or concealed hallway that would have allowed

Rossi to escape unseen. After accepting that his trap door theory was a bust, Martin decided to leave. His first original thought, after many months, provided no answers. Martin thought that he had just wasted nearly two hours with nothing to show for it. Moreover, he realized that Detective Kelly was not showing up. Detective Martin left the church and headed back to the precinct. He needed to talk to Officer Flynn. He also wanted to speak to his secretary who relayed the message to him about meeting Detective Kelly at the church. Maybe there was a miscommunication. That would be the simplest explanation, and according to Occam's Razor, most likely the correct explanation. But Martin had a hunch that things were no longer at their simplest.

Chapter Eighteen

Detective Martin walked up the street to La Prima for some gourmet coffee. It was the middle of the afternoon and the place was packed full of people playing scopa, gossiping in Italian, and dipping biscotti into their espresso. Dr. Abigail Flynn sat at a table by herself. She worked on her laptop and sipped a cappuccino. Detective Martin retrieved his coffee, walked back to his car, and drove to the police station.

Martin found the precinct abuzz with excitement but was too focused to care about why. He was just about to tell the receptionist to call Flynn when Flynn happened to walk by.

"Flynn, I need to speak with you. Please follow me to my office."

"Great, sir, listen, I think I have something."

"Save it for my office."

The two proceeded through the precinct to Detective Martin's office. "Pull the door shut behind you, please," said Martin. He sat down behind his desk and fired up his computer. Officer Flynn remained standing at quasi-attention, fearful of another tongue lashing.

"Officer Flynn, I want to apologize."

"Sir?"

"I was rude and short with you earlier this morning. I know you weren't being critical of my leadership. You're working hard on this case, and I understand that you're just asking questions to learn more and get better. It's a big deal that you, a young officer, are taking the lead on different aspects of this case. And it doesn't help you when a superior beats you into the ground for asking questions," said Detective Martin.

"Sir, it's okay, really, but I think you should –"

"No, Flynn, it's not okay. I was wrong and I'm sorry. I'm embarrassed to tell you this, but for the first time in my career, I really have no idea what's up or down. I'm frustrated. All the hard work usually pays off, but in this case, none of it is leading to anything. The answers to the bigger questions are with Rossi, who's vanished into thin air."

"Sir, if –"

"One thing is for certain, Flynn. There won't be a need for you to do anymore interviews."

"Sir, I don't think you understand. I know where Rossi is," said Officer Flynn.

"Huh? Nicholas Rossi, the person we've been looking for now, for months on end. You know where he is?"

"Let me rephrase. I don't know exactly where he is, but I do know how we can find him. His attorney came in today. She left me her card."

"Nicholas Rossi's attorney came into the station and asked to speak with you. Not me, the lead guy. You. The rookie cop."

"That's what I said to her, but you weren't here, so I talked to her. I thought you would be pretty mad if I didn't."

"You're right, I am glad you spoke." said Detective Martin as he frantically tried to operate his computer and talk at the same time. "What did the two of you talk about?"

"Not a whole lot, she didn't stay long. She just told me that she'd heard we were looking for Rossi. I said yeah, that's right. You're gonna bring him in here so we can talk. She said not likely."

"She said not likely. That's how you left it with her?"

"She gave me her business card, then told me to call her on Friday. Said we could meet, and if things went well, maybe she would tell me where Rossi was. I think she asked me out on a date, sir."

Detective Martin got up from behind his desk and paced around his office. He chuckled a bit as he reflected on the absurdity of it all. "Alright, it's been a long day and it isn't even close to over yet. Let's refresh a bit. The attorney representing Nicholas Rossi comes into our station, tells you that she isn't going to bring Rossi in, gives you her business card, then asks you out on a date with the caveat of that if things go well – on the date, I presume – she will let you know where to find Rossi. Did get that correct, Officer Flynn?"

"Yes, sir. I would say that is an accurate summation."

Heartly Law?

"An accurate summation. Good. This attorney — she is a woman, right Flynn?"

"A very, very good looking one at that. But I guess that really doesn't matter, does it, sir?"

"Not to me. Her business card. Do you have it on you? Can I see it, please," said Detective Martin who was doing his best to fake composure. Flynn opened up his wallet, removed the business card, and handed it to the detective. "Jeannette Royale, Esquire. No office address, no Bar ID number, no phone number?"

"Number's on the back, sir."

"This is handwritten. What is this, a cell phone?"

"I assumed it was," said Officer Flynn who wasn't sure if he should be proud or frightened.

"And this card smells…good."

"I believe it is Chanel No. 5, sir."

"That so. Well, no time like the present. We certainly aren't going to wait until Friday, your date be damned."

"I'm married, sir. I was kinda worrying about the set up."

Martin slid his desk phone around to the front. He picked up the receiver and dialed the number.

"Hello?" said the sultry voice on the other end.

"May I speak with Attorney Jeannette Royale?"

"Speaking."

"This is Detective Martin, Pittsburgh Police."

"I thought you may be calling me. I left my card at your station," she said with a slight chuckle.

"Let me get to the point. If you're representing Nicholas Rossi, you need to bring him in here for questioning."

"I don't think I can do that. So sorry."

"So sorry? Do you know who I am? I certainly don't know you because you're a nobody. I've been around the block and I know every defense attorney in the tri-state area, but I never heard of you."

"Well, that is a pity."

"I'll tell you what is a pity — the fact that I have a warrant for your client's arrest, and if you do not bring him down here to cooperate, I will roll SWAT and perp walk both your asses down here myself."

"Oooohh. You like the rough stuff, huh? Well, humor me, detective. What do you have a warrant for? My client was a victim who was shot in the chest."

"The warrant is for obstruction and conspiracy," said the detective, unaffected by the attorney's tone and comments.

"Conspiracy to be shot in his own chest? My my, that is certainly creative."

"You can challenge the warrant in court all you want, but for right now, the warrant is good and you need to cooperate."

"Else you'll get rough. I get it. I tell you what. Meet me in my office tomorrow. Bring me the warrant. When I see it, I will make arrangements for you to speak with my client. How about that? Then you can save the rough stuff for another time."

"Fine. Where is your office?"

"The Duquesne Club. I will be by the bar in the pool room. I can meet you there at 2:00 p.m."

"Fine. See you then."

Detective Martin slammed the phone down. "That little bitch wants to see the warrant, fine." Martin stuck his head out of the office and yelled down the hall, "Sergeant Allen, print me the arrest warrant for Rossi and bring it to me." Martin feverishly paced the office again and bumped into Officer Flynn during his loop. "What the hell, Flynn? I leave the office for two hours to meet Kelly, and I come back to this nonsense. Jesus."

"Kelly, sir? Retired Detective Kelly?"

"Yes, Flynn. My old partner. I was supposed to meet him at the church, but he never showed."

"He was here, sir," said Officer Flynn as he backed away from the Detective.

"You can't be fucking serious. You mean to tell me that in the two hours I was gone, you spoke to both the attorney representing Rossi and Detective Kelly?" Detective Martin stuck his head back out of his office and yelled for the receptionist, "Marcia! Marcia! Come to my office please. Okay Flynn, what did Kelly say? Did he say anything about meeting me today?"

"No, sir, he did not. It was kind of odd, you know? He, like, just came down the hall, I heard him saying hello to everyone, they all seemed really happy to see him. Then he came to my desk and introduced himself. We talked for a couple minutes, but then I had to go up front to meet Rossi's attorney. He said he would show himself out after talking to a couple more people."

"Yes, Detective, you wanted to see me?" said Marcia, the front desk receptionist.

"Yes, please. I want to be clear —"

"Oh my God, are you alright, Detective? You're sweating like a madman!"

"I'm fine, I'm fine. Just please, when did you talk to Kelly today?"

"I think it was about 1:15 or 1:20. It was right before my lunch. Right before I called you."

"Specifically, what did he say?"

"He told me to pass a message to you. He said meet him at St. Mary's at 2 o'clock. I even wrote it down. I called you right after that and told you exactly what he said. Then I signed you out, just like you asked. Then I went to lunch since it was 1:30 at that point."

"Did he say anything else?"

"No, not really. We chit chatted a bit, you know. I asked him how retired life is treating him, and he said it couldn't be better. I told him I was happy for him but missed seeing him around. That's about it as far as I remember."

"Did you know that he was here today?"

"Yes, I found out after I got back from lunch. Apparently he was here then gone during my lunch hour, so I missed him, which disappointed me. I wish I could have seen that old bugger," said the receptionist.

"So you don't know what time he actually got here?"

"I don't. He wasn't here when I left at 1:30, and I know he was gone before I got back at 2:30. But the exact times, I wouldn't know."

"Don't you find it extremely strange that he would call you to tell me to meet him at St. Mary's at 2 o'clock, but then he shows up here instead, at about the same time he was supposed to be meeting me?" asked the detective.

Marcia gave the detective a wild stare as if she understood what he was saying but still could not make sense of it all. "You mean you never met up with him today? Well, yes, it does seem strange that he said he would meet you at two, then come in here. That doesn't make a whole lot of sense now that I think about it."

"Are you absolutely positive that he told you to tell me to meet him at the church, or is there a chance that maybe the message was confused? Would it be possible that he said he would meet me here at 2:00?"

"Oh, no, sir. I'm sure that was what he said. If you like, I can go get the message to see exactly what I wrote down."

"Who covers the desk when you're at lunch?"

"Cindi, she always covers for me."

"Can you please get Cindi and tell her to come down here now, quickly? And grab the note you wrote down and bring it here."

"Yes, Detective, right away."

"Sgt. Allen, come in. You got that warrant for me?

"Umm, no, I don't. I'm not quite sure I understand what you're asking me, Detective?"

"What the fu–, what do you not understand? I asked you to print the arrest warrant for Mr. Nicholas Rossi."

"I, don't know," the befuddled sergeant stammered.

"Is there a problem, sergeant?" scolded Detective Martin who was losing his battle for composure.

"I think, yes, there is."

"You wanted to see me?" asked the very confused backup receptionist, Cindi.

"Cindi, great! Come in here, join the party!" said Detective Martin who was moving ever so closer to the maniacal side.

"Um, okay."

"Wait. Marcia, anything?"

"Sorry Detective, just like I told you," said Marcia who handed the note to Detective Martin. He glanced at it and threw it away.

"Cindi, my dear Cindi, please tell me, what time did Detective Kelly come in here today?"

"Oh my God, I am so sorry! This is all my fault. I didn't sign him in. I didn't even think of it, you know? I mean, he is – he was a detective, so I didn't even think I needed to sign him in. I am so sorry," said Cindi.

Heartly Law?

"Cindi, I am not mad at you.. This is not about you not signing in a retired detective. I just need you to think, to remember, what time did Kelly come in today?"

"Well, I sat down at 1:30. I wasn't sitting very long. I returned a couple emails. I would say between 1:40 and 1:45. Definitely not later than 1:45. I know I hadn't been sitting there that long."

"Did Kelly say anything to you?"

"We had a little small talk. He was dressed in civilian clothes, so I told him that retirement looked good on him. We laughed a bit. Then he asked who was second in charge of the St. Mary's shootings behind you," said Cindi nervously.

"Go on."

"I said that I wasn't really sure who was second in charge, but that Officer Flynn was spending a lot of time working those cases. He didn't know who Flynn was, so I told him where his desk was, and he said he was going back to speak to him. That's really all that was said."

"He actually asked for the second in charge? He didn't ask for me? And I'm guessing you didn't know that he called earlier, now did you?"

"I had no idea he called earlier. I wasn't on the phones until 1:30."

"Did you know what time he left?"

"No. Come to think of it, he didn't leave out the front, he didn't walk past me. I would have said goodbye. I guess he went out the back or side door."

"So you didn't know that he called earlier and asked me to meet him, and you weren't aware that when he showed up, I was already out of the building?" Everyone else in the office remained silent as Detective Martin pieced the puzzle together out loud. "And he asked to speak to the SECOND in charge, he didn't ask to speak to me, why is that? Why is that, I'll tell you why, it's easy. He knew I wasn't here, because he left a phone message with Marcia to get me to go to St. Mary's at 2:00. He knew that Cindi would be unaware of that fact, and that Marcia would not be at the desk at 1:30. Jesus Christ, what gives?" Detective Martin turned back to the stunned onlookers. "Cindi, what time did that attorney get here?"

"2:00. As soon as she walked in the door, the time clock behind me on the counter struck, loudly. For some reason that old thing tics hard at the top of the hour. She arrived about 15 to 20 minutes after Detective Kelly."

Martin stopped pacing. The office full of people awaited his next move. "Sgt. Allen, the warrant please."

"You try, sir," said the desk sergeant.

"Alright, fine, I'll print the warrant myself. " Detective Martin sat at his desk and typed at his computer for a couple minutes. He paused. There was more typing. Another longer pause. Then one final attempt, "R-O-S-S-I. Nothing. Absolutely nothing is popping up," said the detective. "Sergeant, do you know why the active warrant for Nicholas Rossi is not showing?"

"Try the released section, sir"

"Released section? Here it is. In the released, non-active section. Wow wee, this certainly is not good. Sergeant?"

"Yes, Detective Martin?"

"Can you please tell me what I'm looking at?" asked the Detective Martin who sought confirmation.

"Certainly, sir."

"When it says that this warrant has been released and is no longer active, who does it say did that?"

"That would be you, Detective Martin," said the sergeant.

"I see. And what time does it say this formerly active warrant was released, sergeant?"

"Approximately 14:02 today, sir." There was dead silence in the room. After a long silent pause, the sergeant attempted to explain. "You see, sir, when you asked me to pull and print the warrant, I found that it was no longer active, just like you did. Then when I saw that it was you who released it less than two hours ago, I just thought it was an odd request, thus my confusion. But I didn't know, until just now, that you were not in the building at that time, sir. I had no idea."

"That explains your hesitation, but please continue. Explain to me, as you just pointed out, how could I have released this warrant when I was not in the building. How does this work?"

"Well, sir, it's actually kind of slick. When warrants are issued, the only people who can release them are the lead detectives in the case, the one exception being a court order. If a judge files a court order to release the warrant, then the system administrator could then release it. Short of that, the only two people who could have released this warrant were you and Detective Kelly. But then since Detective Kelly is retired, the system would no longer recognize his credentials. So, absent a court order, which there is none, you are literally the only person who could have released that warrant. It's kind of a safeguard in the system to make sure nobody but the lead detectives can release a warrant without a court order. And a lead detective can only release a warrant after first logging into the system with the proper credentials – which you did, sir, at 14:01 hours."

"And, so there is absolutely no confusion, you all realize that I was not physically present in the building at 14:01 hours, correct?"

"No reason to doubt you, sir."

"Is there any way we can make it active again," asked Detective Martin, who already knew the answer.

"No sir. Once it's released, it's gone for good. Process has to start over. You need a judge to sign off on a new warrant."

Martin began to spin in his chair like a little kid. He stopped just short of saying "wheeee." The onlookers in his office did not know if he was ready to cry, or ready to have a heart attack, or ready for his head to explode. After a few more spins, he addressed them. "Well, thank you all. Thank you all for your assistance. You are all performing your jobs quite admirably, and I am glad we are all working together. Now if you don't mind, please excuse yourself from my office. Except you, Officer Flynn. Please, pull of a chair."

Chapter Nineteen

After the sergeant and the two receptionists vacated the office, Officer Flynn took a seat in front of Detective Martin's desk. Martin reclined in his chair with his feet up on the shelf behind his desk and stared out of the window, motionless. Officer Flynn remained still, though nerves got to him. He tapped his finger on his leg. After five minutes of calm nothing, Detective Martin put his feet down and spun around to his desk.

"You know, Flynn, Kelly always had a pocket flask with him. Always filled with some top-of-the-line hooch. The really, really good stuff. Funny things was, he rarely drank it. Once, maybe twice a year at most, would he take a swig. Only in very stressful times. I really wish he was here now, for many reasons, as I'm sure you've guessed. If he was here right now, I'd certainly ask him for a swig."

"Would you like me to make a run to the store for you?"

"No, but thanks for the offer, because now, I have to grill you. My own subordinate officer whom I've hand-picked to help me. Flynn," said Detective Martin with laser focus, "I need you to be precise with your answers. And just so we're clear, I am not mad at you. You have not disappointed me, and you are doing a fine job. I just need certainty in your response. *Capisci?*"

"Yes, certainly," said Officer Flynn.

"Start by telling me what you were doing immediately prior to your encounter with Kelly, and how that all transpired."

"I was writing a report."

"By hand or on the computer?" asked Martin.

"Computer, sir. I was writing a report from a witness of the church shooting. I heard a little bit of commotion. Well, not necessarily commotion, just an increase in the noise level. I lifted my head from the computer and I noticed him walking down the hall toward me. I didn't know who he was, but people were coming up to greet him and they all shook his hand. After a minute or so, he came over to my desk. He said something along the lines of 'You must be Officer Flynn,' or something like that. So I got up from behind the desk and shook his hand and said 'yeah, that's me.' He introduced himself to me as Francis Kelly, and I said 'Detective Kelly?,' and he said yeah, but now it's Retired Detective Kelly."

"Then what? Did you stay standing, did he stand?"

"I grabbed a chair and pulled it over for him. Then I sat on the front of my desk as we talked for a little."

"Go on, Flynn" said the detective who dissected every one of Flynn's words.

"Like I said earlier, it started to get a little weird," said Officer Flynn as he squirmed in his chair.

"Why weird? How weird? You are just talking. What did he drop his pants or something?"

"No, sir, nothing like that. It was a feeling. It gave me a weird vibe. He started to say some stuff." Flynn paused.

"Okay, good, Flynn, now we're getting somewhere. He was saying things that gave you a weird feeling. That's your cop's intuition. For your generation, it's like Spidey-senses, get it?"

"Yeah, I guess. Well, he started saying that he's heard all about me, that I'm doing a great job and already have a good reputation."

"How is that possible, Flynn? You didn't get transferred here until after the second shooting, when it looked like Kelly wasn't coming back. You were at Zone 3 for the first nine months of your career. Did your paths ever cross when you were at Zone 3?"

"No, they did not. I never met Detective Kelly until today."

"So how is it possible for him to believe that you're doing a great job and that you have a great reputation? You don't know him. You never met him. How would he know that?"

"He said that he heard those things from you. He said you talk me up all the time to him. Said you told him that I was one of the finest young officers you've seen in a while, which I should take as a compliment because you came up through the ranks with some fine policemen," said Officer Flynn, somewhat embarrassed.

"He told you that I said those things to him? That I talk you up to him?" asked Detective Martin.

Heartly Law?

"Yes, sir, and that was the start of my weird feeling. Because, sir, and I mean no disrespect, I told him that hearing that praise coming from you was a bit shocking. I told him that at times, you can get on my case pretty good."

"Okay, well, he broke you down and now you're being honest with him. What did he say then?"

"He kind of shrugged it off and said 'that's just Ben being Ben' and that I should be proud that you've taken an interest in my career."

"Standard playbook is in effect."

"Sir?"

Detective Martin paused for a moment, then chuckled slightly to himself. "There was more to this conversation, right?"

"A little bit more, and that's when it really got weird for me. He said something to the effect of, if I was lucky enough to live as long as him, I would run into people I've known their whole life, as if he was saying he knew me my whole life. Or he at least knew of me and he has kept tabs on me. My older sister, too."

"I'm sure that's what he said," said the now confident detective. "Tell me, Flynn, did he explain how he knew you for your whole life?"

"He said that when he was younger, back when he walked a beat, he befriended my parents. They were younger than him, but he knew them. That's how he knew when my older sister was born and when I was born. Said he's always kept tabs on us both."

Detective Martin slammed his fist on his desk and put his face into his hands as he mumbled "teachable moment, teachable moment, don't be a dick, Martin." The detective sat up in his chair and addressed the rookie cop.

"Okay, Officer Flynn, I am now, slightly disappointed in you. By the looks of you, you still have no idea what happened, right?"

"I'm sorry, sir, I do not. I don't remember a situation like this in the academy."

"Where exactly did you grow up, Flynn?"

"Mt. Lebanon."

"To your knowledge, does the City of Pittsburgh Police Department dispatch officers to walk a beat in a South Hills suburb well beyond city limits?"

"No, sir. I have never heard of such a thing."

"And to your knowledge, does the Mt. Lebanon Police Department dispatch officers to walk a beat?"

"Sir, I haven't lived in Lebo for some time, but to the best of my knowledge no, sir, not that I'm aware of."

"Correct again, Officer Flynn. So please explain to me how it's possible that a city cop walking a beat in the City of Pittsburgh would befriend your parents who lived in Mt. Lebanon."

Officer Flynn sunk in his chair and said nothing. Detective Martin continued his line of questioning. "Did your parents, by any chance, have a job in the city?"

Dry mouth overwhelmed the young officer who struggled to speak. "No, sir. My dad worked in Washington County, and my mom stayed at home with me and my sister."

Detective Martin said nothing for a moment. Flynn wasn't certain if the detective was thinking of more questions or planning on just how he would kill him and conceal the body. After an excruciating pause, the detective continued. "If your dad worked in Washington County and your mom stayed at home, then how is it possible that Detective Kelly would befriend either of them when he was walking a beat in the City of Pittsburgh?"

Officer Flynn sunk lower in his chair and put his head down. He could not even look at the detective anymore. "I guess that means Detective Kelly lied to me, sir. But why would he lie?"

"Son, from now on, you are not permitted to ask me 'why' about anything that pertains to this case. I don't have those answers. But I can tell you exactly what went down here today, pay attention. Kelly calls the station, leaves a message with the receptionist to tell me to meet him at St. Mary's Church at 2:00. That gets me out of the building. Then he arrives shortly after 1:30 when the receptionist who took the message wouldn't be at the desk. Whoever was covering the desk would have no knowledge of the phone call and supposed meeting with me and Kelly at 2:00. Then he comes back here to you and initiates 'Good Cop Bad Cop,' which he executes flawlessly. I've seen him do it hundreds of times, and if you haven't guessed, he's always the good cop. What makes this time especially impressive is that he was still able to make me the Bad Cop even though I wasn't even here. He pumped your ego a little bit, then was ever so slightly dismissive of me while at the same time recognizing that I am tough on you. That made you start to like him because he showed you sympathy along with praise. Then he name-dropped your parents and sister, people you most likely love and trust, as a reference to his good nature. That caused you to trust him. How long did you two talk?"

"Two, maybe three minutes at the most."

"And what were you doing before you started to talk with him?"

"I was on my computer, typing reports."

"How long does it take before your computer times out and you have to log back in?"

"I guess about 10 minutes or so."

"What happened next, Flynn?"

"I got a call from the front. Attorney Jeannette Royale wanted to see me, so I left Detective Kelly and went up front to reception."

"And you did so without shutting down your computer." Detective Martin paused for a minute. "When you left, Kelly was sitting in front of your desk. When you got out of sight, he went behind your desk and jumped onto your computer, which wouldn't have timed out by that point. You got to the front damn near 14:00, and at 14:01 he was using my credentials, which I'm certain he knows, to log into the warrant section, so by 14:02, the warrant for Nicholas Rossi was released, never to return. Then he slipped out the back or side door after shaking a few more hands. Game over."

Officer Flynn sat in shock and horror. After a minute of silence, he tried to speak. "Detective Martin, I am truly sorry. I had no idea. I never would have guessed, never would have seen that coming in a million years. If you want to reassign me or even transfer me, I understand."

"Stop that. I am not pleased, I think you should have picked up on the whole beat cop in Mt. Lebo thing, that should have raised some red flags. But I've seen him work this routine on people who have a thousand times more street smarts than you. He is the master.

And before you ask me why would he do that, because I know you want to, I will simply tell you that I DO NOT KNOW. Now, please get back to work. I need to you do, something. And just to be sure we're covering our bases, call and double check with your sister. Don't bother your parents, no sense getting them worked up. But call your sister just to make absolutely certain that she does not know who Detective Francis Kelly is. Can you do that please?

"Yes, sir. I'll call her now. Sir, I mean it, I am really –"

"GO NOW!" Detective Martin sat at his desk for a few minutes, shut down his computer, and got ready to go home for an early day.

Chapter Twenty

Marcus Flynn limped back to his desk with his tail between his legs, embarrassed by how easily he was duped. "No wonder people don't trust cops," he said to himself. He sat for a minute in his chair before he called his sister.

"Hey, little brother, what's up?" said Dr. Abigail Flynn, still sitting in the La Prima coffee shop in the Strip District.

"Hi Abs. You got a minute to talk?"

"I'm meeting a client in a bit, but I have some time. Are you okay, Marcus? I worry so much about you in your job."

"I'm fine, nothing wrong. I just had a very strange interaction today. I wanted to talk to you about it."

"Do you need to make an appointment," said Dr. Flynn, partially in jest.

"I don't think it's that serious, probably nothing at all. I met a guy today, I swear I never met him before, but he said he knew me. Said he knew you and our parents as well. His name is Francis Kelly. Detective Francis Kelly. Do you know him? Does that name ring a bell?"

"Not off the top of my head? Where is he from? What does he look like?"

"Nothing special about him. He was in street clothes when I met him, looks like a typical grandfatherly kind of guy. Nondescript."

"You aren't giving me a lot to go on. Did he say anything about me?"

"He just said you were smart and you were cute, that's all."

"Clearly he knows me," said Abigail with a chuckle.

"Yes, clearly. Okay, thanks, I know you're busy, so am I."

"Marcus, what is this about? You don't sound like you're alright. Some rando says he knows us, maybe he does, maybe he's confused. What's it matter?"

"It probably doesn't matter, but he isn't really a rando. He's retired from here, and I replaced him when I transferred here. And he's connected to the church shooting I'm working on. So I guess I thought it was important to check in with you, that's all." There was silence on the other end except for the background noise of the café. "Sis, you still there?"

"You're working on the shooting at St. Mary's? With the priest?"

"Yeah, don't worry. It's a strange one, but I don't think it's a dangerous assignment."

"Holy shit. Literally. Marcus, I'm on that case too!"

"What?!?"

"I was retained to be part of the defense team. I'm in the Strip now, and in a couple minutes, I'm meeting with the priest as part of his initial forensic interview. Marcus, are you still there?"

"I said this case is strange, and now it's even stranger. Is it a conflict that you and I are on the same case? I mean, since I'm trying to build the case against him and you're trying to help him out. Is that a conflict?"

"I don't know for sure. But the conflict isn't on my end, he can hire whomever he wants and you guys can't say 'no' to that. Besides, this is a private case. I'm not walking away from it. I need the money."

"Okay, it's cool, do your thing." Marcus dropped the phone from his ear for a second as he pulled his hair back and muttered *Jesus H. Christ* under his breath before he continued. "I'll raise the issue with my superior, no worries. But I think it's wise if we have, uh, no further communication about it, until it's resolved."

"I agree with that. And sorry, but I have to go now."

"Get to it. I'll talk to you later," said Officer Flynn. He ended the call and sat at his desk in silence for 10 minutes. With his courage finally built up, he rose from his desk and walked down to Detective Martin's Office. "Sir," he said, "I think we have another issue."

Dr. Abigail Flynn closed her laptop and placed it in her work bag alongside her multiple notepads. She headed down the block to the rectory at St. Mary's Church to meet Father O'Toole for his first forensic interview.

116

Chapter Twenty-one

"Nice to meet you. I'm Dr. Abigail Flynn, and I'm here to conduct phase one of your forensic interview. Is this still a good time for you?" asked Dr. Flynn.

"Nice to meet you, lass. Yes, now is good. Pretty much any time is good. Not a lot of commitments these days, no pun intended," said the priest. "Please come inside."

Father O'Toole's comment drew a bit of a look from Dr. Flynn as she stepped inside the enormous rectory. "Wow, I had no idea this place was so big."

"Yes, at a time when it was built, there would have been numerous priests living here. Sort of a frat house for the holy. But now, just me. I used to have a secretary who worked here, but she's been dismissed, poor thing. But before we start, I have a quick question. You said you're here for a 'forensic interview.' I'm not sure what that is. My attorney said that I have to talk to you as part of my defense. He didn't say I needed a 'forensic interview?' Is this for the newspaper or something?"

"Not at all. Why don't we go somewhere where you'll be comfortable, and I'll explain the process to you, okay?"

"Let's go to my study. It's cozy there." The two proceeded through the rectory until they came to Father O'Toole's study. There was a couch and an oversized chair with an ottoman along with several shelves overflowing with books. In the corner of the study was an antique rolltop desk complete with an inkwell and quill pen and a half-empty bottle of Jameson with two crystal rocks glasses.

"My dear, can I get you a cup of coffee?"

"No thank you, I just finished one."

"Do you mind if I get one before we start?"

"Please do. Whatever you need to be comfortable."

"Very good," said O'Toole. In a couple minutes, he returned from the kitchen with a steaming mug full of coffee. He walked over to the desk and grabbed the bottle of Jameson.

"Excuse me, Father O'Toole," said the somewhat stunned Dr. Flynn.

"What? Oh, just a little sweetener for my coffee. You said whatever I need to feel comfortable. Just two fingers worth. The nerves, lass, the nerves."

"Just a little. Being under the influence will wreck the whole interview. Fix your coffee, then sit where you feel most comfortable."

"You don't want me to lie down on the couch?"

"You can if you want to, but you don't have to. This isn't like the movies. You can sit, stand, or lie down. Whatever is easiest for you."

"Very well. I choose comfy chair."

"May I sit at your desk?" asked the doctor.

Father O'Toole nodded. He sat in his chair and placed his feet up on the ottoman.

"Here's how this goes. I'm a psychologist, and I am going to give you a forensic interview. It's different from the therapy you'd receive from a psychiatrist. In therapy, you address your problems, your phobias, your mental hang-ups, and you receive therapy in order to try to overcome them. My forensic interview, on the other hand, is used to determine if something happened in your life, as a child or young adult, some form of victimization, some form of neglect, anything that I can uncover that may help to explain your actions. Maybe it will lead to a diagnosis."

"My actions?"

"Yes, your actions," said Dr. Flynn as she picked up some pre-written notes and feigned as though she was reviewing them. "Your action being that you shot a Mr. Nicholas Rossi," she said in a deliberate tone. She stared right at him to gauge his reaction.

"I never shot Nico. Never," said the defiant priest without hesitation.

"Right. Attorney Meyer did tell me that. I wasn't there so I don't know, and I am not here to judge you. I just want to dig into your past a little bit, and when I'm done, I will write up a report of my findings. That report will be given to your attorney as well as the DA's office. How they choose to use the information, that's on them. Maybe something inside the report can help your attorney with a defense strategy."

"And if it can't, it's of no value to him?"

"Then if you're found guilty, and that's a big *if* because you didn't shoot anybody, but if you are found guilty, then the information inside can be used as mitigation at your sentencing hearing. And because the information I gather will be used as either defense strategy or possibly mitigation, it's crucial that you be completely honest with me every step of the way. Do you understand the process now?"

"Yes, I do."

"Great. Then I am going to ask you a few questions. I want you to do most of the talking."

"Irish people excel in that area."

"Tell me whatever is on your mind, and when I need to redirect you or if I have other questions, I will ask them. How would you describe yourself, besides being a priest?"

"I'm not a priest at the moment."

"Until recently, you were a priest. But you weren't born a priest. Who was Thomas O'Toole before he was a priest?"

Father O'Toole paused. "I've been a priest for so many years. So many years that my life before priesthood seems like it wasn't even mine. I was a street kid when I was very young. Then I played baseball for a short time. Then I was a soldier. Then I became a priest, many many years ago. There you have it. Interview over now?"

"Not quite. Few more questions. Did you have a family when you were growing up? Mother, father, brothers and sisters?"

"I did have a family, for a very short time," said Father O'Toole with a touch of sadness in his voice. He took a large gulp of coffee that had cooled from his sweetener.

"Tell me about your family, about being a street kid, what you remember. Seems like a good place to start"

Father O'Toole took another large sip of coffee and set his mug down on the table beside him. He sunk into his oversized comfy chair as his mind started to think about long ago, nearly forgotten times. "Some of what I know was told to me by nuns, teachers. Some of it I learned, and some it, I can remember."

Chapter Twenty-two

Colin O'Toole and Mary Margaret Flaherty were forced to leave Ireland due to a potato blight, and they had even greater fortune to arrive in America just at the start of the Great Depression. The two hadn't known each other in Ireland, and their journey across the Atlantic was separated by two months. Like many Irish immigrants before them, they both settled in the Strip District of the City of Pittsburgh. At that time, the Strip District was nothing more than a shantytown of homemade shacks cobbled together from discarded materials scavenged from adjacent industrial sites. Like Ireland, most shacks had sod roofs and offered little shelter when the rain turned the dirt roads of their foundation into streams of slow mud and industrial ooze. The Strip District of that time was the polar opposite of the half million-dollar condominiums and high-tech office parks that live there today. Back then, child labor-filled sweatshops and factories spewed as much pollution as the unregulated steel mills that dwarfed the shanty shacks in front of them. An endless stream of trains that moved coal from mines in West Virginia to steel mills throughout Pittsburgh and the Mon Valley would nearly topple the shanty shacks from the vibration of their transit. The residents counted themselves lucky when a few pieces of coal would fall from the hopper cars since it was the only source of heating fuel these cold immigrants had to almost warm their shacks to barely above freezing in the winter, which seemed to last about nine months.

Colin O'Toole devoted every waking minute, six days a week, to working or looking for work. But the seventh day was reserved for church. The newly erected St. Mary's Parish, with its Romanesque design and two golden domes, always shone brightly despite the crud in the air or the dismal weather. It was satiation for the spirit and the one beacon of hope in the shantytown. Colin's faith and devotion to God eased his mind and enabled him to keep driving every day when he was hungry and tired. Father Cox, the new pastor of St. Mary's Parish, utilized Colin's volunteer services every Sunday. Colin's duties ranged from repairing or cleaning something in the church to running errands.

One particular Sunday when Colin was running a church errand, his path crossed with Mary Margaret Flaherty. After talking for a couple minutes, Colin invited her to attend Mass with him the following week. She agreed and the two sat together that Sunday morning. A courtship soon followed, and a few months after that, Father Cox performed their wedding in St. Mary's Parish.

In typical Irish-Catholic fashion, the two newlyweds immediately started to grow their family. Within four years, Colin and Mary Margaret had three sons: James, Mark, and Matthew. Although the extra mouths to feed caused additional stress, Colin and Mary felt joyous and truly blessed. To Colin, who was especially in love with his family, it didn't seem quite so dirty anymore, it never seemed to be as cold as it used to be, and his work wasn't quite as arduous as it once was. Their proudest moment came every week when they went to mass on Sunday and sat together as a family.

A couple years later, Colin felt it was time to teach his boys to work so they could contribute to the family. The fact that the O'Toole boys were "babies" by just about anyone's standard did not absolve them from their responsibility. Their first job was to walk along the train tracks to gather the coal that had fallen from the trains and bring it home for the large cast-iron pot that burned in the middle of the house. James O'Toole, six years old and the eldest of the boys, took the lead on all matters regarding coal gathering and delivery. He was quick to show his two apprentices, middle child Mark and youngest brother Matthew, how best to choose from the discarded coal along the tracks. A crumbly piece would burn too quickly and was very dirty, but a rock-hard, shiny black glass-like piece was optimal. James was also the safety supervisor. He demonstrated the proper technique of walking on the tracks so as not to get a foot caught between the railroad ties and risk a sprained ankle, or worse. He also emphasized quickly removing oneself from the vicinity if a train could be heard even in the distance.

Heartly Law?

Colin was a hardworking man who would walk barefoot across the top of the filthy Monongahela River if his family needed it. The only thing greater than the love he had for his family was his desire to make their lives better than tolerable. Colin would do anything from sweeping floors to cleaning out slaughterhouses and everything else imaginable. Every cent he made was spent on food and clothing for his family. But every Sunday was reserved for church work.

With great assistance from Father Cox, Colin secured a job as a laborer on the railroad. Although the pay was only slightly better than what he was earning doing his freelance work, the employment was steady and much more dependable. Mary Margaret also began to earn as a seamstress. It was a trade that she could practice despite her constant state of pregnancy and child-raising. After a few years, the two saved enough money to buy a house in the Strip District. Technically it qualified as a "house" since it had four adjoining walls, although only three of them had brick on the outside and none of them were insulated. There was no running water or indoor plumbing, but there were actual windows with glass that could be opened and closed, and there was a solid roof on top that kept everyone dry inside. There was also not just a pot but an actual pot belly stove inside the living room/kitchen that Mary could use for cooking and that kept the house a bit more above freezing in the winter. Very basic ductwork also ran from the stove into the two other rooms — one bedroom for the children and the other for the parents — so that they too could be slightly heated.

The newly found sense of privacy got the best of Mary and Colin and soon, Mary Margaret was again blessed with child. The family celebrated the pregnancy. The boys hoped and cheered for a little sister, and the parents prayed for health and thanked God for the additional gift from heaven. Colin and family believed that God had personally touched their lives with so much joy and hope for the future.

Although blessed at that moment, all the strength in Colin's back was not enough to prevent the sort of tragedy that only seems to afflict the Irish, especially at those times when much brighter days appear near on the horizon. The midwife whom Colin hired to assist with the birth was one of the best in the area, and the pregnancy seemed rather routine. It was Mary Margaret's fourth child, and there were no issues of any sort with the first three deliveries. The pregnancy was normal. Mary suffered from fatigue and the occasional bout of morning sickness, but nothing unusual. In fact, she continued to sew and mend all the way up to the day of delivery. The nine months' time passed by quickly and uneventfully, both of which were considered blessings.

When it was clear that Mary Margaret was heading into labor, Colin sent James to summon the midwife, who hastened to the O'Toole house. Water was set to boil on the stove and actual clean towels and wash cloths were prepared. The midwife helped Mary deliver their newborn son, Thomas, in a rather uneventful birth. Although Thomas appeared to be healthy, it was clear that he was undersized compared to his brothers at the time of their births.

Colin held his wife's hand throughout the delivery. Matthew and James took turns wiping her face with clean rags. The midwife cut the cord and cleaned the newborn with warm, wet towels, but Mary Margaret could not get comfortable and started to complain of severe pain that she hadn't experienced with the other deliveries. The midwife discovered that Thomas was born slightly smaller than his three brothers because he was sharing space with another child. This baby girl, who was Thomas's twin sister, was breach.

Even the greatest and most talented of midwives could not remedy a breach child. The trauma and the blood loss were too much for Mary Margaret, who died an extraordinarily painful death in the arms of her loving husband amidst the soft cries of her three sons and even softer cry of her newborn child. James held the baby while the midwife scrambled to do something to save the girl. It wasn't long before the unbaptized, unnamed twin sister of Thomas O'Toole suffocated, and all movement stopped. The newborn cried as he sought to be nursed. Colin was paralyzed by the shock and sadness of the unexpected event and was helpless to do anything but hold his deceased wife.

Catholic custom did not allow for an unbaptized child to be buried in a Catholic cemetery, but Father Cox said nothing as the child was laid to rest alongside his mother in the same casket, although the child's name was not put on the headstone. There was no funeral home viewing or even a Mass, just a few prayers said and a blessing with holy water. Colin dug his own wife and child's grave in order to save money.

Following the death of his wife, Colin secured the services of local Irish women from shantytown to help him raise Thomas, the newborn. At times, Colin offered the women slight compensation from his railroad earnings. If he was short on money, he would lend her family his physical talents in some way, usually with a house repair or a collection of coal for their stoves.

Tragedy, however, was just beginning its path of epic destruction over the O'Toole family. Less than a year after the death of his mother, her second born son, Mark O'Toole, was killed by a train while gathering coal from the tracks. Again, Colin secured and comforted himself and tried to do the same for his surviving children, with his religion and faith, both of which waned.

James, the oldest of the O'Toole children, was now eight years old and able to get work in a local sweatshop as a floor sweeper. After a time, the adult workers would tie a thick wool rope around his waist and lower him down through the multiple chimneys so that he could clean them. He acted as a cross between a chimney sweep and a human Q-tip for industrial chimneys. Nobody at that time had a problem with an eight-year old boy working 12-hour days hanging from the waist by a rope in the heart of an industrial chimney. OSHA would not exist for another three decades. Colin thought that hard work would be good for the boy and would keep him out of trouble. And of course, the additional income helped the family.

As time went on, the Colin and his three remaining sons adjusted to loss and survival and continued to trudge ahead. Their days were filled with hard work, except for Sunday, which was filled with both hard prayer and hard work for their parish.

Chapter Twenty-three

Normally Father O'Toole's voice boomed even in casual conversation, but the recollection of his family history had reduced it to a reluctant monotone that at times seemed to fight its way from his mouth. He reached to the table beside him and took another drink of his special coffee. Dr. Flynn eyed the bottle of whiskey and the rocks glass on the desk where she worked. Father O'Toole continued with his tale.

Just when family life for the O'Tooles felt at least regular again, a giant explosion in the Strip District rattled the tin roofs and shook the shacks of the shantytown. Word spread through the rail workers that the enormous explosion came from the fabric mill where Colin O'Toole's oldest son, James, was employed. Colin could not leave the railroad to go to the mill until his shift was over for fear of losing his job. It wasn't as if there was a shortage of Irish immigrant workers willing to take his place if he displeased his employers.

By the time Colin arrived, several hundred mill employees both young and old were scrambling or moping about in search of loved ones and coworkers. The ones who survived the blast appeared even more wretched than usual as they limped and staggered around in circles. Several held dirty oily rags against their head or face in a feeble attempt to stop bleeding. Many a man found that his hair was burned off his head and his clothing was smoldering and full of burn holes from exploding flaming fabric that sprayed the entire area like a double-barrel shotgun blast straight out of Hell. The only parts of their faces and hands that were not caked in dark black soot were the ones where the skin had been ripped or burned off from the explosion. The exposed pink skin juxtaposed to black soot and dirty singed hair made them look like discarded calico cats, only more pathetic.

The "fire department" was nothing more than volunteers who had access to a hand pump that could spray water almost 50 feet mounted on the back of an old wooden wagon towed by an even older horse of some kind. It would be years until the city had an actual professional fire department and first responder unit on the payroll. The hand pump had a small reservoir which required constant refill. Two men operated the pump while a slew of volunteers, both regulars and those who simply jumped in to assist, shuttled wooden buckets of water 200 yards from the river to the wagon. The water pump was ineffective, and the fire would have burned itself out with or without the modest amount of water it sprayed. Still, the firemen were ceaseless in their efforts due to a subconscious need to try to help and not just sit back and do nothing.

As Colin navigated through the chaos, he looked up at the factory to find that half of it was blown away while the other half smoldered and crumbled before his eyes. St. Mary's Church could now be seen in the background. As far as Colin could see, the church was undamaged since the brunt of the explosion was directed away from it. Colin stared at the church through thick black smoke, and his eyes immediately focused on the two golden domes that shone brightly. For a brief instance, Colin had hope that God had protected his son and that maybe for the first time in his life, Colin and James would have received the Luck of the Irish.

As Colin searched for his son, he could not avoid the pungent smells of burned hair, burned flesh, and burned fabric as well as the sulphuric smells from all the burning oils, grease, and solvents inside the factory. It had been years since Colin had experienced this odor, but it was something he was all too familiar with. It was the smell of death. Colin first smelled the unmistakable and unforgettable scent of death as it hung in the air over the blighted potato farms and poured out of the rustic cottages with sod roofs. No matter how hard the wind blew in Ireland, the smell of death never retreated. The smell he experienced at the factory was even worse than Colin remembered, as though he was standing in the middle of Hell and the smell had come from Satan himself. Unfortunately, he'd become an authority on how Hell smelled and looked.

Heartly Law?

On a small hillside away from the din and chaos laid a small body covered by a greasy burlap sack. Colin approached the body and drew down the burlap to reveal the badly burned face and broken limbs of his first son, James O'Toole, whose body still smoldered. James was inside a chimney at the time of the explosion, and the force of the explosion on the floor of the factory sent him up and out of the chimney like a human shotgun slug to his landing place about 200 yards from the site. Colin could only hope that his son died instantly and did not experience the flight through the air and crash to the ground. The explosion in the sweatshop had taken his life along with the lives of many other immigrant children and adults. Colin covered his son's face with the burlap sack, hoisted his limp body over his shoulder, and trudged to St. Mary's. This trek was all too familiar for Colin, who could do nothing but pray the entire way to the church. The realization that more than half his family would soon be in the cemetery was more than even a hard-bitten Irish immigrant could bear.

Colin began to sob. He attempted to pray away the flow of tears, but instead his sobs grew into a full-blown weep. He wept for his young wife, for his three dead children, for the home and family farm he left behind in Ireland, but mostly he wept for his acceptance that all the hopes and dreams of a better way of life in America would never come to fruition. He found the strength to keep walking, and when he arrived at St. Mary's rectory, he rang the bell and waited for Father Cox to open the door. Father Cox arrived at the door, and neither man spoke a word as Colin entered the rectory with his dead son in his arms.

Chapter Twenty-four

"You see, lass," said Father O'Toole with a matter of fact tone in his voice that seemed impossible to resonate from a human being under his circumstances, "I had to learn that piece of my family history. I was too young to know any of it as it happened. It was told to me in pieces and bits over the years by the nuns, my teachers. But Matthew...I lived through Matthew. Sweet Jesus, do I miss him still."

Matthew O'Toole was the youngest of the three original O'Toole boys and was not quite three years older than Thomas. He was bright, kind, and pleasant despite living most of his short life in gloom, tragedy, and desperation.

Colin's financial struggle escalated after his wife's seamstress money and James's child labor wages ceased. It became difficult for Colin to make the mortgage payment on their "house," and food was now a luxury. The income loss led to cutbacks in staff, thus the neighborhood ladies who aided Colin in raising his boys were let go. Some ladies offered their services free of charge, but Colin's Irish pride would not allow him to become a charity case under any circumstances.

Even though Matthew was old enough to get a job in a mill or factory, Colin decided that Matthew would instead stay at home to be the one to tend to Thomas. Colin figured that the little money that Matthew could earn in a mill or factory would only be enough to pay the wages of a sitter for Thomas. It did not seem wise to make Matthew risk his life in horrid conditions only to use his wages to pay others. And more urgently, Colin could not bear the thought of losing another son in an industrial accident. Thus, Colin decided that after his shift on the railroad ended, he would do additional odd jobs, while Matthew's job would be to tend, or rather raise, little Thomas.

Matthew's day was filled with duties and obligations and began by taking his younger brother to St. Mary's Church for a hot bowl of soup and a couple pieces of bread from the soup line. Colin did not see that as a handout and justified it based upon all the volunteer work that he had done for the Church. It was a rather long walk to the soup line for two small boys, and oftentimes they were both hungry again by the time they returned home.

Matthew's second duty was buying and preparing dinner for the three of them with whatever change his father would leave for him. Any scraps not eaten at dinner would be packed up in the same brown paper bag used over and over again for Colin's lunch the next day.

Matthew learned to go to the soup line later in the day instead of first thing in the morning. If it looked as though not all the bread would be consumed that day, soup line workers often gave extra to Matthew. If his father ever asked him about it, he would lie to him and tell him that he was able to buy it with the money his dad left for him. He knew his dad would not approve of a handout.

But many times, there was no extra bread. And sometimes, the money left for Matthew was not enough for one meal, let alone three. When this situation arose, Matthew had no choice but to steal food, and Matthew was a horrible thief who was often caught in the act. But as soon as a shopkeeper or street vendor took one look at Matthew's malnourished face and that of his younger brother Thomas, they would allow Matthew to keep what he took as long as he promised that he would not steal again. Matthew always kept that promise, not because he actually meant it, but rather because he did not want to press his luck by being caught by the same shopkeeper twice.

One time, after getting caught trying to steal a can of beans, a shopkeeper was so moved by how wretched Matthew and Thomas appeared that he gave Matthew enough food for one decent dinner, free of charge. Matthew took the food home and hid it from his father. He then spaced it out for "dinner" and "lunch" for almost two weeks. He saved all the change that his father would leave for him and instead of buying more food, he bought Thomas a new pair of shoes.

Matthew had enough sense to buy the shoes bigger than needed — almost four sizes bigger. He stuffed them with old newspaper so that they would stay on Thomas's feet, then he scuffed and dirtied them so that his father would not be suspicious. It was the first new pair of shoes Thomas ever wore. Previous shoes were first worn by his three older brothers, so by the time they made it to Thomas there was not much left of them. Oftentimes the shoes had already fallen apart. If he was lucky, the makeshift repairs made by his mother would hold up. If not, his feet would get soaked when it rained.

Matthew grew tired and lonely. He missed his sweet mother and his older brothers, and he was scared. He was no longer a happy and pleasant child. He was anxious because he was running out of places to steal food. The stress of this existence, if you could call it that, was making him sick. It was more than any seven-year old could endure, even if the seven-year-old was the son of a tough-as-nails Irish immigrant. He missed his father. The image of a kind, sweet man who laughed and smiled when he bounced his children was just that – an image, a sad dream that haunted him even after waking up.

Colin was doing no better. He was rarely home because of his odd job work schedule and his regular railroad job. He was missing out on watching his two remaining sons grow up as the entirety of parenting was left to Matthew. When he was home, he would sleep in the living room on an old couch — a dirty, tattered, deteriorating mess that was bought second or third hand right before his wife died. Each boy now had their own bedroom, for whatever that was worth.

One rare sunny day, while Thomas was taking a nap, some neighborhood kids convinced Matthew to come outside to play with them. Desperate to get out of the house to interact with anyone other than his toddler brother, Matthew followed the neighborhood kids outside. Knowing not to wander too far from his house and not out of earshot of his sleeping brother, the boys played with rocks and sticks in the street. They played leapfrog, it-tag, and other assorted poor street kid games. For a brief moment in time, Matthew was a seven-year-old boy again. Not a surrogate father, not a would-be bread thief. He felt the sun's warmth and enjoyed it, sometimes even laughing and smiling.

As per the O'Toole legacy, all good things must come to a tragic end. Matthew did not see the jagged piece of splintered streetcar track sticking up from the ground until it damn near went through his foot while he ran and chased with the other boys. His worn-out shoes, first worn by his two older brothers, were no match for the sharp rusted piece of iron which tore a deep cut into him.

Although it caused excruciating pain and bled profusely, Matthew was more worried about what his father would say for having disobeyed him by leaving his brother at home. He did not want to be the cause of additional stress in his father's life. Matthew limped back home as best he could.

Upon his return, he found Thomas still napping in bed. Figuring that he was in the clear, Matthew bandaged his foot with an old rag he found on the street near his home. That would at least stop the bleeding. He put his shoe back on and hid the injury from his father.

A couple days later, Matthew developed a fever, and while his father was at work, Matthew died from the massive infection that spread throughout his frail, tiny body. Colin returned home after working to find Thomas lying in bed beside his dead brother. Nobody knew until afterwards what had caused Matthew to die.

Chapter Twenty-five

Colin O'Toole tried to keep it together for his last remaining son, but nightmares about his wife and children and premonitions about Thomas's impending death made it impossible for Colin to sleep. Eventually, Colin succumbed to the Irish scourge. At first, he would take a drink to help him sleep, but soon he was drinking all day. No amount of faith, no amount of prayer, and not even Father Cox could not stop the inevitable. He was, after all, poor, Irish, and heartbroken.

Functional alcoholism worked for Colin for a short time, but after a while too many mistakes on the railroad cost him his job. He returned to his old ways of walking, or rather staggering the streets to look for odd jobs that would pay a few cents. But mainly he worked for booze. He became a full-blown booze whore. He would go days without returning to his house. Lord knows how Thomas survived those days without a parent.

One day when Thomas was five years old, he woke up and found that there was not a solitary scrap of food in the house. He walked over to his dad who had passed out on the couch late in the afternoon the day before. Thomas gently woke him and helped him to get dressed for "work." Before Colin left, Thomas gave his "Daddy" a kiss on the cheek and told him that he loved him very, very much. Hearing his young son call him "Daddy" was the last remaining thing on this dreadful, God-forsaken planet that could bring a smile to Colin's face. He said nothing to Thomas and used what little strength remained in his boozed-soaked body to hold back his tears. He took a knee and hugged Thomas for several minutes. The sensation of that embrace reminded Colin of hugging his wife and other children at a time when things were tolerable. The found memory turned to razor-sharp pain and forced the beaten-down man to release his hold on his young son. He kissed Thomas on the cheek, said "I love you," and staggered out of the house. That was the last time Thomas ever saw his father.

Later that morning there was a knock on the door. Thomas answered it and found Father James R. Cox, who told Thomas that he needed some help at the church and that Thomas could earn some money. Thomas left with Father Cox. That was the last day Thomas was ever in his family home. The abandoned house was squatted in by other poor Irish until it was razed by the city in the name of urban redevelopment.

Nobody ever saw Colin O'Toole alive after that day. His body was discovered in an alley on the other side of the city, far away from his house and far, far away from his son. The only thing found in his tattered canvas wallet was a disintegrating black and white photo of a young man, a young woman, and three little boys who were diaper age. Although the picture was in very poor condition, two things were clear – the young man and woman had enormous smiles on their faces, and the picture was taken in front of St. Mary's Church.

The police officer who found the body contacted Father Cox at St. Mary's and asked if he could come down to the city morgue to identify a John Doe. Upon first look, Father Cox had no idea who he was looking at. When the police officer showed Father Cox the old picture from the wallet, Father Cox burst into tears – tears for the unrecognizable condition in which he'd found his friend; tears for the years of pain and anguish Colin endured; tears for Colin's one remaining son who would never know his father or how great a man and husband and father he was; tears for that brief instant whereupon Father Cox questioned God's plan and what was to be gained from an entire life of suffering; and even tears of joy for at last, the suffering was over and Colin was with most of his family in a far better place than a blighted farm in Ireland or a filthy infested shantytown of pain and despair in the most abandoned part of Pittsburgh.

Father Cox explained that Colin O'Toole had no remaining family except one very young son who was already in the church's custody. He told the officer that he would send for the body in the morning so that Colin would receive a proper Catholic burial. Father Cox paid the burial expenses himself and helped to dig the hole to save money. Father Cox wanted to ensure that Colin was buried beside his wife, his daughter, and his three sons. Colin O'Toole was 34 years old.

Colin was one of many unfortunate immigrants who had no choice but to abandon their family farms and escape to a distant land with nothing more than hope. Colin knew nothing of America other than the phony belief that America welcomed immigrants from all over the world, and with hard work and determination, everyone could succeed. That is, of course, if one could survive the discrimination, squalor, and lack of food. Despite his unwavering faith, his rabid devotion to his family, and his unworldly work ethic, Colin never got to experience what the Golden Door of the Statue of Liberty promised as the entrance to a land full of freedom and a better way of life. Instead, he only got to experience being tired, being poor, and being one of the huddled masses yearning to breathe free from oppression. He died alone. Welcome to America, kid.

No one but Father Cox ever knew how or why the priest showed up on that particular day to rescue Thomas. In later years, Thomas liked to believe that seeking out Father Cox on Thomas's behalf was his father's last attempt to provide for him and to do whatever he could so that Thomas might avoid the curse that decimated his family. But the Irish tend to be romantics. Even a drunken, penniless death in a cold, wet, back alley gutter can be romanticized by an Irishman with the gift of gab. Perhaps it was just luck. Lord knows, the O'Toole family was due for some luck at that point. Thomas was already poor, Irish, and heartbroken well before his sixth birthday.

Chapter Twenty-six

"That look and that hug from my daddy, I will never forget that. I don't know if you'd consider that a traumatic experience. I do not, but that image and feeling, it's like a scar on my brain that won't fade. But it's a good scar, at times, if there is such a thing," said Father O'Toole as he took another drink of coffee. "One thing is for sure. I believe the stories about my father, about how good of a man he was. But I barely remember him. I just have that feeling of his hug and that look in his eye to hang onto. I'm certain he was a good man. Wonder what he thinks of me now? Talking to a doctor one-third of my age as part of my criminal defense."

Dr. Flynn wiped her nose with a tissue, cleared her throat, and sat up straight in her chair. "After your father, you said that you were raised by a Catholic priest. Tell me about that. Did anything happen to you while you were in his care? Were there other priests or other adults? Sorry, just, you were about six years old when Father Cox took you in. Tell me about that. Hopefully you have better memories – I mean, firsthand knowledge," said Doctor Flynn who struggled with the exam.

"I remember all of it." Father O'Toole got up from his chair and went to his closet where he removed a piece of some kind of antique leather. Dr. Flynn couldn't identify it until the priest slipped it over his hand and pounded the open baseball glove with his other fist. He sat back down in his chair, put the glove over his face, and inhaled deeply through his nose. "Still smells like victory. Like freedom. Like regret," he said before he continued his story.

As Thomas grew up and developed his personality, he displayed what many a prejudiced man would say were "typical Irish" traits. It was most likely typical teenage angst, and the overwhelming Irishness of his life magnified the already intense feelings that grew inside him.

Father Cox loved Thomas and treated him like a son. And Thomas loved Father Cox, but he was still his parish priest. Thomas missed his "Daddy." He strained to remember something more specific about him, but it was like trying to remember a vague and disconnected dream. Only the scar of the last look and hug remained certain. He remembered how much his Daddy loved him and how much he loved his Daddy, and not having him to love anymore made him sad and sullen at times. The only thing that made Thomas sadder was the fact that he had no recollection of his mother at all. Sometimes he just wanted a Mommy there to hold him.

He also missed his brother, Matthew. He missed how his brother would try to teach him to read from old newspapers despite the fact that his brother could barely read himself. He missed the long walks with his brother and the stories he used to tell. Thinking back on it, Thomas could not decide if those stories were real or just something his brother would say to distract him from the long and painful daily walk to the bread line.

Thomas did forget what it was like to be hungry and cold and wet all the time even while inside his house, as well as how much the oily puddle water would flood his shoes and soak his feet when it rained. He remembered those conditions but somehow forgot how bad it truly felt. He recognized that he was in a better, safer place, and he knew that there were still people in shantytown who were envious of him for the mere fact that the roof over his head kept the water out and allowed him to sleep when it was rained. Still, he did live in a church, with a priest. Despite knowing full-well how much better things were for him, he would feel dreary when he grasped his situation. The amount of loss was never nullified by all the good that was now in his life.

Thomas was encouraged to talk to people about his feelings when he started to act particularly Irish, but the nuns who taught him were especially useless in this regard. All that they said was to pray to God and seek guidance. Thomas wasn't quite 15 years old but had already experienced a tremendous number of life-altering events and enough suffering to last a lifetime. He did not want guidance. He wanted answers. He wanted comfort. He wanted one day without pain. He wanted help.

Heartly Law?

Father Cox was a bit more pragmatic. He actually knew Colin O'Toole and his wife, and he knew Thomas's brothers and the conditions Thomas lived through. He could provide actual insight to Thomas. Talking to Father Cox on occasion stemmed the suffering. Father Cox drummed into Thomas's head that both his parents went through Hell and back to provide a life for their children that was significantly better than their own. Father Cox insisted that Thomas should not be ashamed of how Colin died but rather proud of how he lived, what he accomplished despite of his suffering, and his relentless effort to improve the situation. Father Cox was clear with Thomas that no matter how much faith a man has, no matter how hard he tries or what efforts he puts forth, sometimes a man will hit a breaking point. Once that happens, a man is like a ship lost at sea, and only the grace of God Almighty can give him shelter. Colin did find his shelter at long last.

Thomas always remembered those words. They would comfort him even when he was very low. Thomas was bright, and all the suffering of his childhood provided him with a perspective that adolescent boys, even the Irish ones, shouldn't possess at such a young age. He was able to take comfort in Father Cox's words because when he would think about how much suffering his father endured, he realized that he was just sad, right or wrong, but that he was far from reaching his breaking point. Thomas thought his Daddy would be proud of him if he used this guidance from Father Cox to move on, even at times when he didn't feel much like doing anything.

One day Thomas's English teacher gave the class an assignment. Thomas was to write about a person he truly admired using primary sources. Father Cox was the obvious choice, but that didn't quite seem fair to Thomas, almost as if it was too easy. He then considered writing about his Daddy, but there were no primary sources other than Father Cox. So, Thomas chose to write about his other actual hero, Bob Feller of the Cleveland Indians.

Chapter Twenty-seven

Bob Feller was in the twilight of his career when Thomas discovered him. He first learned of him in the *Sporting News* which he would read in his school's library, when permitted. Bob Feller was the most dominant pitcher in Major League Baseball throughout the 1940s. In later years, baseball historians would argue that Bob Feller was the greatest pitcher of all time and that, but for World War II, Bob Feller would have put up numbers and statistics that would never again be achieved in any level of baseball.

As a teenage boy, Thomas believed that baseball was more than just a game or the national pastime. Baseball was the greatest sport ever created. For Thomas, baseball was competition and release at the same time. It soothed his soul and had no equal in that regard. What fascinated Thomas most about Bob Feller was how such a dominant pitcher in the prime of his career could walk away from the game to enlist to serve in a world war and risk getting himself killed. Finding the answer to that question led Thomas down the path of research and discovery.

Thomas was a voracious reader. He searched through every single issue of the *Sporting News* in his school's library and read every single article that mentioned Bob Feller. He compiled quotes from other players about Bob Feller. He acquired all his statistics throughout his career and documented them. Thomas was pleasantly surprised to learn that Bob Feller grew up as a poor and simple farm boy in the very nondescript town of Van Meter, Iowa. That was the first commonality that he and Feller shared – both were sons of a farmer.

Thomas's school began to get a newer sports magazine, *Sports Illustrated,* which provided pictures of Bob Feller that Thomas could trace and color with pencils. Thomas thought that adding pictures to his report would impress his teacher. He even found articles that covered Bob Feller's time in the Navy as an antiaircraft gunner aboard the USS Alabama. Thomas wasn't surprised to learn that Bob Feller was just as successful and decorated as a sailor as he was as a ballplayer.

Thomas acquired and compiled a lot of useful information about Bob Feller — about how he grew up, his performance in the major leagues, his military service – but he could not find the specific answer to why Bob Feller took four years off from baseball during the prime of his career to serve in the military during a war. Thomas was forced to use his own slowly developing logic to answer that question. Thomas concluded his report with the following theorem based upon his own deductive reasoning: 1) Bob Feller is the greatest baseball player to ever live and play the game; 2) Bob Feller stopped playing baseball for four years so that he could protect and serve his country, the United States of America, during World War II; 3) Therefore, it is a greater honor to serve and protect the United States of America than it is to be the greatest baseball player ever.

Thomas earned an A+ on his report. The conclusion of the report brought several nuns to tears despite the fact that they had no idea who Bob Feller was prior to Thomas's assignment. The grade, however, was not the greatest benefit Thomas gained from the assignment. His love for the game of baseball grew deeper the more he read about Bob Feller and the other ball players in the major leagues. Thomas further recognized how great this country must be if the greatest player in the major leagues was willing to walk away from the game to risk his own life in defense of his country. Thomas never again questioned why his parents came to this country. Bob Feller helped him to understand. Thomas also never thought the same about the soldiers and police officers who defend his country daily. His respect and admiration for them was just as high as it was for Bob Feller, even if their collective stats couldn't hold a candle to those of Feller. Moreover, he started to develop his own identity, and he now believed that he had a place in this country, even if it didn't work out so well for the rest of his family.

There was one additional tidbit that Thomas learned from his Bob Feller research that did not make the report. Buried in a *Sporting News* article in which Bob Feller was interviewed to talk about his team, the Cleveland Indians, and their rivalry with the New

York Yankees, was one tiny paragraph in which Bob Feller described how he would hold and throw a two-seam fastball. Feller described in detail how, with a slight adjustment to the grip but with the same exact throwing motion, he could take several miles per hour off the fast ball to produce a changeup that caused batters to become unbalanced and make wild swings with no hope of connecting to the pitch.

Thomas did not include this information in his report because he did not want the "secret" getting out. He committed the information to his memory. Thomas could not wait for the dreary, dirty, smog-colored snow of Pittsburgh to melt so that he could get out on the sandlot to practice throwing with Bob Feller's technique.

Chapter Twenty-eight

The church was Thomas's home, and his family was Father Cox, but his sanctuary was the sandlot. The same plot of now vacant land where a child labor-filled textile mill hastened the decimation of his family had been reclaimed by neighborhood kids as a source of joy. Thomas lived at that sandlot. Even when his teammates were otherwise occupied, he spent endless hours there just him throwing at cans.

Thomas knew that a hitter could change the game with one swing of the bat, but in his mind, nobody had more influence over the outcome of a game than a pitcher. A dominant pitcher made up for substandard defense, slow players, and a more talented opposition. Thomas loved the way it felt to lead his team on the field. He relished how he could control the speed and tempo of the game. He felt the tangible support of his teammates who focused behind him on his every movement. He felt like Bob Feller every time he took the mound, and he had good stuff for a kid. There was his regular fastball that threw with pinpoint accuracy. He had a "Bob Feller two-seam" fastball that had a natural sink to it, tailing away from right hand hitters and diving at the knees of a lefty. He also had a completely nasty changeup in his repertoire, but he rarely took it out. Observers in the community took notice of Thomas. Some would say that the Irish kid threw so hard because he would release all the inner turmoil and suffering from his life with every pitch, but those people were idiots.

The pitching mound was the only place where Thomas didn't think about his Daddy, his family, his loss, or the pain. He didn't think about growing up cold, hungry, and poor only to switch lives almost overnight and complete his childhood in a church being raised by a priest. His focus was on the batter in front of him. He was determined to be better than the hitter on every single pitch. His extraordinary focus drove the intensity with which he threw. That intensity struck most batters out before they set a single cleat into the batter's box. As Thomas's ability and reputation grew, more and more players on the opposing teams became "injured" and unable to play if he was taking the mound, a precursor to "Ryanitis."

When Thomas was 18 years old and in his senior year of high school, rumors of an Irish kid from the Strip District who threw harder than most professional pitchers made their way to the offices of the Pittsburgh Pirates. Unbeknownst to Thomas, a scout for the Pirates went to the sandlot to see him pitch. The scout watched him pitch an entire nine-inning game in which he gave up only two flukes, both of which were infield singles where the speed of the batters was not matched by the dreadful infielders. Nothing left the infield, not one foul ball or even a lazy pop-up. Thomas wore out three catchers who had to change positions because their hands were hurting from his pitches. The scout introduced himself to Thomas after the game and offered him a minor league contract on the spot. After a brief discussion with Father Cox, Thomas decided to accept the contract, to begin after he finished high school.

In Thomas's day, graduating from high school was a big deal. Most kids left after the eighth grade to start their careers in the steel mills or factories that dominated the area. For those students who did complete high school, the pomp and circumstance of the graduation ceremony carried well into the night with parties and gifts galore. Moms and Dads attended the commencement in their finest suits and dresses. Little brothers and sisters were dressed in their Sunday best and mindful of their behavior that day. Thomas was alone. Father Cox had a last-minute funeral mass at St. Mary's and thus was unable to attend.

When Thomas found himself alone amongst a group of people, often he would become sullen and withdrawn. He never felt sorry for himself, but he was still an emotional teenage Irishman, and thinking or reflecting upon any sad situation would get to him. Thomas was sad at first that Father Cox would not get to see him receive his diploma, which was only possible due to Father Cox's efforts. But Thomas understood the business of the church, and he understood that funeral masses were not planned ahead.

Despite the fact that nobody was there to congratulate him or celebrate with him, Thomas thought about one thing and one thing only — playing ball. He marched across the stage, shook his principal's hand, flipped his tassel, and joined the rest of his graduating classmates for group pictures.

Thomas walked back to the rectory to meet Father Cox for dinner. Unbeknownst to either, this would be their last supper. With the help of several nuns, Father Cox had prepared Thomas's favorite dinner — baked ham, mashed potatoes, green bean casserole, and apple pie with ice cream. The two talked about old times, about the future, about baseball, and even a little bit about God, faith, and love, and how a blessed person cannot separate any of the three. As the dinner wound down, Father Cox spoke less and less, and Thomas, despite his natural gift of gab, felt odd having to carry the conversation.

When the meal was over and the two had finished their coffee, it was time for Thomas to go. Father Cox had packed Thomas's bag for him. He walked Thomas to the front door with his hand on Thomas's shoulder. Thomas felt a slight tremble in Father's hand. He bent down to pick up his bag, then turned to say goodbye. Father Cox stood there speechless.

Father Cox devoted almost the entirety of his adult life to ministering to the needs of hundreds of dirt-poor and hopeless families from Europe: Irish, Polish, Czech, or Italian, the only difference between them was language. The immigrants' universal need to lessen the desperation and extreme poverty amongst the masses made ministering to them all the same. Hunger was hunger, death was death, cold was cold, and heartbreak was heartbreak no matter in what language it was expressed. Having grown up in that environment and immersed himself into the multiple ethnicities and cultures, Father Cox had developed an unequal proficiency in communication. His language skills rivaled that of any ivy league linguist. Yet at this instant, he gazed upon Thomas and was unable to speak even the slightest word. He was paralyzed by the immense emotional weight that bore down upon him.

Thomas stared back at him, afraid to make a move. In that brief moment of silence, Thomas comprehended all that Father Cox was communicating with his paralyzed stare. Thomas was not looking into the face of a priest, but rather a distraught parent. He was witnessing firsthand the anguish of a parent watching a child leave home and head into uncertainty when there was nothing more the parent could do to further protect his son, except hope and pray — hope that the father was effective in teaching his son lessons that would help him to survive with minimal damage.

The pain on Father Cox's face reminded Thomas of the look on the face of his natural father. Thomas now understood sacrifices that Father Cox had made over the past 13 years. He pulled Thomas out of the gutter and off the street and for some reason gave Thomas the opportunity to grow and develop and not fall victim to shantytown, all the while running a church and ministering to all the poor, tired, huddled masses on a daily and nightly basis.

Thomas lowered his eyes. He reached out to Father Cox and hugged him tightly. All he could say to Father Cox, in a voice slightly above a whisper, was "thank you for everything, Daddy."

Thomas turned and headed out the door with his bag in his hand. He walked toward the bus station and said prayers in his head. He prayed that he would not suffocate from the giant lump in his throat.

The bus pulled into the terminal, and Thomas boarded. It was less than half full, so Thomas did not have to share a seat. He put his duffle bag on the seat beside him and opened it. On top of the packed clothes were a couple graduation gifts Father Cox sneaked into his bag. There was a new Pittsburgh Pirates baseball cap, an old set of Father Cox's favorite rosary beads that were given to him years ago by a family who brought them from Ireland, a St. Christopher medallion on an inexpensive chain, and a graduation card. Inside the card in very shaky writing were the words, "Be amazing in whatever you do. God's peace and all my love. I believe in you, Thomas. F.C."

Thomas put the new cap on his head and pulled the brim down low over his face. He leaned back in his seat and softly cried until he put himself to sleep.

Chapter Twenty-nine

Thomas moved up the ranks in the minor league system. His velocity and control improved every day. Pitching coaches taught him to use his tree-trunk legs to push off the mound for added velocity and to keep his arm "live" a bit longer. His overhand style of throw served him well as he learned to throw a 12-6 curve ball. This curve ball was only slightly slower than his fastball, which he was not afraid to throw inside and high if he thought the batter was crowding the plate. When seeing a 90-mph curve ball come at his head, many a hitter would dive for cover only to watch the ball drop across the inside corner of the plate for a strike.

In 1954, at the age of 20, Thomas found himself in the AAA minor league of the Pittsburgh Pirates. He didn't know if he was more excited to be playing for Danny Murtaugh or to be playing on the same team that once fielded such great players as Dazzy Vance, Earl Weaver, and the legendary "Shoeless" Joe Jackson. His excitement level peaked when he was told he would only be on that team for a short time before being called up to the Pirates.

On one of the first days with the team, Thomas was scheduled to pitch against the Montreal Royals, the AAA farm team of the Brooklyn Dodgers. Roberto Clemente was on the Royals, and he was generally regarded as the best all-around player in the minor leagues. Had it not been for his nationality, he probably would have been called to The Show much earlier. Thomas faced Clemente in the first inning and wanted to send him a message that his accolades did not intimidate him.

Thomas's first two pitches against Roberto were fastballs, and the Great Clemente didn't even come close to either of them. Thomas decided it was time for the curve. He dug in deep with his back foot, pushed off hard with his leg, and hurled a wicked curve that moved in a way that seemed to defy the laws of physics as they pertain to round objects and short distance traveled. He knew the instant the ball left his hand that it was the hardest pitch he'd ever thrown. Clemente's swing was late, clumsy, and nowhere close. The only sound louder than the pitch slamming into the catcher's glove was the sound of the ulnar collateral ligament in Thomas O'Toole's elbow popping and blowing out. Thomas's arm hung useless at his side as Clemente tipped his hat to the pitcher on his way back to the dugout in the classy style that was Clemente.

Just before that season even ended, both players were in Pittsburgh. Roberto Clemente went to Pittsburgh to become an all-star rookie, World Series winner, Hall of Famer, and member of the 3,000-hit club for the Pittsburgh Pirates. Thomas O'Toole went to Pittsburgh to find work on the docks or maybe a steel mill. It was either more "Luck of the Irish" or the fact that he threw far too many pitches at an early age, but Tommy's baseball career was over before it got started. If appropriate medical treatment had been developed by that time, perhaps the surgery needed to repair his arm would be known as Tommy O'Toole Surgery today as opposed to Tommy John Surgery. As his Irish luck would have it, that surgery was 20 long years away. His arm would heal in time, but it would never be good enough to pitch again. At least he struck out Clemente.

Chapter Thirty

"I thought I was going to catch a break when you started to talk about baseball, but even that ended tragically," said Dr. Flynn as she wiped her eyes.

"I thought so too, at the time," said Father O'Toole as he finished his coffee. "But losing out on a baseball career led me to my true calling. I guess the good Lord had a different path for me."

"So, after baseball, you went into the priesthood?"

"Not at first. I still hadn't received that call. I came back to Pittsburgh and got a job at J&L mill for a short time. I even took some college classes at night. I did well with my coursework, but I couldn't stand being in that mill. The thought of my brother haunted me. I was anxious, hesitant. I had to get out of there before…anyway, I looked for the best opportunity to get away. I had few options because I had little money, so I enlisted in the Army. My arm wasn't good enough to throw a baseball anymore, but it could still pass an Army physical. I became an MP."

"Military Police?"

"Correct."

"So that uniform that you were wearing, when you shot Nicholas Rossi…"

"I never shot Nicholas Rossi," said the priest.

Dr. Flynn paused and attempted to jot down a note. Her page was smudged from tear drops that rolled down her face and onto the ink. She flipped to a clean dry page. "The uniform that you were wearing at the time of the shooting, that was your MP uniform?"

"It was."

"And it still fit you, after all these years?"

Father O'Toole chuckled a bit. "It was a little snug, but I did lose quite a bit of weight leading up to the…you know, it was a very stressful time."

"During your years of service, and I'm almost afraid to hear the answer, did anything traumatic happen to you?"

Father O'Toole paused. "You know, nothing bad happened during that time. I did sustain one serious injury, but maybe it was a blessing, or maybe in light of my current situation, it was the curse. Those were some of the best years of my life. I loved the comradery with the soldiers and even the officers. I had lots of friends. I even met a girl. It was the first time in my life I ever had a girlfriend. She was quite a darling. Good lookin', too. I really loved her, very much so," said the priest with a slight tone of regret.

"Let's back up a minute. I'm confused as to why the injury was either a blessing or a curse. Tell me about your time in the service as an MP," said Dr. Flynn.

"I thought I had the greatest job in the world. I was serving and protecting those who defend our country. I didn't realize at the time that most MPs were so disliked. They were the meatheads of the Army. Not me though. I went out of my way to help people because it was just the right thing to do. The soldiers warmed up to me and the officers really took care of me. I constantly lent them a hand with whatever was needed and went beyond my duties as an MP. They started inviting me into the Officers Club for drinks. I usually stayed away from the booze because I saw what it did to my dad, but in time they taught me how to drink in moderation. For the first time, I felt like my life had a purpose. I often talked to the officers about being career military. I thought that was going to be my job for the rest of my life, and I was fine with that. And in that Officers Club, that's where I first met my girlfriend. She worked on the base as a civilian employee."

"What happened to her?" asked Dr. Flynn, fearing that some traumatic event occurred that ripped her away from O'Toole.

"What happened to me, more like it. We got really close and we spent a lot of time together. One night I got permission to take her to the Officers Club on my own. We had a grand time together. After our dinner, when I went to the bar to grab a couple drinks, an officer I never met before moved in on my girl. Before she knew it, he had his hands all over her, so I went back to the table, grabbed him, and told him in no uncertain terms that she was with me and to back off. He said something to me, I can't really remember what, but he had a Polish accent. I used my Strip District upbringing and hurled a litany of Polish swear words at him. I must have said something worse than I thought because he charged me. Instinctively I pushed off my back foot like I was pitching and came across with an overhand right that caught him square in his forehead. I knocked him out cold, but I also broke my hand in a couple different places and would need surgery. Serves me right. I should've known better to hit a Pollock in his head. They're the only people more hardheaded than the Irish."

"I thought it was going to be the end of me. But one of my officer friends wrote up a favorable report that exonerated me. While I was recovering from the surgery, that's when it happened. That's when I received my calling. It was so powerful, there was no way I could ignore it. I was never more certain of anything ever in my life. I felt the suffering and loss from childhood, but this time, it was different. The pain had become a positive, driving force inside me. And I felt my Daddy beside me. He was happy I would be doing work for the Church and for others who needed me. He was proud of me. I knew at that moment that I had to come back to Pittsburgh and go to the seminary. I just knew it was the right thing to do.

While I was in recovery, I spoke to the Army chaplain. He gave me good information and we even talked about me coming back to the Army as a chaplain. My girlfriend was not as understanding. I tried my best to explain it to her. I tried to be gentle, but I was honest too. I remember how sad she was, and it made me feel awful to break her heart. She protested and I tried my best to let her know that it was my decision, it wasn't her."

"You actually said that?"

"Yes, unfortunately I remember that conversation vividly," said Father O'Toole.

"I think I've just documented the first time in history when a guy said 'it's not you, it's me' to a woman and was being completely honest."

Father O'Toole gave the doctor a glance. "Keep going," said the embarrassed doctor.

"I do think about her on occasion, much more so in recent years. Sometimes when I'm standing at the altar and I look out at the families, the ones with small children, I wonder what it would have been like to get married and have a family. I think I would have made a good husband. Probably a better father. I know I would have enjoyed playing catch with a little boy, or girl. But my calling was overwhelming. I couldn't ignore or deny it. Anytime I think of what might have been, I take refuge in the fact that it was the correct decision. It was the right thing to do. But then again had I married, we wouldn't be here today, now would we? So, you tell me, doctor, was it a blessing or a curse after all?"

The two sat silence for a moment. Dr. Flynn thought that she should be following up with more questions but wasn't certain which direction to take.

"My life as a priest was uneventful until those damn protestors took the wind out of my sail. Imagine, I work tirelessly to bring St. Mary's back from a nearly defunct parish to the jewel of the Strip, like it was when I was a kid, and those protestors deemed me the problem. Why, because Catholic dogma is always right? Because I preached loving all people, not just a select few? Because sometimes people deserve a second chance? Up until then, I think I was good at being a priest. I tried to be like Father Cox, to help as many people as I could, through ministry or in other ways. I tried to help Nico, I really did, like Father Cox helped me. When he came back home, he was just a shell. All that brilliance, all that potential, that kid could've saved the world. I thought it was the right thing to do to help him, but I was too late. Now I realize this is all my fault," said Father O'Toole.

Dr. Flynn sat up straight in her chair. "When you say that this is all your fault, what exactly do you mean?"

"I mean what has become of Nico. I tried to help him, but I failed, and my failure opened up a very bad door."

"I don't quite understand. Let me ask you a few more questions. Now I know that you did not shoot Nicholas Rossi, right?"

"You are correct."

"But your MP uniform, you admit that you were wearing it on the morning of the shooting?"

"Yes."

"And the gun, did it belong to you?"

Heartly Law?

"Same gun I used when I was an MP. I hadn't holstered it since the last time I wore that uniform during my active duty. But I always kept it with the uniform."

"So, you admit to putting on the uniform and taking the gun with you to church," said Dr. Flynn as she chose her words with care. "Did you shoot the gun in the church that morning?"

"I most certainly did."

Dr. Flynn paused. "Why did you shoot the gun in a church full of people?"

"Because it was the right thing to do."

Father O'Toole's response struck a chord with Dr. Flynn. She glanced down at her notes and adjusted her glasses. "Father, you just said a couple of minutes ago that when you received your calling, you just knew that you had to become a priest because 'it was the right thing to do.' Did God tell you, like he did when you received your calling, that you needed to shoot the gun? Did God tell you that it was the right thing to do?" asked Dr. Flynn, thinking that she might be getting somewhere.

"Are you suggesting that I'm hearing voices? That certainly was not the case. Not God or any angels or even the devil himself, nobody told me to shoot. I just knew it was the right thing to do. It had to be done."

Dr. Flynn removed her glasses and shut her notebook.

"Tell you what, Father, that's enough for today. I may need to come back and talk to you some more. Would that be okay?"

"Certainly. I'm pretty much free all day, except for Thursday between 1 and 4 o'clock, when I get my window," said Father O'Toole as he pointed to his ankle bracelet. "I do my food shopping at that time."

"Not sure I'll have to come back, but I'll call if I do," said Dr. Flynn. She stood up from behind the desk.

Father O'Toole pulled himself up from the chair and walked her to the door. As she was about to walk out of the rectory, she surprised herself by giving Father O'Toole a big hug. When she made it to her car, she called Ari.

"Dr. Flynn, to what do I owe the pleasure?"

"I just finished a session with Father O'Toole."

"Working a bit late, huh? Glad I'm not the only one," said Ari.

"I need to see you. I mean, I need to meet with you to talk about this, the sooner the better, like now, if you aren't busy?"

There was a short pause on the other end. "Okay, sounds important. Guess you got some good stuff for me. Tell you what, I was just about to order some Chinese food, and I'm guessing you didn't eat dinner. How about I pick you up something and you can meet me in my office in 30 minutes?"

"Where is it?"

"It's a little whole-in-the-wall in Bloomfield, but the food is great."

"No, your office. Where is your office?"

"Oh, yeah. 331 Green Way, in Churchill, two minutes from the exit. What would you like to eat?"

"Surprise me."

"Okay, well then, how about –"

"See you in 30 minutes," said Dr. Flynn. She ended the call and placed her head on the steering wheel.

Chapter Thirty-one

The forensic interview with Father O'Toole overwhelmed Dr. Flynn. She took several minutes to regain her composure. She fixed her makeup and headed down the parkway to Churchill. She was surprised to find herself in a residential community rather than an office complex.

"Dr. Flynn, what's up?"

"3-3-1 Green Way, did I get that correct?"

"Yes, ma'am, you did."

"Then I'm here."

"Come on inside," said Ari. "The front door is unlocked."

Dr. Flynn gave a polite, gentle knock and stepped inside. Ari was in the kitchen plating the Chinese food. "Have a seat on the couch. I'll bring your food in there." Dr. Flynn remained standing in the doorway when Ari approached. "But first," he said as he handed her an unsealed envelope, "This is what I owe you at your private rate. Just let me know if there are more costs involved, like if you have to testify, I'm good for it."

Dr. Flynn cracked open the envelope and saw several bills, although she did not bother to count them. "Where did you get this money? It stinks!" she said with a scowl on her face as she put it in her purse.

"It all spends the same. But if you like, I can spray it with Cool Water?"

Dr. Flynn chuckled. "No thank you, that won't be necessary."

"Come into the living room, sit down. I'll pull the coffee table over for your food. Sorry, I don't have a proper dining room. I just use that room to fold laundry, do some ironing, exercise there sometimes, yoga and what not."

"You do yoga?"

Ari laughed. "I was joking."

"Could we please talk about Father O'Toole?" said Dr. Flynn. Ari sensed the agitation and desperation in her tone.

"Are you okay? You look shaken."

"I am not okay, with any of this. And I'm sorry to intrude. I know it's after working hours and this could've waited until tomorrow, but I just had to talk about this. About O'Toole, I had to decompress," she said with a slight sniffle.

"Don't worry about it. We attorneys don't keep normal hours. No big deal."

"Are you sure? I should leave, we can talk tomorrow. So unprofessional, but this whole day has been unprofessional."

"No worries, doc. You need to get something off your chest, and I need to hear what you have to say, so go ahead. But if – holy hell. Look at you, you're shaking."

"I'm sorry," said the embarrassed doctor.

"How about a drink? I know I want a highball. You want one?" Dr. Flynn nodded. "Come into my kitchen so I can fix you what you like." The two walked into the kitchen. "My liquor cabinet has three shelves, bottom, middle and top, see? Now the bottom, that's for girls — for anybody who isn't all that good but for one reason or another is here and wants a drink. The middle shelf is for friends and family who stop by. You know, people I hold in higher regard. But the top shelf, well that is for special gir— special people. What would you like?"

"Whatever you're having."

"A highball it is."

"I never heard of anyone but my grandparents drinking a highball. How old are you?"

Ari laughed and reached for a bottle of Crown Royal from the middle shelf and a bottle of Seagram's 7 from the top. He grabbed two tall, thin glasses and dropped some ice from the freezer and pre-cut lemon wedges into both glasses. "This one's yours, doc," said Ari as he brandished the bottle of Crown Royal.

"I see. I'm not top shelf girl, huh? At least I'm not on the bottom."

"Some people believe Crown is better than 7. I'm not one of them, but I thought you might be."

"Make me what you're having, please."

"Sure, doc. You might be alright after all." When Ari finished making the drinks, the two went back to the living room. "Tell me what you got."

Dr. Flynn took a sip of her drink. "I'll just continue on my path of being unprofessional," she said as she looked at the drink in her hand. She took another sip.

"Not bad, huh?"

"Quite good. But if I may return to my unprofessional manner — Ari, you don't have shit," said the doctor. She took another drink and set the glass on the table.

"Not what I expected to hear. Care to elaborate?"

"For starters, I believe he is 100 percent sane. You could send him to a psychiatrist for a second opinion, but I didn't see anything that would make me refer him up the food chain. Your choice, but I think you'd be wasting time and money. He demonstrated an accurate understanding of his legal situation and everything that led him to this predicament with complete clarity."

"Did he tell you that he didn't shoot Rossi?" asked Ari.

"I'll get to that. I found him to be exceptionally sharp. He may be old, but his mind is quite sound. He remembered names, dates, events from his past."

Ari switched into lawyer mode and began to cross examine Dr. Flynn. "So what? He's sharp. Because he's sharp, he can't be insane? Doesn't that make him a psychopath? Isn't that a typical trait of a psychopathy?"

"Typically, psychopaths possess great self-awareness. They tend to be astoundingly perceptive. But I don't think he's a psychopath either."

"Can you make that determination after only one visit?"

"In this case I can," said Dr. Flynn.

"How can you say that after only one visit?"

"Because he's brutally honest. And I don't think that has anything to do with the fact that he's a priest. It's just his nature, not to not lie. He was direct with his answers, he didn't hesitate, no typical physical indicators, a 'tell' so to speak, that even psychopaths can't avoid when they lie or try to manipulate. Nothing there. He was telling the truth."

"So, if he's telling the truth, what'd he say about shooting Rossi?" said Ari with a little more fire.

"I'll get to that, please let me process."

"Please continue," said Ari. He knew he had to keep his cool and not further upset the only ally he had for his criminal defense strategy.

"O'Toole's childhood was brutal, and that's being kind. He came up in abject poverty, in shantytown. Constantly cold, wet, hungry, just like everyone else who lived there. He never knew his mother because she died during his childbirth. His father struggled to keep it together and did the best he could to raise him and his brothers. One by one, every one of his brothers died, each worse than the one before him. His only saving grace was that he was too young to know any of them and didn't really experience their deaths or how they died firsthand. He only knows of them through stories he heard growing up. He does remember one brother who died when he was about five, but that's it. He barely remembers his father. Not long after his last brother died, his father disappeared. That's when Father Cox, the local Catholic priest, took him in and raised him."

"A priest? He was raised by another priest?" asked Ari.

Dr. Flynn took a sizable sip and nearly finished her drink. She continued to process out loud. "Yes. But the one thing missing from his childhood is some sort of triggering event. There was not one specific mention of abuse or victimization of any kind. One could argue that the deplorable conditions and constant heartache might be enough to turn him into a psychopath, but I just don't see it. For one, he was removed from that situation before he was old enough to fully absorb how dreadful things were. And two, if there was a triggering event that he suppressed, or if the collective dread was enough to turn him into a psychopath, it would have manifested much earlier in life: torturing animals, alcohol or drug abuse at an early age, setting fires, cutting himself, something. But in fact, he turned out quite the opposite. He was well liked by many and played team sports, so he wasn't even a loner or antisocial. He did show indications that he may have suffered from depression, but we could chalk that up to him realizing that he wasn't like 'normal' kids who had a mother and father — being raised by a priest would have seemed odd even back then. But despite this nontraditional

162

upbringing, he grew up with love and support and certainly was not neglected from that point on. So, I'm confident that he is not insane. Nothing in his childhood could be used as a potential cause for his shooting."

"Fair enough, nothing from his childhood. But what about later in life? Could all that sorrow and suffering serve as a base? Or like a seed that's dormant for years, but when exposed to water and sun it grows? Forgive my bad analogy, just thinking out loud," said Ari.

"It's a fine analogy."

"Well, then, thank you."

"It is possible that a seed was planted, and maybe there was a triggering event later in life," pondered Dr. Flynn.

"For example?"

Dr. Flynn paused. "Baseball."

"Baseball is a trigger? I don't get it," said Ari with confusion.

"Baseball was the first thing in his life that he was passionate about. It motivated him, it was a release. He enjoyed playing on a team, he practiced pitching by himself any chance he had. No real coaches, no overly involved parents, just him and some other kids on the sandlot. According to him, he was quite good. He said that he signed a minor league contract with the Pirates, and after he graduated high school, he played in their farm system. He said that he was about to move up to the pros, but he blew out his arm pitching against…" Dr. Flynn stopped speaking for a moment to review her notes. "It was against someone named Clementine. No wait, someone named Clemente. Sorry, my notes got smudged."

"Did you just say, 'Clemente?'" asked Ari.

"Yes, Clemente. Don't know him. Was he good or something?"

Ari said nothing and gave her a look of disgust. "So, what happened with Clemente?"

"He said that he struck him out, but the last pitch he threw blew out his elbow. It ended his baseball career."

"The last batter he faced was Roberto Clemente and he struck him out. Way to go out on top, kid," said Ari as he stood up from the couch. He paced about the living room and pulled back his hair. Dr. Flynn sat in silence. After a minute pacing, Ari continued.

"I don't think I can argue to a jury that my client had a promising baseball career until an injury robbed him of his dream, and thus you must find my client not guilty. Injury is a part of all sports; thousands of people's careers get cut short from injury. That doesn't give them the right to shoot people, at least not in the eyes of the law," said Ari. He sat back down on the couch.

"Not just with sports, with other careers too," said Dr. Flynn. "People pick up a path and see their life headed on one direction, then things happen: sickness, family issues, injury, and their path changes. But again, O'Toole seemed to handle the life transition well. He moved back to Pittsburgh, he worked in a mill for a short time, then he left after he enlisted in the Army. He was Military Police."

"That explains the uniform. Anything happen there? PTSD?" asked Ari.

"No. He described his time in the service as some of the best years of his life," said Dr. Flynn. She paused, looked directly at Ari, and said, "He enjoyed helping others."

Ari picked up on her pause and stare. "You got something, doc?"

"Not sure yet. He injured his hand while on duty and was honorably discharged. He said he got his calling while recovering from hand surgery, so he went to seminary. No PTSD or anything else of value for you in any of that. But let's talk about the shooting."

"Finally. I mean, yes please."

"He admits to dressing in his military uniform on the morning of the shooting. He admits the gun was his. He even admits that he shot the gun, but he is steadfast in his belief that he did not shoot Nicholas Rossi."

"If he's as sane as you say, if he's not psychotic or a psychopath, then why can he not admit he shot Rossi?"

"Because he genuinely believes that he didn't."

"Then he must be insane, psychosis, no other explanation. I'm not the doctor here, but 'you don't need to be a weatherman to know which way the wind blows.' The only aspect of this case which cannot be debated is the fact that he shot Rossi, period. That is our starting point. That is reality, not a legal fiction, not a church miracle. It is a fact. And if he cannot grasp that fact, then he is struggling to grasp reality, which, makes him insane."

"You'll never get that diagnosis. As far as a temporary insanity, nothing there either. He was too deliberate, too methodical in his planning. He didn't snap. This was a planned—" Dr. Flynn as she cut herself off mid-sentence.

Ari stared at her. "Go on. It was a planned hit. It was premediated. If he was successful, it would have been First Degree murder."

"But this wasn't a hit. This was his attempt to help. That's was why he was wearing the uniform. He helped people when he was an MP. He was trying to help."

"Who was he helping? How was he helping? It wasn't self-defense or defense of others. How is shooting an unarmed man helping? If he shot Rossi in order to help, then how is that, by definition, not insanity?" said the exasperated attorney.

"There's more to it."

Ari got up from the couch and picked up his empty glass along with Dr. Flynn's. As he headed back to his kitchen, Dr. Flynn spoke loud enough for him to hear. "I can go back, if you want me to?"

Ari returned with two fresh drinks, his a little darker than hers. "Go back if you need to. Not my job to tell you how to do your job or to write a report."

"These are just the highlights, in advance of the actual report."

"He's not insane. He's not a psychopath. He didn't snap. He might have been trying to do a good deed by shooting Rossi, which he still denies. That will not help me at all, now will it."

"Only at sentencing. I think it is pretty strong mitigation."

"But not strong enough to keep him from dying in jail." Ari paused and took a drink. "If I can convince him to plead, maybe we can get an agreed-upon sentence that keeps him out of jail? If I try the case and lose, well…" Ari took another sip.

Both sat in silence for several moments. "Alright," said Ari, "Let's eat. You'll get loopy from those drinks if you don't put some food in your belly." Ari brought out two plates, and when he sat down beside her, he noticed that she had taken off her shoes and glasses and let her hair down.

Their conversation continued into the night. Dr. Flynn asked for one more drink. Ari obliged her but was sure to give her more ginger ale than whiskey this time.

"It's cold in here," said Dr. Flynn.

"You probably didn't eat enough. You hardly touched your plate." Ari pulled at the afghan draped over the couch and wrapped it around Dr. Flynn.

"I shouldn't have bothered you tonight, but I just had to process."

"I already told you it was okay. We all have bad days. Sometimes this stuff hurts," said Ari.

"With all my training and all my experience with victim advocacy, I thought I was past getting overly emotional. Emotion clouds judgment."

"Okay Yoda, if you say so."

"I'm serious, today was rough. And you're being so sweet to me," said Dr. Flynn. She leaned into Ari with her arms wrapped up tight in the afghan. Ari put his arm around Dr. Flynn, and the two sat in silence for a couple minutes until Dr. Flynn spoke again.

"What do you do when you have a bad day, Ari?"

"I pull a bottle off the top shelf and I listen to Mac Miller records until I cry myself to sleep on this couch."

"Seriously?"

"Or pass out."

"That is so unhealthy."

"My whole life is unhealthy. Bourbon and Mac Miller are probably the least of my concerns. But if you want to be my life coach?"

"Maybe. I'll think about it."

"I'm serious. But I won't do yoga." The two laughed.

"You are too much, Ari," said Dr. Flynn. She put her legs on the couch and sunk deeper into him. "You surprise me a little bit, too, Mr. Attorney Meyer."

"How so?"

"Well, you let me come over just to process the greatest tale of woe I've ever heard, you bought me a yummy dinner, you made me nice drinks from somewhere other than the bottom shelf. You don't seem that sweet and kind when you're in court."

"I'm kind of a jagoff in court, but there's no room for kindness in our court system."

"And this house, I never pictured you as a suburbanite. I would have thought you'd be living somewhere cool, like Downtown or Lawrenceville maybe?"

"This house is strategically located between the two best pool halls in the area. That's why I bought here."

"Again, a little odd, not many people buy property based on their proximity to pool halls. Schools, maybe," said Dr. Flynn. She struggled to keep her eyes open. "You have very little furniture. A small TV, lots of books — I kind of expected that — and a record player with what, about 200 records over there. I didn't picture you as a record playing hipster."

"First of all, that is not a record player. It is a Technique 1200 Turntable, the finest turntable ever made. A high performing piece of art. And there are 235 records over there, but I have many more in my office. Any more questions, Dr. Flynn?"

"Yeah, what's up with the chess board covered in dust in the corner?"

"I'm in the middle of a game right now, I don't want to disturb it."

"Only the first move has been made. What are you waiting for?"

"Well, Dr. Flynn—"

"Please call me Abby," she said with a slurred yawn.

Ari was taken aback by her request until it dawned on him that he couldn't remember exactly when he'd begun to run his fingers through her hair with gentle strokes.

"My partner disappeared on me, but I am expecting him to return. One day. At least so we can finish our game." Ari looked down and found Dr. Flynn fast asleep. He remained on the couch for a few minutes until he got up to get another blanket. He covered her and put a pillow under her head, then headed to his office and turned on his computer.

Chapter Thirty-two

The next morning Ari picked up jeans from the floor, threw on a hoodie, and grabbed a handful of money from his sock drawer. He planned to grab a bite to eat before heading to Sally Billiards for some quality research time. Ari pushed aside his bedroom curtain for a quick peak outside. He knew from the shallow puddles on the street that it must have rained overnight. Ari could smell the heavy petrichor that would blanket the regular stale Lucky Strike odor inside Sally Billiards. This unusual scent combination, which only occurred after a rain, was soothing to Ari for some reason. He thought that with any luck, he might be able to hustle a few bucks this morning. He reached back into his sock drawer and removed another short stack of bills.

He sneaked through his house and peeped in to find Dr. Flynn still asleep on the couch under the two blankets. Ari softly closed backdoor behind him and got into his car. He sent a quick text message to Dr. Flynn: "Dear Dr. Abby, please lock the front door behind u. There is oj & toaster waffles in the fridge. Help urself."

On the other side of town, Detective Martin arrived early to work. The short day yesterday allowed him to catch up on some sleep and spend some good family time, which gave a boost to his step. He made a fresh pot of coffee and sat down at his desk to read the morning paper online. Officer Marcus Flynn joined him.

"Good morning, sir. What would you like me to do today? Want me to meet—"

"I want you to game plan with me right now. I'll meet this attorney in the afternoon."

"Okay," said a hesitant Officer Flynn.

"I'm not going to yell at you, but we need to understand what's going on before I meet this attorney. We lost the warrant, so we can't force Rossi to come in without going before a judge, which she would fight," said Detective Martin. He stared out the window and thought out loud. "I can't help but think there's something connecting these two shootings, and we're just missing it."

"Sir?"

"Besides the obvious, that Rossi and the priest were in both shootings. There's something else, bigger than that. Let's brainstorm, what do we got? First shooting, in the church, O'Toole is target. Dylan Ray, religious nut-job, pulls a gun and shoots at O'Toole. Thinks he's doing his religion a favor by assassinating the priest. But gun fails or bullets fail, don't know which. Either way, priest survives. Nut-job claims Rossi turned into Jesus and stopped the bullets by putting his hands out. Claims it was a miracle. Nut-job admits to everything, open and shut case, except we still have no idea why the gun or the bullets failed. See, there. There's something there that's bigger than this case. We can get a conviction for nut-job based upon his confession without knowing why the failure." said Detective Martin. He paused for a moment as Flynn listened intently.

"Let's move on. Second shooting, same church, same Rossi, same O'Toole, first nut-job is in jail. This time, O'Toole pulls the trigger. This time, he actually hits Rossi. But the bullet doesn't kill him because it gets stopped by an old church key in his pocket. Rossi vanishes into thin air. O'Toole's lawyer hasn't even attempted a guilty plea negation yet, so presumably O'Toole wants a trial even though 500-plus people were in the church at the time shots were fired. But we don't know why O'Toole would shoot Rossi."

"Kinda makes O'Toole seem like the nut-job now. Insanity, maybe?" asked Officer Flynn.

"Agreed, and I thought of that, yet no notice of any kind of affirmative defense. No insanity or diminished capacity. And his attorney, that little jerk, he's good. And now your sister, it seems, is helping him."

"I don't know this attorney, but my sister is smart. She wouldn't miss something so obvious to you and me. If this priest suffered from something even close to that, my sister would know," said Officer Flynn.

"Where are we now? We got nut-job number one from the first shooting who admitted to everything, but he's in mental health jail doing his best Woody Woodpecker impression, so he isn't going to trial anytime soon. Then we have case number two, whereupon the victim of case number one has turned into the shooter and defendant. That has to suck for the DA. The priest is wearing an ankle bracelet, and no continuances for extensive mental health evaluation are even hinted at. Looks like he gets to go to trial first."

"Seems unfair, doesn't it, sir?" said Officer Flynn.

"Unfair?"

"I mean, I am following you. Both cases seem related to one another on some kind of level, as if the first shooting is the cause of the second."

"Go on," said Detective Martin, hoping the brainstorm session would lead to something.

"Father O'Toole was almost shot, and because of that, he suffered trauma which he couldn't deal with. And because of the trauma, he snapped out and shot at Rossi. So, there you have it. And priest or not, this guy has a zero-prior record score, not even traffic tickets, and he served in the Army. Sounds like snapping out to me. So, it's unfair that the cause of the whole mess, nut-job Dylan Ray, won't be going to trial, but the real victim, Father O'Toole, will be," said Officer Flynn.

Detective Martin was glad that he decided to seek the young officer's input, even if he didn't agree with the conclusion. "Good job, Flynn. But you sound more like a defense attorney than a cop. Maybe it is unfair to O'Toole, maybe he is a victim of some kind, although that's not for us to say. And besides, if your sister is even average, she would pick up on him snapping due to some trauma. That first shooting wasn't so long ago, so it's not like he'd be dealing with deep-rooted trauma. I think if there was anything psychological there, we would have heard about it by now. Then again, maybe I'm looking at things too deeply. I need to step away, stop asking why, and focus of what we know. Do we have enough evidence for a conviction? Leave the why and issues of fairness for the court to sort out. Maybe Meyer is just stringing this out. You know how attorneys like to play those little games. Maybe he's waiting 'til the 11th hour so he can plead out? Maybe that's his game," said the detective.

Wil 3

But the only game Ari Meyer was playing that day was 9-ball. In typical fashion, he was doing quite well, petrichor and all. His defense strategy for O'Toole, not so much.

Chapter Thirty-three

Detective Martin sat in the relative silence of his office. His mind was adrift in thoughts of both shootings, the lack of progress in either, what he would say to this mystery attorney in a couple of hours, and fairness. *Maybe Officer Flynn did have a point? Maybe fairness and equity should factor in? I never arrested someone out of spite, just to jam them up. That's fair, right? Go on the facts and evidence, make the arrest, aid in prosecution. If there is explanation or reason for leniency, fairness or otherwise, that's for the attorneys and the courts to decide. But maybe Flynn had a point? Maybe O'Toole shooting at Rossi was caused by trauma O'Toole suffered from the first shooting? Maybe that shooting flipped his switch? Is it fair that O'Toole will go on trial, be found guilty, and die in jail while the true cause, Dylan Ray, lives out his days in a mental hospital?*

Detective Martin's mind kept drifting. He hoped that examining both cases through the lenses of fairness and equity would lead to better questions and maybe even some answers. In the end, the mental exercise only offered a slight respite from the x's and o's of criminal investigation and prosecution. He emptied his head of all collateral thought and focused on Jeannette Royal, Esquire, and what he wanted to say to her. She was as close to Rossi as he'd come in the past year. He grabbed his suit coat and headed out the door.

Detective Martin pulled in front of the Duquesne Club. An attendant was immediately at his door. Martin gathered his belongings, climbed out of the car, and put on his jacket.

"Valet, sir?" asked the attendant. Detective Martin shot him a look of disgust.

"Yes. Please valet my cop car," said the indignant detective. "On second thought, I think I'll park right here in the front of the building." Martin reached into his car and flipped on the blue and red lights. He shut the car door and entered the club. Once inside, his car's security system loudly chirped for all to hear. "Hate this place," he mumbled under his breath.

Detective Martin walked down the long corridor of French oak paneling and marble floors. His advancement was stopped just short of the threshold to the billiards room and bar by a vision he would never have anticipated. Attorney Royale was dressed in a tight red pencil skirt with a long slit in the back that revealed a glimpse of her sculpted leg while she moved around the antique slate table. One by one the pool balls dropped with a dull thud into the old leather pockets. The "gentleman" playing at her table and his googly-eyed friends didn't seem to mind losing to her, especially when her shot required her to bend over the table. Her cream-colored sleeveless silk blouse pulled slightly away from her chest and shoulders to reveal just a little bit more.

"Tough luck, cupcake. You made the shot but didn't give yourself a good leave," said the old man with a lecherous smile. He chalked his cue almost indecently.

Attorney Royale strolled around the table and stretched as far as she could across it, sure to hold her position for a few extra moments while her opponent got a good look. She exaggerated a fake pout.

"Just short. You're going to have to use a bridge. Good luck with that," said the dirty old man.

Attorney Royale stepped away from the table and in one fell swoop wound her long hair into a messy bun held together with her Mont Blanc pen. She slowly approached the old man. "Tell you what, sugar," she purred as she tugged at the old man's collar, "Double or nothing says I sink this 8 right now and win this game. What do you say?"

The smitten old man did not think straight. "I feel bad taking your money, cupcake, but okay," he said. He turned to his onlooking friends and remarked, "This'll be something to see."

Attorney Royale leaned her cue stick against the table and walked toward the rack of house cues and bridge. She walked right past them until she came to her corner table, where she sat down and slid on her five-inch patent leather ribbon heels. She sauntered back to the table and now found that she had plenty of reach without the need of the bridge. She gave a devilish kiss in the air to her opponent and shot the 8-ball into the corner pocket with another dull thud.

"Oh my. Sorry sugar. Looks like you owe me $400. But grab a drink on your way out, it's on me." The dirty old man wasn't sure if he was more disappointed that he had to pay her or that the show was over. He paid up and moved along with his friends to another part of the club. Detective Martin moved as Attorney Royale made her way back to the corner table. She put on a black blazer to complete her outfit, which now resembled something professional.

"You Jeannette Royale?" asked the detective.

"I am," she said. She stood up to shake his hand. "You must be Detective Benjamin Martin. Please, have a seat." Detective Martin sat down and scanned the artwork adorning the walls in the billiards room of the historic club.

"You an attorney or some country club hustler?" he asked.

"Your Hendrix and tonic, madam," said the waiter. He set the drink down on the table in front of her.

She smiled at the waiter and took a small sip. "One in the same," she said to Martin before she put the drink down on the table. "Care for a drink, detective?"

"No thank you. I'm working right now."

"So am I," she said. She took another drink.

"You call this working?"

"I'm making money, so I'm working. Thank you, James, we're good for now," said Attorney Royale.

"Yes, madam," said the waiter. He removed himself from her area.

"Are you going to bring in Rossi for questioning or not?"

"Detective, I thought you told me that you had a warrant? If you have a warrant, then you want me to turn him in. That's a little more than questioning, isn't it?" said the attorney. She removed a pair of shiny black framed Chloe glasses from the pocket of her blazer and put them on.

"I no longer have a warrant, but I'm certain you're well aware of that," said the detective. Attorney Royale pushed her glasses down onto her nose and looked at him but said nothing. "I don't know what your game is or what you're up to, and I certainly don't know how Kelly is involved in this mess. But if you don't bring Rossi in and let me talk to him, I'm going to make your life difficult, to say the least."

"Back to the rough stuff again? Well, sorry to disappoint, but no warrant, no talking to my client. Simple as that," said Attorney Royale.

"Fine. You want to keep playing games? I'll have a warrant by the end of the week. Then you better be ready to—"

"I don't think you want to do that," said the attorney. "Let me be absolutely clear with you, sir. My client is the victim of an attempted homicide. The law does not require the victim to participate in the prosecution of the defendant, especially when participating in trial will only re-victimize and traumatize him. You try to get a warrant, and I will go before the judge to explain my position, which is neither unique nor original. Granted, your position is original, albeit completely absurd. The fact that you would try to obtain an arrest warrant for obstruction or conspiracy against my client, the intended victim of the shooting, will not be well received by even the farthest of right-wing judges. Sorry, no rubber stamp on that warrant now," said the confident attorney.

She took another sip of her drink before she continued, "I promise you that if you try to get an arrest warrant for my client, the jury pool in this county will not be tainted, it will be flooded. Once I let the victim advocate groups know that my client, the victim of an attempted homicide, does not wish to participate in the trial, but the government is forcing him to do so based upon the threat of arrest, well sir, there won't be protests, there will be marches. The media frenzy will be so overwhelming that you just might have to go to Texas to pick 12. And once my client lets that jury know that the only reason he's there is because you threatened him with an arrest, well, the DA will lose the case against O'Toole. Whatever the evidence, however many eyewitnesses, won't matter. They will lose the case based upon nothing more than the fact that you, sir, are a dick. Now please ask yourself, do you want a conviction against O'Toole, or do you want to try to speak with my client and risk everything, including quite possibly, your career." said Attorney Royale. She removed her glasses and put them into her blazer. She picked up her drink and slouched back in her chair. "Unless you have money and want a game, I believe our time here has concluded."

Detective Martin said nothing. He stared at her for 10 long seconds but remained quiet. He rose from his seat and walked out of the Duquesne Club.

Martin sat in his car, still parked in front of the Duquesne Club, and called back to the precinct. "Flynn, wrap it up, all of it. Finish the interviews you have scheduled, but don't set up any new ones. I'm going to speak with the DA, tell him we're done investigating. Give them everything, finish all reports as soon as possible, but no more interviews. Got it?"

Detective Martin rarely felt dejected at any point during his professional career. He had his highs and lows, but he'd was always maintained an even keel. He never had such an extended period of despondency as the one he'd experienced for the past year. His mind had become dull and blurry and at times made him spiritless when his subordinates deserved leadership. These two cases had become a cancer inside him, devouring his mind, moving onto his soul, and he could do little to stop the ravenous spread. Even the feckless attempt to gain information from Rossi's attorney went from futile to painful in seconds. She was sharp, she knew her stuff, but he was an All-Star, a future Hall of Famer. He should have been able to push back a little bit. He tried to convince himself that walking away without argument was the smart play, but he knew that he was just too anemic to do anything more.

He thought, for the hell of it, that he should drive past St. Mary's since he was close by, to pretend like he was still putting forth effort. He crept up slowly on the old church and seized upon the glowing police tape. This time it was not a giant highlighter pointing out something important. It was a giant middle finger, and it was pointing at him.

Chapter Thirty-four

Hurry up and wait. Nothing happens until it happens, then all Hell breaks loose. Typical adage for any case in litigation headed for trial. Ari never appreciated any of that sentiment. As a public defender, he was in court constantly, so the downtime void of any particular case was readily filled by the Hell breaking loose on another case at hand, which was nearly every day. With only one client as a private attorney, Ari finally understood what hurry up and wait meant. He was waiting for discovery from the District Attorney's Office, he was waiting for his expert report from Dr. Flynn, he was waiting for O'Toole to call him and tell him that he wanted to plead guilty as long as he could remain out of jail, he was waiting for something, for anything, to happen.

The initial flurry of activity was maddening — a bond hearing for O'Toole, his resignation from the Public Defender's Office, numerous meetings with his client and one with Dr. Flynn, followed by his waiving of O'Toole's preliminary hearing, which he did by paper. But now there was nothing, just time, which felt as uncomfortable as dead air to a disc jockey. The inactivity in his life was stressing him out. He felt lazy, uninspired, common, and mundane. He wore the same clothes he went to sleep in, sometimes for a couple days in a row. He only showered to buy Chinese food with enough extra for three days.

Due to either a subconscious need to start doing something constructive or out of complete boredom, he called Dr. Flynn.

"Hi," said the bashful voice on the other line.

"Hello Dr.– Abigail. How are you? Been awhile," said Ari.

"I know, I'm sorry. I got really busy with some crazy fires that needed my immediate attention, and O'Toole is more complicated than I first thought. I've been going through my notes, the ones I can still read, and it's taking longer than I thought to write up. It should be done soon. Sorry, I will call you as soon–"

"Hey, it's okay, no big deal. I think I know what it's going to say."

"Thank you for understanding, I just need to–"

"I didn't call you just about the report. It's just been awhile since we talked," said Ari in an attempt to gauge her temperature.

"It has," said Dr. Flynn in a hesitant tone.

"So…thank you for locking the door behind you."

"Ari, I was hoping you were going to be cool about that and not bring up my indiscretion."

"Indiscretion? Nothing happened. You were exhausted and had a couple drinks. You did the smart thing by sleeping on the couch," said Ari.

"I'm so embarrassed. I hardly know you, I fell asleep in your lap. That is terrible."

"Maybe for you."

"What?"

"I enjoyed our time together, outside your report, of course. That was a bit rough, but otherwise, I enjoyed your company."

Dr. Flynn paused for a few moments. "Thank you?"

"So now you know me a little better, right? Maybe I'd like to get to know you better?"

"Maybe."

"Maybe? You better, for your own good. There's so much I can teach you," said Ari.

"Oh, really now? What could you possibly teach me, besides how to make a highball, which you already showed me."

"For starters I could teach you to appreciate the beautiful elegance of a Mac Miller love song, and how they sound best when played on vinyl."

"Okay."

"But then, if you're good–"

"If I'm good?"

"If you're good, I can teach you how to shoot stick."

"What?"

"Play pool. You know, billiards."

"Wow, Ari, you are quite the charmer now, aren't you?"

"Was that a laugh, or maybe a little giggle I heard?" said Ari.

"Maybe a little one. You do crack me up sometimes."

Heartly Law?

"Do I now? Well, you don't say." Ari's call waiting beeped on his phone. "This is the district attorney calling me. I have to take this call. Maybe when this case is over, we can get Chinese food or something?"

"Maybe. If you're good," said Dr. Flynn back to him.

"Got it. Thanks. And get me that report!" said Ari. He clicked his phone over to the other call.

"Hello?"

"Attorney Meyer, this is Assistant District Attorney Lindsay Kennedy from the Allegheny County District Attorney's Office."

"Good morning Ms. Kennedy. How are you today?"

"Your discovery is ready. You may pick it up at your convenience."

"Ok, well, thank you. I will probably swing past this afternoon."

"Fine. And Attorney Meyer, you are aware of reciprocal discovery, aren't you?"

Ari was annoyed by the young prosecutor. "Um, not sure, what ah, what is that?"

"Sir, that is when you need to provide our office with your discovery, as in your expert report. We have not received it yet," said the terse ADA.

"Oh, yeah, that. I think I'll get it in about two weeks or so. Don't get yourself into a tizzy and get all worked up there, sweetheart. I'll make sure you get it," said Ari with deliberate condescension.

"Thank you," she said. She ended the call.

"What an angry little bitch she is," said Ari as he looked at his phone.

Ari jumped in the shower, shaved, and for the first time in a couple months, put on a suit. He arrived at the District Attorney's Office and found that his discovery was packed into three full banker boxes.

"I wasn't expecting this much. Can I borrow a cart?" Ari asked the discovery clerk.

"No."

"Okay, give me a minute." Ari stepped out of the office and called his former secretary.

"Hey Sarah, how's my number one girl doing?"

"Praise be, you're alive. I didn't know for sure, you never call me."

"I'm sorry about that. It's just this transition has been crazy, setting up a new office, clients, the whole shabangy-bang. But I am sorry, I should have called," said Ari.

"What do you need, Ari?"

"Maybe I just wanted to talk to you?"

"I know you too well, Mr. Meyer, and that is why I love you so much, sweetie."

"Thanks, I do need a favor. Do you think you can snag a pull-cart out of the office and sneak it down to the DA's office without Vince seeing you? Promise I will bring it back. I need it to get some boxes to my car."

"What's in it for me?"

"One big wet sloppy kiss, and I'll mess your hair up, too, while I'm at it."

"Now how can I resist that! Just don't tell my husband," she giggled. "Vince isn't in today, so I'll bring it down now."

"Thanks, mamma, you're the best."

Chapter Thirty-five

The literal mountain of discovery was overwhelming at first, even for a seasoned veteran like Ari. At least it gave him something to do. He opened the first box and reviewed the cover sheet that indicated the contents: one expert report from the Allegheny County Crime Lab detailing one .38 Special revolver, one spent .38 caliber shell casing found inside said .38 Special, and one .38 caliber mushroom slug recovered from the crime scene. And 93 statements from witnesses.

Ari took out the expert report and glanced at it for 20 seconds. He set it aside and dove into the witness statements.

"Okay, what do we have here," he said out loud to himself. "A statement from Detective Benjamin Martin, Mr. Law and Order himself. If that flattop-having prick testifies as an actual eyewitness, get used to prison life, O'Toole. Who is this? Detective Kelly. Nice enough guy, for a cop. He's older, if I remember. Maybe his age and eyesight will be something to explore. Oh, great, he was 20 feet away. Who are these people: Italian guy, Italian guy, Italian guy, Italian guy. Oh, these guys are from the Vatican. Really? That's kind of odd, isn't it? Better ask a Catholic about that. They must be back in Rome now. Are they really going to fly back for this?" said Ari as he flipped through the eyewitness statements.

Ari reviewed witness statements and took notes for the rest of the day and the entire next day and night, though actual note-taking stopped after the 30th or so statement. Every statement said pretty much the same thing: "Heard a loud gunshot, then saw Nico Rossi fall to the ground." The only real difference was the location of the witness. Some were closer than others, some had a clear view, other views were partially obstructed by church pillars or other people in the front.

Ari paced in his living room and said to himself, "The DA is not going to call 93 witnesses, otherwise this trial would take four months, so they'll limit their witnesses to the best ones, which would be those closest to the shooting. Yeah, got to hedge the bet a little." Ari moved his coffee table and arranged it to be parallel to his couch. He grabbed the first album from his stack.

"*Mind Games*, John Lennon. Perfect." he said to himself, noting the irony. "John Lennon is Rossi, he goes up front." Ari spent the entire week, morning through evening, reading and re-reading every statement. When he was sure that he'd gleaned all possible information, he placed the statement on the floor in position according to where each witness was at the time of the shooting in relation to Lennon/Rossi. He used his coffee table and couch to represent the locations of the witnesses who were seated in the balcony.

Meanwhile, in the District Attorney's Office, a small task force of assistant district attorneys was working day and night to prepare the case. They were determining the strengths and weaknesses of each witness. Those witnesses whom they intended to call would need to be interviewed again by the lead prosecutor. It was a daunting task that would easily allow for a continuance to be granted based the necessity for more time to prepare. But the DA did not want a continuance. Everyone realized that Father O'Toole's physical condition may have been exaggerated at the time of his bond hearing, but several months had passed since then, and it was an undeniable fact that O'Toole was very old. The DA wanted his conviction before anything happened to the old man, so no continuance would be sought by his office.

Chapter Thirty-six

After a couple months of trial preparation, the Discovery period closed. With no motion for a continuance from either side, the long and grueling process of jury selection began. It was difficult to find people who did not have strong opinions on the case. Father O'Toole joined Ari for jury selection, and he argued hard to include any person on the jury who wore a crucifix. The Deputy District Attorney, who was lead prosecutor, argued just as hard to keep them off the jury. It took a week to select 12 jurors and two alternates. The trial was scheduled to begin in a month.

After the last juror was chosen, Ari drove Father O'Toole back to the rectory. The two did not speak a word the entire trip back. Ari parked in front of the rectory and broke the silence. "I don't know how confident I am with that jury."

"Thank you for the ride home. I'll wait to hear from you," said the tired priest. He made his way into the rectory and shut off the outside light.

Ari drove to his house/office. He was careful not to disturb his living room which was modeled after the inside of St. Mary's Church. He stood at the threshold and looked out over the lifeless stacks, many of which now had a filmy layer of fine dust on the top sheets. Ari knew he put the time into this case, moreso than any other case he'd ever had. He immersed himself in the depths of witness statements and his own expert report, yet he still felt unprepared. He had no trial strategy, no plan of attack, no defense, no opening, no closing, no nothing. With a month to work with, he had time to pull a rabbit out of his hat. He just needed to figure out exactly how.

"What am I missing?" he said to himself. "Nothing. I am not missing a damn thing. There is nothing here. There's no defense, no strategy. I got shit. Maybe a few witnesses can be challenged on what they saw based on their location, but nothing short of a miracle is going to stop this conviction. Even this DA can't screw this one up. No chance. This is asinine."

The next morning Ari drove back to the rectory to speak one more time with Father O'Toole. He'd barely kept open the lines of communication, and though O'Toole joined Ari for juror selection, the two did not discuss anything meaningful regarding the case. Ari knocked on the priest's door.

"Do you have a few minutes to talk?"

"With my lawyer, on the proverbial eve of a trial that may cause me to die in prison? I think I can spare a few moments," said the priest. He let Ari in. "Let's talk in my study."

Ari took a seat on the couch but stood right back up to address the priest who sat behind his desk.

"I've been working my a–, my tail off to get ready for your case. I have reviewed and re-reviewed and re-re-reviewed all of the eyewitness statements."

"How many eyewitnesses against me?" asked the priest.

"Ninety-three," said Ari. O'Toole nodded, seemingly unfazed. "And all of them are consistent. All say that they heard the gun shot, then watched Rossi fall to the ground right after that. There is no variation, no inconsistency that I can exploit to cause doubt in the mind of a juror. And yeah, some may have had a bad perspective, maybe their view was partially blocked and maybe I can knock out one or two that way, but not 93 of them, two of whom are Detective Kelly and Detective Martin. My personal feelings aside, they are good cops. They've spent as much time in court being cross-examined as I've spent in court grilling witnesses. They won't rattle. They had a front row seat, so they have no perception issues. And there is no dirt on either of them that I can use to impugn their credibility, none. The jury will believe them."

"And they will also believe the crime lab expert, Dr. Victor Chan. Simple, routine, clear-cut, no nonsense report. The slug recovered from the scene is a .38 caliber slug that matches the .38 caliber revolver removed from your hand by Detective Kelly. We have no defense to that."

Ari paused. O'Toole sat in silence and listened. "Now for your expert report. That, sir, was like pulling teeth. You did a number on Dr. Flynn, that's for sure. The report is well-written. It is sad, even heartbreaking. But before you even say it, I know you're holding to the position that you did not shoot Nicholas Rossi. So, I figure, hey, 93 witnesses can't all be wrong, so if you can't admit that you shot him, then clearly you're suffering from some psychological disorder, insanity or some kind of diminished capacity. But no, according to Dr. Flynn, you are probably saner than I am. So that is not going to help us in terms of a defense strategy. In other words, we have no defense strategy, and how we proceed is rather limited. Can you see that?"

Father O'Toole sat and pondered for a moment. "Attorney Meyer, do you need more money for the defense? I have it if that would help?"

Ari laughed out loud. "You think this is about money? I couldn't care less about the money. A million more dollars doesn't change the facts of this case, and it won't buy you an insanity diagnosis. But you know what comes to mind, now that you mention money? What is that story, that passage, from the Bible, about how it's easier for a camel to pass through the eye of a needle than it is for a rich man to get into Heaven. Do you know what I'm talking about?" asked Ari.

"Surprising you would bring up New Testament verse. Impressive."

"It's a pretty well-known story that people use to teach their children not to grow up to be greedy. It goes beyond the Bible in many instances," said Ari.

"It certainly does."

"You are like the rich man trying to get into Heaven. You can't do it. Like the rich man loaded down with money and riches, you too are loaded down. Maybe not with money, but with facts and evidence against you. It is overwhelming," said Ari with a sad tone in his voice.

Father O'Toole pulled himself up and moved away from his desk. At that moment, for the first time, Ari noticed his true presence. He felt his being, he saw his aura clearly. He was no longer looking at a broken-down old priest or hard-luck client. He was looking at a fearless street-fighting warrior. Ari got a bit emotional at that moment, which was a great surprise since he'd been practicing criminal defense long enough to divorce himself of any emotional entanglement.

"Sit down, son," said Father O'Toole. He removed the cork top from his bottle of scotch and poured a drink into the heavy crystal rocks glass. He handed the glass to Ari and moved back to the front of his desk. "I know this case is stressing you out, I can see it on you. I know you're working as hard as you can, probably even more than I deserve. I never doubted you in that regard, ever. And I know you have a huge heart. It's buried under your fancy suits and brash demeanor, but I know it's there. So, tell me, son, what's troubling you?"

"What's troubling me?" asked Ari. He took a gulp of the scotch. "Where do I begin?" he said. He took another gulp. The scotch warmed his whole body, but it did little to steady his shaky voice. "You used to be called Tommy. I never saw you as a Tommy, or as a little boy. But your dad, your brother, your teachers, all called you Tommy. That report by Ab–, Dr. Flynn. My God, I had no idea what you lived through. How you are still even here? That may have been the worst thing I've ever read. I can empathize with a couple parts, but most of it, shit, I don't even think empathy is strong enough," squeaked Ari. He finished the last of his drink. Father O'Toole sat back on the edge of his desk and listened.

Ari cleared his throat in attempt to regain his composure. He stood up from the couch and continued. "Let me use that report. Let me share your pain, your suffering as a child, all that heartache and loss with the DA. Maybe that, along with some favorable reports from your doctor friend at Mercy, maybe I can use that to convince the DA that your life does not equate to one single bad decision, a decision made under severe stress caused by the protestors, by the Vatican who demanded a miracle, and from the trauma suffered by nearly being shot on the altar a year ago. Maybe I can convince them to see it my way. I don't need to be a Christian to recognize and appreciate your entire life of service, or what it means for you to help so many desperate people, or to give to others before yourself, and to protect our country. Before this whole shooting, your life was beyond admirable. Despite one heart-wrenching tragedy after the next, you continued to get up to serve others. That must count for something. I'm not promising you that I'll be successful. But I think there's a good possibility that we could plead guilty in exchange for you staying out of jail. Maybe. I'll try my damnedest to make that happen. But one thing I promise you is that if you go to trial against this evidence, you will die in jail."

"So, you want to know what's bothering me? The fact that you have lived a life beyond remarkable with humility and kindness and grace, and you will die in jail beside some mafioso or rapist or drug dealer, and that is not what you deserve. That is not justice. Shit, dying drunk on some back alley on the North Side is more dignifying. And not only am I the one leading you to the gallows, I'm also putting the noose around your neck with a jury trial instead of a plea deal," said Ari. He gulped the remaining scotch in his glass and slumped on the couch with his face in his hand. He waited a moment for Father O'Toole to respond.

"Son, I know I am your client, and it is not my place to second-guess your legal strategy. What you propose does make a lot of sense. But my case, it is different. I can assure you that you've never had a case like mine. Guilt or innocence is not the ultimate goal. Here, I must face the demon." Ari lifted his head from his hands upon hearing that comment. "I need you to be strong for me, son. Do not lose your heart. It is your greatest weapon. In the end, it's God's will."

"Mr. O'Toole, likewise, it is not my place to second-guess theology with you, but I promise you that your faith cannot save you from a guilty verdict," said Ari.

"That is where you're wrong. My faith has already saved me. That's why I am content with any outcome. But you must help me face the demon. You must not lose your heart."

Ari stared at Father O'Toole in silence and struggled to comprehend what he said. He started to second-guess himself and his abilities. He couldn't convince Father O'Toole to plead guilty in the face of overwhelming evidence and the certainty of a prison death. He even implored him with honest emotion, but to no avail. It was like the time in high school when he poured his soul out to a girl he liked only to be pushed aside for the captain of the football team who drove the Z-28, only it was even worse this time. Ari rose from the couch and stepped toward the door. Father O'Toole stopped him.

"Son," he said, "in any of those statements you read, did anyone say what happened to Nico after the shooting?"

Ari pondered for a moment before he answered. "I don't recall anyone saying anything about that, but so what? He could have gotten up and danced a jig, or God himself could have reached down and pulled him up to Heaven, it still doesn't matter. Actions after the fact, after the shooting, don't matter. Doesn't change the charges against you."

"Oh," said Father O'Toole, "doesn't matter, huh? I just thought maybe there was something there. Interesting, though, don't you think?" Ari headed for the door of the study. "Ari," said Father O'Toole, "do not lose your heart."

Ari exited the study and walked through the rectory by himself. He pulled the front door behind him and got into his car.

Chapter Thirty-seven

A failed attempt to implore Father O'Toole to see things his way rendered Ari emotionally exhausted. He reviewed his encounter with O'Toole while he drove home. "Why did he say he had to face *the* demon?" said Ari out loud to himself. A deluge of random and chaotic thoughts clanked around his head as he struggled to assemble them into something meaningful. It wasn't until Ari pulled into the gravel parking lot and put his car in park that he realized he didn't drive home as intended. Lost in his own thoughts, he realized that he drove to his second home – Sally Billiards. "Well, since I'm here," Ari said to himself.

"Well, sonofabitch, look who decided to grace us with his presence," said the belligerent old man. Ari said nothing and walked inside. The money table immediately emptied before he got to it. Ari grabbed a house cue from the rack and approached his table. He racked a 9-ball and placed the break cloth on the table. Ari laid his stick on the table, then with both hands on the rail, stared across the table in silence, almost as if he was meditating. After several minutes of absolutely nothing, Ari picked up his cue stick and readied himself for the break. The smooth house cue slid effortlessly across his bridge hand. Ari focused and struck the cue ball with a thunderous blow – far off-center and low. The errant strike launched the cue ball off the table and across the room. It crashed down on the petrified oak floor with a tremendous thud like the shot heard 'round the word. All action in Sally's immediately ceased as the players readied themselves for the impending volcano of obscenity that was ready to explode.

Sally, from the opposite side of the pool hall, spun around so quickly that he seemed more like Yoda with a light saber than Mickey with a rusty nine-iron. "MOTHER FUC–," he started to scream, but he cut himself off when he saw that it was Ari who caused the damage. Sally used his nine-iron cane and limped over to Ari. "Son of a bitch – you okay?" he asked.

Ari lifted his downtrodden head and looked at Sally. "No Sal. I'm not okay. I think you better give someone else this table today." A patron retrieved the cue ball and sheepishly approached the table, setting it there gently before returning to his own table.

The stunned onlookers in Sally Billiards remained motionless as they watched Ari walk to the refrigerator. He opened it to find several open cases of beer. He took four cans from somebody's case and replaced them with a $20 bill. He walked out of the parlor and down to the riverbank behind the old pool hall with his head hung low.

Years of industrial waste rendered the riverbank like old asphalt in stark contrast to the sandy banks across the river. Ari walked up and down the shore while he slugged his beers. Still unable to decipher his conversation with O'Toole, Ari called Dr. Flynn.

"Hey Ari, what's up?" said Dr. Flynn.

"Abby, you're Catholic, right?" asked Ari.

"Yeah? Why do you ask?"

"I just met with O'Toole. He said some things, I dunno. I can't understand what he meant. I thought maybe it was a Catholic thing."

"Ari, are you alright? You don't sound good," said Dr. Flynn.

"He said he can't take a guilty plea, even if it keeps him out of jail, because he has to face *the* demon. Don't most people say they have to face *their* demons? I can't make sense of it, so I thought you could shed some light?" said Ari. His head spun from confusion and a few beers.

"I understand that as an attorney, words are your weapons. I know how important precision in word choice can be to a case. But don't you think maybe he misspoke, or maybe you didn't hear him correctly?" said Dr. Flynn.

"I am certain that's what he said. Besides, it's the only thing that makes any sense to me. It's not about guilt or innocence with him. Hell, it isn't even about dying in prison or not. It's about going to trial to face *the* demon. What I don't understand is what that means. Why would he say that?" Ari stopped his stroll and sat down on a fallen tree to listen.

"Let's talk this through logically," said Dr. Flynn, transitioning into clinical mode. "Priest or not, all people can have demons. Drugs, alcohol, gambling, but nothing suggests to me that he suffers from any of that. He likes to have a drink on occasion, but I don't think that's a problem for him. Based upon his traumatic early years, if he did suffer from psychosis of some sort, it would have presented much earlier in his life. A demon is just a colloquial categorization of some psychological, or sometimes physical, problem that a person has. It's their way to segregate the negative aspect of their life from the positive parts. A person says they need to fight their demons when they take ownership of the issue and address it."

"So, you're saying that demons are intrinsic?"

"Exactly."

"But that can't be correct. He never said he had to face *his* demons, it was always *the* demon, I'm sure of it," said Ari. "Could there ever be an extrinsic demon?"

"I'm not sure what you are getting at."

"Could there be a driving force inside him that makes him fight a demon on the outside?"

"Do you mean an *actual* demon? I never expected you to ask a question like that. You don't seem like one to believe in the supernatural."

"Well could there?"

"You're really getting out of my wheelhouse now. There are some, a very small percentage, of Catholics who believe demonic possession is real. The book that *The Exorcist* was based on was supposedly inspired by real events. The freezing cold room, the head spinning, the enormous spew of vomit, all that was documented by medical professionals outside the Church. But that is not the norm. Even the most devout Catholics today think that demonic possession is blaming the boogeyman, a way for a person not to be held accountable for certain acts. But exorcism is still practiced by a handful of very specific priests. That said, IF Father O'Toole does believe that he needs to fight a literal demon, then he would surely recognize the futility of doing so in a court of law. Not the right venue, as lawyers would say, to have that fight. It would be a useless endeavor."

"So, the hamster keeps running on the wheel, not going anywhere. He can't admit he shot Rossi, he won't take a plea to avoid dying in prison, and now he wants to face down some demon with a jury trial. If I didn't know any better, I would say the guy is insane. But I trust your assessment. So where does that leave me?"

"I would never tell you how to practice law, but it's very concerning to me that you're going down this path. I understand that it may be helpful to get into your client's head, I do it all the time. But why ask these questions of faith? People say all the time that they have faith in the system, or they have faith in the jury, but you know that's just lip service. Those people aren't talking about the deeper faith that you're asking me about. That all stops when the jury is seated. Your faith, my faith, Father O'Toole's faith, it doesn't matter in the end. The jury will hear the evidence and they will decide the case on the facts, not based upon their faith. You know this. It really sounds like you're not in a good place, Ari, but that's understandable. You quit the only job you ever had to hang a shingle to practice law out of your house, and you're stuck in a rut with a client who has no defense, I get it. But if you don't start dealing with this case based upon the evidence you have and move past it, I'm afraid that Chinese food and a highball won't be enough to heal you."

"I don't know where this leaves you," said Dr. Flynn. "My question for you is, why are you beating yourself up when you know that, demon or not, it will not affect the outcome of this case?"

After listening in silence, Ari tried to respond. He felt the lump in his throat grow as a tear formed in his eye. "I'll tell you why," sniffled Ari. "My house, my chess game, my dad, it all makes sense to me now."

"I don't understand."

"I think I was five when my sister was born. I remember all the excitement, but that's it. I never saw her. Never saw my mom after that, either. She took the baby and left. Didn't say goodbye, didn't tell me or my dad, nothing, just left. So, my dad raised me. But then he lost his job, so we had to move to low income housing and eventually I was taking more care of him than he was of me. But

Heartly Law?

that was fine, I was cool with it. We talked, you know, about what was going to happen when I graduated school and got a Big-time job in a corporate law firm, about how we would move somewhere nice with a yard and maybe a man cave in the basement. But when I graduated law school, things weren't good for new attorneys. Law firms were laying people off. The PD's office was the only place that would hire me. I figured, it's okay, work here a year or two, when things pick up, leave for a better place, right? Two months into my job, my dad disappeared. No note, no voicemail, no discussion, he was just gone. I spent the next couple months looking for him, driving to all the dive bars he worked, checking in with some of his friends, but nobody had seen or heard from him. Not knowing what happened to him drove me crazy, but then Vince, my old supervisor, thought I was ready to try my first case. So, I focused all my time, outside the office, preparing for it. The more I focused, the less I worried about my dad. I tried that case and got a win. As a reward, I got two more cases. Soon I had a case load that was three times larger than any other PD, but I never complained. In fact, every time Vince assigned me another case, I viewed it as him doing me a favor. I was being productive instead of being consumed with grief and questions."

Ari choked back his tears as he continued. "I bought my house in that neighborhood because that's where we used to live. I thought maybe my dad would get word of it and show up. I even started a chess game. I thought maybe he'd feel the vibe or something. It didn't work out that way," said Ari as he wiped his nose with his sleeve.

"I didn't realize it until I read your report. All the people I've represented, O'Toole is the first client I can truly relate to. He lost siblings, his mom and his dad. So did I. He grew up as a scrapper, just like me. He had it a lot worse than I did, but still I can relate. And I can help him, I can help my fathe–...I can help Father O'Toole if he'd just let me. Why won't he give me a chance, Abby?"

"Ari, sweetheart, why don't I come see you tonight? We can talk some more. Maybe we can figure out a way–"

"I don't want to see you tonight. I mean, I always want to see you, just not right now." Ari stood up and cleared his throat. "I guess I should say it's not necessary. You've actually helped me already, a lot. You're right, focus on the evidence that I have. I've spent too many days on this case and I have very little to show for it. Thank you for reminding me that I no longer work for the government."

"I'm serious Ari," said Dr. Flynn.

"I know. Thank you, I mean it. But I do have a lot to do. Thank you for listening. And I am sorry."

"Please don't be."

"Gotta go, thanks again." Ari hung up the phone and started his walk back to Sally's gravel parking lot.

The long sobering walk back to his car helped to clear his head. As he drove home, he re-focused on his last discussion with O'Toole. But not about demons or guilty pleas. Instead he focused on why O'Toole asked him what the victim did after the shooting. *Was that important? Is there something I missed? Maybe I missed what isn't written, not what's written down?*

When Ari arrived home, he retrieved the mail. Mixed in with the bills and junk marketing was a mailing from the District Attorney's Office. Ari opened his front door and tiptoed to his kitchen to open the letter. It was the District Attorney's witness list. It contained all 93 witnesses. Not in any sort of order or priority, just a list of all available who could possibly testify.

Ari took the list and a pen and stepped into his living room. He collected his witness statements from the floor and organized them by priority based upon what he believed would be the most logical order in which the DA would call them. He knocked the dust off each statement and re-read it to see if any spoke of Rossi post-shooting, but none did.

Ari worked late into the night. One witness statement remained on the floor. It was from Detective Kelly, who was not listed as a witness. All witnesses were numbered on the DA's list, except for one — Nicholas Rossi. He was listed as a witness but still had no statement. Ari took a beat to sit back and think on that.

Chapter Thirty-eight

Father O'Toole sat patiently in his study and waited out the last few minutes before his 1 o'clock window to leave the rectory for his three-hour trip to the grocery shop. Just before he was ready to leave, there was a loud knock at the rectory door. Father O'Toole opened the door to find the stunning and immaculately dressed Jeannette Royale, who stood taller than he in her high heel boots. A car idled behind her.

"May I help you?" asked Father O'Toole, not knowing who she was.

"Hello, Father O'Toole. My name is Jeannette. I'm an attorney, and I need you to come with me, please."

"If it is about my case, you need to speak to my attorney. I am currently represented–"

"I know who your attorney is, and he is very good, but this doesn't involve him. It does involve your case, so you need to come with me."

Father O'Toole looked confused. "I can't go anywhere. This is my window—"

"I know that, too. 1:00 p.m. to 4:00 p.m. You'll be back in time so as not to violate, I promise," said Jeannette.

"I need to get my groceries. If someone needs to meet with me, they can come over here any day of the week except now." At that moment, Retired Detective Francis Kelly got out of the car from behind the driver's seat.

"Good afternoon, padre. Been awhile, huh?" said Kelly as he walked toward the front door.

O'Toole looked at him in disbelief. "Detective Kelly, is that you?"

"Retired now. No longer on the job."

"Again, not to be rude, detective, but I don't think my attorney would like me talking to police officers without him here."

"Again, I am retired. And this isn't police business. If it makes you feel any better, don't say anything at all. But you need to come with us. It's important, padre."

Father O'Toole peered at both for a moment. "Against my better judgment, for the love of Pete," said Father O'Toole. He walked to the car. "If you don't mind, I'll sit in the back seat."

The three of them traveled quietly down the road. Father O'Toole broke the silence. "And just where are we going?"

"Riverview Park," said Kelly.

"I didn't bring any bread to feed the ducks," said O'Toole, "If you'd let me get to the store first, I would have picked some up."

"No ducks today, Father," said Jeannette, "There's an important person who needs to meet with you."

"Who would that be?"

"You'll see shortly. Relax and enjoy the drive."

After a short ride through the city, they arrived at Riverview Park. Jeannette Royal remained in the car while Kelly and O'Toole walked into the park. It was the middle of a Thursday during the school year, so Riverview Park was completely empty. Kelly and O'Toole reached the end of the park where a dilapidated, poorly poured set of concrete steps traversed the hillside to the riverbank below. Kelly helped O'Toole down the steps and lead him along the riverbank until they were beneath the Hulton Bridge.

"Okay, Father, I don't expect your meeting to be very long. When you're finished, walk back up through the park to the corner of the boulevard. You can catch a bus there to bring you right to the rectory," said Kelly while he pointed directions.

"You're not staying for the meeting?"

"This is all you. You'll be fine. Great to see you again, glad to see you're still well." Kelly turned and headed back toward the park. O'Toole watched him until he disappeared. There was no one else in sight. The river was calm and quiet with no barge traffic. The only sound was from an occasional car that passed high above on the bridge. Bad thoughts filled the priest's mind, like bodies attached to cinder blocks at the bottom of the river or buried in the sands of this very bank. Out of the emptiness, a figure appeared on the riverbank and walked toward the priest from the opposite direction. Father O'Toole stared, and as the figure got closer, he was able to identify him – it was Nico Rossi. Father O'Toole began to tremble. The last time he saw Nico, O'Toole was looking at him through the iron sight on his pistol. The closer he got, the more he shook. He thought about fleeing, but he knew it was useless. He could never outrun Nico in perfect conditions, so the rocky sandy bank of the river ensured the futility of escape. He tried to steady himself and started to pray.

"Father O'Toole," said Nico, "so good to see you again." Nico gave the priest a big hug. Father O'Toole said nothing. "What, you aren't happy to see me?" Nico noticed that O'Toole was shaking. "Relax man, it's me. Nico, your buddy."

"I…I dunno what to say," murmured the priest.

"That's okay, you don't have to say anything. I brought you here so I could say a few things."

Father O'Toole caught his breath. "I suppose you're going to tell me that you'll be at my trial to bury me with your testimony."

"I hadn't even thought about going to your trial. But you got, what, two more weeks? Maybe I'll change my mind. I brought you here so that I could apologize to you."

"Apologize to me?" asked the priest.

"I am sorry. I drove you crazy and stressed you out what with all that business of being a priest and getting the Vatican all riled up. Those newspaper interviews sure didn't help, and the street ministry was even worse. The errors of youth and indiscretion, huh? Had I listened to you, none of this would have happened. You never would have shot me. But God protected me with the church key in my pocket. God's will, Father. God's will," said Nico.

"I don't think it was God's will. I know who you–"

"I forgive you for shooting me," interrupted Nico. "I know I just apologized to you for causing you to shoot me, but I want you to know that I do forgive you, just in case there's any tiny part of you that feels a little guilty," said Nico. He backed up a step from the priest.

"Ok, well, fine. I'm sorry for the shooting and I accept your apology. Now, I have to catch a bus."

"One more thing before you leave," said Nico. He reached into his pocket and pulled out a deck of playing cards still in the plastic wrap. "Pick a card, any card." He unwrapped the plastic, took the cards out of the box, and fanned them in front of the priest with both hands.

"What is this? You want to show me a card trick?"

"You'd better hope it works," said Nico in a cold tone. "Now, pick a card. Please."

Father O'Toole made his selection with a shaky hand. "Show me your card," said Nico.

"What kind of trick is it if you know my card?" asked Father O'Toole.

"You'll see. I think you'll like this," said Nico. He piled the remaining cards back up in his hand and held out the other hand for the card O'Toole chose. Nico examined the priest's card. "The King of Hearts? You got to be kidding me. Fifty-two cards and two Jokers, and you choose the Suicide King? Kind of ironic," said Nico with twisted lilt in his voice.

"So, I'm here to kill myself? That's your trick?"

"Hardly. Just watch. I'm going to take your Suicide King and put it on the back of the deck like so. Now keep watching me. I place the cards back into the box with your card as the very last one. Now Father, put the box of cards into the left pocket of your shirt, making absolutely certain that the King of Hearts is the closest to your chest. The trick won't work if you mess up the order."

Father O'Toole unzipped his jacket and placed the box of cards inside his shirt pocket as instructed. "Zip up your jacket," said Nico. He turned and walked 20 feet away from the priest.

"Okay, now what?" asked O'Toole.

"Stand perfectly still," said Nico in a cold inflection. Nico pulled a pistol from his pants pocket. O'Toole froze at the sight of the pistol. No need to worry about standing still. His breath escaped him as Nico drew back the hammer and took aim.

The hammer dropped onto the steel with a snap, but without the thundering sound of a bullet firing. "Bang!" said Nico. He took a few steps toward O'Toole.

The stunned priest shook. "It didn't fire," said the priest with trembling voice.

"That's odd," said Nico. "With a gun this old, I guess sometimes they don't always work so well. You can have it back, it's yours anyways," said Nico. He handed the .38 Special to the priest. "I'll be seeing you around. Thanks again," said Nico. He turned and disappeared under the Hulton Bridge at the turn of the riverbank.

Father O'Toole held the gun in his hand until he lost sight of Nico. He looked down at the old pistol and opened the cylinder. He saw that there was one spent shell casing inside, although he never heard a shot fire. O'Toole stood in shock and grasped both the grip of the pistol and the fact that he was holding his own gun, the same gun he'd used to shoot Nico at St. Mary's Church. The same gun that would be used against him as evidence during his trial. Father O'Toole looked around. Still, nobody was there. He looked out across the river and in his mind's eye saw Roberto Clemente standing at the plate. With every ounce of strength in his old body, he pushed off his back foot and hurled the gun as far as he could muster toward Clemente. He watched and heard it splash down into the murky depths of the river. It was probably not the first gun was thrown into the Allegheny River from the Hulton Bridge, but it was most likely the first time that a priest threw a gun, as well as a key piece of evidence in an attempted homicide case, into the river.

Father O'Toole walked to the bus stop at as quick a pace as he could manage. He waited a few minutes for the bus to arrive as scheduled, and he boarded it. There was only one other person was on the bus. The other passenger sat up front, so Father O'Toole made his way all the way to the back of the bus. He still shook with every step.

O'Toole caught the breath he'd lost from both the "card trick" and the brisk walk. He noticed a bulge inside his jacket pocket. He unzipped his jacket and reached inside to find a half pint of Johnny Walker. "How did that get there?" he said to himself. "It certainly wasn't in my pocket when I put the jacket on. It isn't even the scotch that I drink." He chose not to discriminate and opened the bottle for a large swig, followed by another. The scotch calmed his nerves just a bit.

By the time he finished the small bottle, he noticed something else – a small hole on the front of his jacket. He investigated further and found another hole, a tad larger, on the pocket of his shirt. He pulled the deck of cards out from his shirt pocket and saw a hole on the card box. He opened the box and removed the deck. Each and every card had a hole in the exact same place. The holes got larger on each card until they reached the end. The very last card in the box was the card he chose– the King of Hearts, the "Suicide King." It was unscathed, not even a scratch on it. He placed the cards back into the box and put them back in his pocket. The scotch no longer prevented his shaking.

The bus arrived at Father O'Toole's stop only a short distance from the rectory. He checked his watch and saw that he'd arrived in plenty of time so as not to violate his window. As he walked up to his front door, he could see that something was left there directly in front of it. There were three bags filled with groceries, including bread. He scooped up the bags, went inside, set the groceries down, and crawled into bed.

Chapter Thirty-nine

The two weeks leading up to the trial were polar opposites of approach. The District Attorney's Office was in constant motion. Teams of assistant district attorneys and investigators interviewed witnesses, prepped several of them for testimony, and issued subpoenas to ensure that all witness would be there for trial. The notable exception to the witnesses list was one Retired Detective Francis Kelly. Detective Martin convinced the District Attorney that Kelly had become a sympathizer with Father O'Toole either due to choice, old age, or the blow he took to his face when they banged heads during his attempt to put him in hand cuffs. Because of his current stance on the subject, Francis Kelly would not be a good witness. The District Attorney did not understand Martin's rationale but figured that the testimony from Detective Martin in itself would be enough to carry the day, so he agreed to remove Kelly as a witness.

Ari, on the other hand, did very little in the waning days before trial. He found himself in a constant state of anxiety over the fear that perhaps his best days as an attorney were behind him. It was a tangible weight on his back. He doubted his skill, and he couldn't understand how ineffective he had become. He could not fathom how he failed to be persuasive enough to talk O'Toole into pleading guilty, especially when a plea could result in a suspended sentence or extended probation.

He slept very little, and he drank slightly more. He watched TV, played some of his records, and on occasion, he ate a meal. He tried to focus enough to prepare for the case but was unable to find anything that grasped his attention. Instead of his typical trial binder, he had one page of handwritten notes, most of which was gibberish.

On the eve of trial, he called Father O'Toole.

"Are you ready, Mr. O'Toole?" said Ari with the outside hope that O'Toole would change his mind and plead guilty.

"I won't be testifying, so all I have to do is show up on time, right? I'm ready for that. I suppose the real question is are you ready, counsellor?" said the priest.

"Tomorrow will most likely be a media circus. I've spoken to the judge's staff, and they've directed the sheriffs to let us into the courtroom immediately upon our arrival. How about I pick you up tomorrow around 6:00 a.m.? I know it's early, but we might avoid the cameras that way."

"Considerate of the judge. Is he a friend of yours?"

"Not at all. But he doesn't envy the media circus, and the last thing he wants is for you to say something on camera that might impact the trial, or more likely the appeal. He's trying to shield you, that's all," said Ari.

"I see, fine then. Six o'clock tomorrow morning it is." Father O'Toole hung up the phone, lit a candle with a picture of St. Michael the Archangel behind it, and resumed his rosary. Ari poured one more drink, made sure his suit was ready, and laid down in bed. He listened to his clock radio.

Chapter Forty

Ari arrived on time at the rectory. He and O'Toole made the short drive downtown well before the sun had risen. They parked in the empty garage and walked to the courthouse. Only one reporter was on the scene, but she was the one who gave the obligatory morning report on nothing in particular "Live from Downtown" as part of the 6:00am news coverage.

A sheriff met Ari and Father O'Toole at the side door of the courthouse. He wanded both of them and lead them to the courtroom. It was still too early in the morning for conversation, so the sheriff said nothing during the brief procession. The uninspiring courthouse seemed even more bleak at this hour. With no sign of any life within, save for the random sheriff or janitor, the dank unlit walls oozed depression, as if to smother and suffocate the will to live out of any passerby. Ari thought it was a perfect place for this trial.

The sheriff unlocked the door, turned on the lights, and left Ari and O'Toole alone in the empty courtroom. He locked the courtroom door behind him and returned to his solitary corner to enjoy his newspaper and coffee on the clock until regular courthouse visitors start to arrive in a couple of hours.

"What do we do now?" asked Father O'Toole.

"We wait," said Ari, not even bothering to look at him. He set his briefcase on the table. "You can sit, stand, walk around, go anywhere you like as long as you stay inside the courtroom. When the trial starts, you'll sit beside me here at counsel table."

Father O'Toole milled about the courtroom. It was the first time he had ever been in any courtroom before. "I recognize some of these black and white pictures of the old judges. I know their names at least. I read them in the papers over the years. It's a shame – first time in a courtroom and I'm the defendant. I do like the feel of this room. I think I'd enjoy watching things unfold and justice being administered, if only it wasn't me. Pictures of the judges hang on the wall like saints. The old wooden-style benches remind me of pews, and look up there, where the judge sits. It's like the altar. I do feel more comfortable," said the priest out loud.

Ari did not respond. He sat at counsel table with his eyes closed. He was not trying to sleep, or plan trial strategy, cross-examines, openings or closings. He wasn't thinking about anything. Not this trial, or his career, or what life might be like if this trial proved to be as disastrous as he was sure it would be. He just sat there, being peaceful.

"Counselor, do you want to discuss, talk about anything?" asked the priest from across the room.

"No, I'm good," said Ari.

"What are you doing?" asked the priest again, a bit disturbed at the lack of action from his lawyer.

"Mindset. Enjoy the few moments of calm before all Hell breaks loose," said Ari, annoyed that his temporary respite was interrupted.

"You don't know how right you are, son," said Father O'Toole under his breath. He took a seat in the jury box to give Ari his space. From one of his pockets he pulled out his old set of rosary beads. From the other pocket, a box of cards with a bullet hole almost all the way through them. He placed the cards in his shirt pocket underneath the jacket of his working-man's suit coat, with the King of Hearts closest to his chest.

Ari's peace and calm came to an end at 7:50 a.m. when a large crowd started to assemble outside the courtroom. Some were witnesses, but from the sound of metal tripods snapping into place and banging off the tile floor in the hallway, Ari could tell that there was also a large media presence. No cameras were permitted in the courtroom. At 8:00 a.m. sharp, a sheriff unlocked the door but kept it closed. He stood as gatekeeper at the door to ensure that only people with business before the court could enter. Most of the media would be kept out except a handful of the seasoned veteran reporters. The courtroom was not big enough to accommodate any nebby onlookers.

Immediately after the door was unlocked, Assistant District Attorney Lindsay Kennedy entered the courtroom. She pulled a roll

Heartly Law?

cart filled with three large boxes behind her and wheeled her way up to the prosecutor's table. She turned to Ari.

"Good morning, Attorney Meyer," she said in a cold infliction.

"Well, hello sunshine! How's my girl today?" said Ari with a cheesy grin. Ms. Kennedy said nothing. She rolled her eyes and started to unload her boxes. When she was finished, she moved to the back of the courtroom. The prosecution's witnesses were trickling in, and Assistant District Attorney Kennedy directed them to their temporary seats. Witnesses normally report to a separate room prior at the start of trial, but the Deputy District Attorney wanted them to assemble first in the courtroom. Ari knew this was the Deputy DA's attempt at a show of force, but he also understood that it amounted to nothing more than lame gamesmanship. The Deputy DA knew that Ari would motion for all witnesses to be sequestered before trial, and that motion would be granted. Nonetheless, the DA's Office took every opportunity they had to intimidate Ari and Father O'Toole. "It won't work on me," Ari thought, "but maybe it will on O'Toole. Maybe the sight of all these witnesses will lead to a last-minute plea?'

Father O'Toole joined Ari at the defense table. "Is she the one trying the case?" he asked.

"I wish. You might've had a chance if she was. Instead, it'll be Deputy District Attorney Nathan Blake, head of the homicide unit. You know, he only tries homicides these days, but he's good. Really good. I guess the DA didn't want to take any chances, so he's using his big guns, so to speak. Even though this isn't a homicide case," said Ari. He was taken aback by the palpable sound of defeat in his own voice.

"I see. Very well," said the priest. He sat back in his chair and held onto his rosary beads.

Deputy District Attorney Nathan Blake entered the courtroom, followed by Detective Martin right behind him. Detective Martin carried the evidence box. "Good Morning, Meyer. Quite a crowd out there already," said the smug Deputy District Attorney. He and Detective Martin approached their table.

Ari looked at Blake and replied, "Good morning." He turned back to resume his direct stare at the judge's bench in front of him.

Detective Martin said nothing. He placed his box on the table and took a seat at the far left.

Ari cracked the gold laches on his briefcase and reached inside to remove his sterling silver Tiffany "Trial Pen." He placed it in the outer pocket of his suit coat. Ari stared for a moment at the two faded Polaroid pictures that he taped to the inside of his briefcase. After a heavy moment, he shut the briefcase and put it on the floor. He was ready for trial.

About 8:30 a.m., Dr. Abigail Flynn unexpectedly entered the courtroom and approached the defense table.

"Well, good morning, Dr. Flynn. How are you today? I do hope you're well," said Father O'Toole.

"I am fine, thank you. How are you, my friend?" she asked.

"As good as possible, I suppose. All things considered. But I know I'm in good hands," said Father O'Toole. He placed his hand on Ari's shoulder.

"Abby, I didn't expect you this week. I hope I didn't give you bad information. We have openings and the DA has a lot of witnesses. I won't get to you for at least a couple weeks," said Ari.

"You were clear. I understand I'm not needed. I just thought I should be here, for the both of you. I can't stay past today until I'm needed, but I just thought, well, you know."

"Cool. If you're going to stay, why don't you sit at counsel table with us?"

"Sure," she said. She took a seat on the other side of Ari.

The three of them sat at the table and said nothing. The stream of humanity continued to flood the courtroom. The judge's tipstaff brought each table a pitcher of water with some paper cups. Ari started to fidget. He removed his pen from his pocket and tapped it on the table like a spastic drummer, out of time and out of sync. Dr. Flynn reached over to his tapping hand and placed hers on top of it to calm him. Ari turned to her. Dr. Flynn's usual look of admiration for Ari was replaced by sympathy, as if to say, "I am so sorry for you." The warm touch of her hand did soothe him, even if just for a second, and even though he realized he was getting pity.

"I'm okay. It's cool. The judge will be on the bench soon. Just kinda' getting anxious a little, you know. Let's get this party

Heartly Law?

started, right?" said Ari. Father O'Toole squeezed his rosary beads harder.

Wil 3

Chapter Forty-one

At the same time Dr. Flynn entered the courtroom, another unexpected group was making its presence felt. Crowds of people hustled to their jobs along the sidewalks in front of the courthouse on either side of Grant Street, as usual for a workday. The melodic sound of a well-tuned engine filled the air. It wasn't brutal and clumsy like a Harley, and it wasn't high-pitched and screaming like a sport bike. It was the sound of perfection just short of divine, and it matched the look of the brand-new carbon black and metallic BMW R1250RT touring motorcycle that cruised down Grant Street. As if some great force just hit the pause button, everyone on the street stopped at once.

The driver appeared not to be concerned about getting ticketed or towed since he pulled the bike beside the courthouse in a spot reserved for city-owned vehicles on official business. The only thing more beautiful than that motorcycle was the back passenger. She dismounted, unzipped the saddle bag, removed her briefcase, and took off her helmet to let all her long blonde hair fall out and over her shoulders. Her hair moved slightly in the breeze coming off the river. She removed her black leather jacket and stuffed it into the empty saddle bag along with her helmet. She stood beside the motorcycle in a navy blue Zadig & Voltaire pinstripe pants suit. The suit combined with her Sainte Laurent Brown Freja leather boots with the high pink heels made it appear as if she'd stepped out of a Bloomingdales magazine. The driver of the bike also resembled a model with his tie-free custom Brooks Brothers suit and highly shined Bacco Bucci ankle boots. Such a presence of unabashed elegance did not belong near a courthouse anywhere in America, let alone on Grant Street. These two unforeseen visions entered the courthouse together.

Ari and friends heard the din from the outside grow larger. It sounded to them as if people were scrambling to get to their cameras or possibly running out of the way. The three of them joined the rest of the courtroom crowd in turning toward the back of the courtroom to witness the arrival of the Jeannette Royale, Esquire, followed by Nico Rossi. Jeannette strolled with jungle cat swagger to counsel tables and directed Nico to sit in an empty seat at the back of the courtroom. Her eyes met Ari's and she gave him wink and a smile, much to the chagrin of Dr. Flynn. Attorney Royale proceeded to the prosecutor's table. All parties walked off to the far side of the courtroom to conference.

Ari strained, but could not hear what they were talking about. He understood in short order without words what was happening. The prosecution looked back to see Nico Rossi sitting quietly. They turned to flash devilish grins at Ari to suggest "Game Over!"

"This is why I listed Rossi as a witness, Ms. Kennedy. Didn't hurt us to do so and look, we caught a break with the star-witness now in the courtroom," said Deputy District Attorney Blake. "I will direct him when the time is right."

"Is that Rossi back there?" Ari asked Father O'Toole.

"It appears so, damn it. He said he wasn't coming," said Father O'Toole.

"When did he say that he wasn't coming? Did you talk to him?" Father O'Toole did not respond, but the embarrassed look on his face was enough to answer the question.

When the prosecutors finished their conversation with Royale, they returned to the table. Ari rose from his table and stepped into the aisle to force a conversation with this woman who had no choice but to walk past him. Ari stuck out his hand and said, "I'm Ari Meyer. I represent Thomas O'Toole. And you are?"

"I know who you are; I know all about you. You should know me, but it looks like you don't. Pity." she said.

"How do you know all about me?"

"Well dear, I am Attorney Jeannette Royale, and I'm your number one fan. I've followed your career since your first jury acquittal," said Attorney Royale with pride.

"Remind me. Which one was that?" Ari asked to test her.

Heartly Law?

"The one where the prominent socialite was robbed of her purse in Market Square, and the cops tried to pin it on a homeless guy. That was an impressive win. Afterall, he did have the purse on him when the cops popped him."

"Yeah, he had the purse, but there were no contents. The actual robber kept the good stuff and threw away the purse. My guy found it, stuffed it with leaves, and was using it as a pillow. Sad how that little fact never made the police report."

"Jakes can be a bitch like that. But that's why we do what we do."

"What's your deal? Are you representing Rossi in some way?"

"I am. And you know what, I'm sure I could teach you a thing or two," said Royale. She stepped even closer to Ari.

"Not likely," said Ari, "but just for laughs, what do you think you could teach me?"

"You got the lawyer thing down, but I could help your pool game," she said with a smile.

"I don't play girls. It's bad luck."

"Number one rule at Sally's – No girls by the desk."

"That's the second rule, the first is–"

"Hit balls easy or leave," they said in unison. Ari was about to smile at her before he caught himself. How did she know he played pool? He'd never seen her at Sally's before? He'd hardly seen any women there over the years, and the few he had seen looked nothing like her. "Who was this girl?" he thought to himself.

The judge's tipstaff then took center stage. "May I have your attention. The judge will be taking the bench momentarily. All those who have business before this court on the matter of Commonwealth v. O'Toole should take your seat. All the rest of you need to remove yourself from the court."

"Catch you later, sugar," said Attorney Royale. She proceeded to the back of the courtroom to sit beside her client.

Ari returned to his table in a state of utter confusion.

"Well?" said Father O'Toole.

"I got to get to know that girl," said Ari.

"I bet you do," snipped Dr. Flynn.

At the DA's table, the two prosecutors readied themselves.

"Kennedy, you ready for Dr. Chan's direct?" asked Deputy District Attorney Blake.

"Yes, sir. I am ready," replied ADA Kennedy.

"After I open, you'll direct Chan. So, get the evidence ready."

Assistant District Attorney Kennedy went into the evidence box and she pulled out the expert report from the Allegheny County Crime Lab which she intended to hand to Dr. Victor Chan, author of the report and the Commonwealth's expert. She had her own copy with her that was marked up with notation. She searched through the evidence box for the gun, but she couldn't find it there.

"Ahh, sir, where's the gun?" she said in slight panic.

"What do you mean, 'where's the gun?' It's in the box," said Deputy DA Blake.

"No, it isn't," said Kennedy. Detective Martin jumped up to look inside. He found nothing.

"Martin, did you leave the fucking gun in the evidence room?" snapped Deputy DA Blake.

"No chance. The gun was in the box after it came back from crime lab, and the box was sealed until Kennedy broke it and opened it up just now," said Martin.

"I didn't break any seal. The lid was on the box, but it wasn't sealed," said ADA Kennedy.

"All rise, the Honorable Judge Nelson is now presiding. May God save the Commonwealth and this Court," said the tipstaff.

"You may be seated," said the judge. Everyone took a seat. Commotion escalated at the DA's table. "Counsel, please identify yourselves for the record."

"Deputy District Attorney Nathan Blake for the Commonwealth."

"Assistant District Attorney Lindsay E. Kennedy for the Commonwealth."

"May it please the Court, and counsel, Attorney Ari Meyer, for the Defendant."

"Thank you all," said the judge. "Are there any motions that I need to rule upon before I bring in the jury?"

"Your Honor, may we approach?" asked Deputy DA Blake.

Heartly Law?

Ari was puzzled by the disorganized scene across from him. He joined the other two attorneys at the judge's bench.

"Your Honor, please forgive my request, but I need a few minutes. It seems a key piece of evidence wasn't retrieved from the evidence room. We need to go back to get it," said the embarrassed Deputy DA.

"I'm not sure I understand," said the judge.

"Your Honor, may I please come forward, sir?" asked Detective Martin. "It's my fault, your Honor, completely my fault. I trusted a new officer to bring the evidence and I guess I failed to properly supervise him. The fault is on me, not the DA. If you could give me a little time, I will personally go back to get the gun and bring it here, your Honor."

"The gun?" Ari thought to himself. The judge looked at Ari to see if he had any comment or objection. The normally verbose attorney said nothing and just shrugged his shoulders.

"Very well. Highly unusual. Let's try again after lunch. Take your seats," said the judge. "Ladies and gentlemen, it seems that we will be slightly delayed in the proceeding. We shall reconvene after lunch," said the judge. He hit his gavel and got up from the bench.

Detective Martin ran full speed out of the courtroom without so much as a glance in the direction of Nico Rossi and his runway model attorney.

Ari jumped up from his seat and bolted back to Rossi and Royale before they left. "Hold on," said Ari. "I have a few more questions,"

"Yeah, I don't know," said Royale.

"Are you Rossi?" asked Ari.

"He is I and I am him," said Nico smugly.

Ari chuckled. "Heard a lot about you, Snoop. How did you get out of the church after you got shot, without anybody seeing you?"

"Excuse me, Attorney Meyer," said Jeannette Royale who stepped in between Ari and her client, "This is highly inappropriate. You cannot come over here and start crossing my client."

"You know what is inappropriate? You and your whole plan, whatever it is. You cannot come into court on the day of trial and bring in the suspected victim of a shooting to testify against my guy.

I have been given no notice, no statements, no discovery of any kind. If he is a witness, he will need to be sequestered just like the other witnesses will be, in which case neither of you will be in here. And if the DA tries to call him, I will pitch such a bitch for discovery violations, the court will have no choice but to declare a mistrial." Ari assumed that she knew there was little merit to his argument. He was saying whatever he could to force her to talk to him so that he could figure out just who she was.

"One question. And only one," said Attorney Royale.

Ari turned to Nico and anticipated his explanation. "Well?"

Nico responded in a calm voice. "Easily. People were running around, knocking each other over, it was bedlam. I went right out the back door at the exact minute the PAT Bus pulled up to the corner. I hopped on and rode it to Oakmont. Nothing more than that," said Nico.

"Occam's Razor, huh?"

"That's right," said Nico.

Attorney Royale grabbed Ari's hand and pulled him away from Nico. "Okay, sweetheart, you got your answer," she said as she held a tight grip on his hand. "There are only two things with which you need to concern yourself."

"They are?" asked Ari.

"First, if it don't fit, you must acquit."

"Brilliant, but I've heard that before," said Ari. "Try again. What's second?"

Attorney Royale took her free hand and placed it with her other hand on top of Ari's. She brought Ari's hand up to her face and softly grazed her cheek with it. She closed her eyes and she affectionately kissed his hand. She released her grip and got close enough to Ari to place her hand on the back of his head and pulled it toward her mouth. She whispered in his ear, "Second is that I know where our father is," she said. She kissed him on the cheek. Attorney Royale motioned to Nico, and the two exited the courtroom in the flow of the other people. Ari stood there motionless for several long seconds before he dragged himself back to the defense table.

O'Toole was about to speak, but Ari held up his hand to silence. He needed to think. What in the blue Hell, he thought to himself? Never in a million years did he envision himself having such a cryptic conversation, and that was saying something, considering past conversations he'd had with O'Toole. At least he now better understood a part of the story of Nico Rossi. He wasn't a miracle man; he was a bus rider. What did she mean by "if it don't fit, you must acquit?" He understood the reference, but was it relevant? And what did she mean by "our father?"

He turned to Dr. Flynn whose body language portrayed both jealousy and anger over the kissing scene at the rear of the courtroom.

"I think I love her," said Ari to Dr. Flynn.

"Why wouldn't you? She's tall, super gorgeous, a lawyer, what's not to love, right?" said Dr. Flynn.

"No, not like that, not like how I love you – I mean, strike that. No, wait, don't strike that," said Ari. "Look, Abby, we got a break. I need to think, by myself. You stay here with O'Toole, if you don't mind, and I'll swing past Nicky's to grab you both some brunch. I just need an hour or so. Please, Abby.

Dr. Flynn offered a reluctant nod. Father O'Toole sat quiet and looked more confused than ever as he strangled his rosary beads. Ari sprinted out of the courtroom.

Chapter Forty-two

Ari returned to the courtroom an hour later. He brought a container of French toast sticks and some coffee for Father O'Toole. He wanted to know exactly how he knew, or thought he knew, why Rossi wasn't supposed to show up for trial. But instead of asking, he dropped off the food and headed back outside to stroll around the city for a couple hours before the start of the afternoon session. Discussions had never been particularly fruitful with O'Toole anyway, and now Ari doubted his honesty, even more than he did with the whole "I didn't shoot Rossi" drum that he kept beating. For the first time since very early on, Ari wanted to think about the case.

"What does the evidence say? What does the evidence say?" he kept repeating in his head. "What the hell was up with all that confusion at counsel table and delay to the start? That was completely out of character for Blake and his OCD'd Assistant DA. There's no way they could have possibly lost evidence. Drug evidence disappears sometimes, but not guns? Probably just didn't grab it, like the detective said. Still..."

Ari pondered and talked out loud to himself. "What's the deal with this chick and Rossi? Is the plan to put Rossi on the stand to testify? His testimony combined with any of the witnesses will make this a short case and a quick deliberation. Why did O'Toole think Rossi wasn't going to show? If his plan is to testify, why not cooperate at jump street? Why wait 'til the morning of trial? Maybe that isn't their plan? Maybe Rossi is some kind of wildcard that I can exploit? But if he wasn't planning to testify, why bother even showing up?"

All of his thoughts and all of his experience didn't help him make sense of the situation. He was no closer to a viable defense strategy or even a plan of attack. He felt the physical pressure of frustration and dread while he trudged up the steps of the courthouse feeling as though both feet were in two buckets of poured cement.

Ari made his way back into the courtroom and took a seat at his table. The opposite table was empty. The two attorneys and the detective were huddled up back in their corner. "What's going on over there?" asked Ari.

"I've been trying to listen," said Dr. Flynn. "There's is an occasional raised voice, but I can't really tell. Agitation is high, though."

"They came in about half an hour ago," said Father O'Toole, "When they saw that I was already sitting here, they took their conversation over there. Been there ever since."

A few minutes later, the tipstaff called all to order.

"Ladies and gentlemen, please be seated. The judge will be taking the bench momentarily. Again, if you have no business in the case of <u>Commonwealth v. O'Toole</u>, you must now leave the courtroom," yelled the tipstaff over the noisy courtroom. The two DAs and the detective took their place at the table. A few moments later, the tipstaff bellowed again, "All rise." Judge Nelson took his spot on the bench.

"Please take a seat," said the judge. Everyone did so except the two district attorneys.

"Commonwealth, are we ready to proceed?" asked the judge.

"Thank you, your Honor. Unfortunately, no, we are not ready. At this time, we must motion for a continuance, your Honor," said Deputy DA Blake.

Ari looked at them with disbelief. He stood up to address the court. For the first time in the entirety of this case, everything made sense to him. He understood Royale's reference to Johnnie Cochran. He realized that he only had a brief moment to make his point.

"Are we on the record, your Honor?" asked Ari.

"C'mon, Meyer, it's a Motion for a Continuance," said the vexed Deputy DA.

"Your Honor, pardon my desire to adhere to proper procedure, but for the sake of posterity, the Commonwealth is making a Motion and as such, I think the interest of justice requires it to be on the record, your Honor."

The judge gave Ari a quick glare before he nodded to the court reporter. She pulled her machine in front of her and started to record for the transcript.

Heartly Law?

"Very well. Counsel, we are now on the record. The Commonwealth may proceed with its motion," said the judge.

After a deep exhale, Deputy DA Blake began, "Thank you, your Honor. Unfortunately, the Commonwealth is not fully prepared at this time. I do acknowledge that my request is unusual, but unfortunately, we need more time to prepare, sir," said Blake.

"Attorney Blake, correct me if I'm wrong," said the judge, "but didn't we delay the start of the trial today because the Commonwealth failed to bring evidence to the courtroom? Evidence that I can only assume is essential to this case?"

"Your Honor is correct," said the Deputy DA.

"And didn't you assure me that you would be bringing it here for the start of the trial, sir?"

"Again, your Honor is correct."

"Well, what happened?" asked the judge.

"Your Honor, if I may, we started to search through all the boxes of evidence—" said Detective Martin. Ari held out his index finger and started to shake it in the "no-no-no" motion, which the judge recognized. The judge snapped on the detective.

"No, you may not, detective. There will be nothing from you. We are on the record and you haven't been sworn in. This argument is for the lawyers," scolded the judge. He turned to his court reporter. "Would you kindly strike anything that the detective said from the record."

"Yes, sir" said the court reporter. After a few quick beats, she replied, "Record stricken. Ready to proceed"

"Very well. Commonwealth, please explain yourself," said the perturbed judge.

"Yes, your Honor. My understanding is that a very solid attempt to retrieve the evidence was undertaken by Detective Martin and others in the precinct. But, as I am sure your Honor can appreciate, there are many, many boxes of evidence, and the evidence we need could have easily been placed into any of them by a misfiling. And the time allotted simply wasn't enough to search all the boxes. We are asking this Honorable Court to grant the continuance requested and allow us the time to fully search for the misplaced evidence. Point of fact, your Honor, when this case does proceed, the Commonwealth intends to call Dr. Victor Chan from the Allegheny County Crime Lab. He will testify, consistent with his expert report which we will also offer into evidence, that he personally tested the .38 Special revolver, retrieved from the crime scene, as well as a bullet slug recovered from the scene which ballistic tests will indicate is a perfect match and was, in fact, fired from the same .38 Special recovered at the crime scene."

"Attorney Meyer, response?" said the judge.

"Many, many, many boxes, your Honor. So expansive. Sooo many boxes. Let's be realistic here: the evidence room is just that, a room. A room in a small precinct. We aren't talking about Iron Mountain, your Honor. It shouldn't take a continuance to find a piece of evidence that is essential in this case. And what are we talking about? We are talking about a gun. It isn't a piece of paper. It's not photographs. The Commonwealth is talking about misfiling a gun the same way they would a misfiled an expense report. And yes, they have an expert report, I read it. It says they tested *a gun* and that the slug recovered was shot from the same gun. But so what? If they don't have that actual gun to enter into evidence, then their testing and reports are of no probative value. That's rather important, considering that they'll have a hard time showing that my client attempted to shoot and presumably kill the victim in this case when they can't offer the gun into evidence and have absolutely no explanation for why it is missing. So, if the Commonwealth is looking for my consent to their Motion for a Continuance, then respectfully, your Honor, I will have to deny my acquiescence. Furthermore, I want an offer of proof."

Father O'Toole knew where the gun was. He knew that in a lifetime of continuances, they would never find it if they limited their search to the evidence room. But he said nothing. He was exercising his right to remain silent. Nobody asked him if he knew where it was, so he wasn't lying.

"The victim. Of course. Well, there you go," said the Deputy DA. "We don't need the gun if the victim testifies that he was shot by O'Toole."

"Where is the victim?" asked Ari.

"The victim, one Nicholas Rossi, is sitting right back–" The Deputy DA and all others turned around to look where Nico had been sitting, but his chair and the one occupied by his lawyer were both now vacant. "Jesus Christ! Kennedy, go out in the hall and see if he is out there and bring his ass back in here, now please," said Deputy DA Blake under his breath, not loud enough to get on record. "Yes, your Honor. Mr. Rossi, the victim in this case, was here this morning. Furthermore, he is being represented by an attorney, Ms. Jeannette Royale. Both were here this morning, your Honor. They must not have made it back from the break. We expect them back."

"Give me a minute," said the judge. He motioned for his law clerk, who came behind the bench. The judge turned off his microphone, and the two had a brief discussion.

A minute later, Assistant District Attorney Kennedy came back into the courtroom. "He is not out there, sir. And nobody out there has seen either one of them since this morning."

"We are back on the record," said Judge Nelson. "Attorney Blake, I am very hesitant to grant a continuance based upon your failure to bring necessary evidence to court, especially because the easiest thing to do would be to call your witnesses in a different order, thereby giving you more time to get organized and bring what you need. However, if the victim has failed to appear, well, that would be sufficient reason to grant the continuance. Mr. Meyer?"

"Thank you, your Honor. I agree," said Ari. The Deputy DA breathed a sigh of relief. "Failure of an essential witness to appear at this proceeding would warrant a continuance. Assuming, of course, that the witness was properly subpoenaed."

"Attorney Blake, was the victim properly subpoenaed?" asked the judge.

"And we are on the record, right your Honor?" asked Ari.

"Yes, of course, Attorney Myer," said the judge.

"Go ahead, Deputy District Attorney. And please, pardon my interruption."

Deputy DA Blake flipped through a large stack of papers to appear as if he was looking for the subpoena. He knew that he wouldn't find it. He was just trying to buy some more time. After about two minutes, the judge moved him along.

"Well, counselor, was the victim subpoenaed or not?" asked the judge.

"It seems he was not, your Honor. But look, that wasn't our fault. We knew who the victim was and we made several attempts to locate him with the detectives and other officers, but we couldn't find him, so he never got served," said Deputy DA Blake who dug himself into an even deeper hole with the judge.

"Hold on now," said the judge with disgust, "you have got to be kid–, you mean to tell me that the Commonwealth is accusing this defendant of attempted murder but that you don't have the weapon, even though it was recovered from the crime scene and you had a full crime lab analysis run on it? Then you are telling me that the victim of this shooting was never given a subpoena because his whereabouts were unknown, even though you just said that he was here today, for some reason, and that he had his own lawyer? But yet, when he was here, with his lawyer, you didn't think to give him a subpoena at that time? Is that really what you're telling me?" asked the judge.

Blake looked at the judge and put the papers in his hand back on the desk. He had a quick, quiet word with ADA Kennedy. "Your Honor, my most sincere apologies. I am not certain what happened here or why we are so unprepared. But your Honor, I have appeared before this court numerous times. I am sure you will agree with me that such unreadiness and confusion on my part is not the norm, not ever. That said, for what has happened, I apologize to this Honorable Court. Your Honor makes a valid point. The most sensible thing to do would be to call other witnesses. Move out of the order we preferred, but start things moving. While other witnesses are testifying, my office, along with the detectives, can locate the missing gun as well as the missing victim so that we can call the victim to testify, as well as Dr. Chan, at the end of the trial rather than the beginning. So, with that, your Honor, I respectfully withdraw my Motion for a Continuance and ask that we move into opening arguments."

"Very well. That can be arranged. Attorney Meyer?"

"Thank you, your Honor. I take no position on the Commonwealth's withdrawal of the Motion for a Continuance. However, I have asked for an Offer of Proof, which I believe would now be proper at this time," said Ari.

"Are you serious, Meyer?" snapped Deputy DA Blake.

Ari did not reply to this outburst but instead addressed the judge in a calm and methodical manner. Ari used the chaos of the scene to make argument before the judge, which was unconventional, if not completely irregular, but that was Ari.

"Here me out, your Honor," argued Ari. "First, let me start by stating that the date on this crime lab report is from 10 months ago. To me that suggests that if somehow the police or the DA or the crime lab lost the evidence, or perhaps misfiled it, it has been so for at least 10 months. That also suggests to me that it isn't going to be found by the time the last witness is called. Second, this incident happened almost a year and a half ago. Like the DA said, they knew who the alleged victim was, but they never questioned him, never took a statement. They had no idea where he was, they couldn't even send him a subpoena. We all know Detective Martin over there. We are all very much aware of his stellar reputation. If he can't find someone in a year and a half, then that person simply will not be found. So to me, that suggests that the alleged victim is an unwilling participant who does not want to be found and does not wish to participate. Yes, he was here today. I have no idea why. I tried to talk to him after the break, but his attorney would not allow it. Now, once again, he is gone. And nobody has a clue as to his whereabouts. If he wasn't readily found in a year and a half of looking for him, I would suggest that the Commonwealth would make a stronger argument by suggesting that this trial may drag on for three months, so maybe at some point the alleged victim will stagger back into the courtroom. But that is a colossal maybe."

Ari continued as the Deputy DA chomped at the bit to respond. "Three months, your Honor. On one hand, I am strongly suggesting that will not be enough time for the DA to collect their lost evidence and find their missing witness in light of what we have seen here today. But on the other hand, your Honor, I am suggesting that three months of trial is far too long to keep this jury hostage."

"Your Honor," interrupted Blake, "I don't see the point in what Meyer is trying to say here. We agreed to withdrawal our motion for a continuance, and he is well aware of the evidence the Commonwealth will be putting forward, so I would ask–" said Blake.

"And I would ask, your Honor," said Ari, "to please direct the Deputy District Attorney to show some courtesy and respect and not interrupt me as I did not interrupt him. Also, could you kindly inform the distinguished gentleman that I have, in fact, passed the Bar Exam, and as such I should be addressed as Attorney Meyer or Counselor and not '*Meyer.*' What he chooses to call me off the record is another matter, your Honor."

"Noted," said the judge. He gave a stern look to Deputy DA Blake. "Please continue."

"As I was saying, your Honor," continued Ari, "the Commonwealth has provided a list of 93 named witnesses, not counting Dr. Chan. In those boxes are 93 alleged eyewitness statements. If a jury has to sit through all of those witnesses, we will be here for three months, easily. And that's even before we put on our defense. So to avoid that potential, I am asking for an Offer of Proof. Quite simply, your Honor, if you look at those statements, they all say the same thing, with slight variations based on vantage point, obstruction, etc. They all basically say that the alleged witness *heard* a loud noise, like a gunshot, then they *saw* the victim fall. That is what they basically all say. But what is *stated* in those witness reports is not important. What is *missing* from each of those reports is the real issue. And what is missing is the fact that not a single one of those witnesses ever said that they saw Mr. O'Toole pull the trigger. Nobody. Not one single witness."

Ari rolled on: "And you know what else isn't included in the mountain of supposed evidence provided by the Commonwealth? Blood. There is no blood anywhere. Not a single drop. Now the Commonwealth is alleging that my client shot the victim, thus knocking him to the ground, yet not one single drop of blood spilled in the process. How is that even a remote possibility? What we *do not* have is actually far more significant than what we *do have*, allegedly, before us today. Not to digress too far off the road, your Honor, but personally, one of the things I was most looking forward to in this trial was to see what really happened. This story the Commonwealth is telling is completely fascinating. We have a priest who supposedly shoots a victim, yet nobody sees him do it. The victim is allegedly struck by the bullet and is knocked to the ground in full view of a few hundred people, yet we have no blood. We have a victim, then we lose the victim, then the victim shows up, then he disappears again, then the gun is lost. I don't know what's happening here. Thus, I want an Offer of Proof, on the record, from the Commonwealth, because at this point, I can't even see how a person was shot, but didn't bleed, let alone see how a jury could find that my client pulled the trigger on a gun allegedly recovered, then lost. As such, and I thank this Honorable Court for granting me leeway thus far, I want to know which one of their witnesses will testify, under oath, that he or she personally saw my client pull the trigger. And if the Commonwealth is not directed to provide this Offer of Proof, they will parade 93 witnesses before this Court who are going to say they heard a loud noise and then saw a body fall. But if they can't identify a shooter, if you don't have a gun, if you don't have a victim, if you have not one drop of blood from the scene of an alleged shooting, in the end, the jury doesn't even get to render a verdict. If that is the best the Commonwealth has, I believe my motion for a judgment of acquittal will succeed before the jury even gets its chance to deliberate, after three months of sitting here. Three months of being away from their families. Three months of being sequestered in the cheapest hotel our Commonwealth is willing to pay for. Three months without work."

"So your Honor," concluded Ari, "I ask you, please direct the Commonwealth to provide me an Offer of Proof whereupon they identify at least one witness who will testify under oath that he or she saw my client shoot the alleged victim. If they can meet this minimal burden, we can use the rest of the trial to deal with the missing gun and missing victim. But I need at least one person to identify my client as a shooter, your Honor."

The silence in the courtroom was surreal, like the quiet, uncomfortable moment when a person opens his eyes just before the alarm clock blares. Nobody moved, mumbled, or twitched. All eyes were fixed on the judge.

"Attorney Meyer, you raise a lot of valid points. You raise even better questions, and like you, I too would like to learn exactly what happened at St. Mary's more than a year ago. But the best point you raise is the fact that this trial may take almost three months, and it may very well be a fruitless effort if the Commonwealth cannot provide a victim or a weapon. I very much agree with you that it would be an extraordinary waste of time and significant disruption in the lives of our jury and two alternates who will miss work and miss time from their family. In light of that fact, Mr. Meyer, I am inclined to Order a Continuance in this matter so that the jury does not have to sit through efforts in vain."

Ari fired back at the judge, "Your Honor, you can't do that, not at all."

His reply startled the judge. "Oh really?" said the indignant Judge Nelson. "Do you forget who you're talking to, sir? Do you mean to tell me that I lack the authority to Order a Continuance, that somehow I cannot manage my courtroom? After all, this would be the first continuance in this whole proceeding."

"Your Honor," stated Ari, "with all due respect, you cannot grant a Continuance because of the sign on your door. On your door and on every single door on every single courtroom in this courthouse, the sign is clear – 'No Continuances will be granted on the day of trial.' I have seen numerous defense attorneys try to get continuances on the day of trial, in this courtroom and in others. Many of them even had valid reasons, but all judges held to the same sign on the door. 'No Continuances will be granted on the day of trial.' With all due respect your Honor, if you Grant or Order a Continuance in this Matter, I will immediately file an Interlocutory Appeal based upon the arbitrary and capricious manner in which it was Ordered, and I will tie this case up for so long in the appellate courts that it will never see trial, your Honor."

The judge sat motionless. He signaled for his law clerk once again. The law clerk approached, and the judge turned off his microphone.

"Abby, hand me one of those blank forms in the desk drawer beside you, please," said Ari. Dr. Flynn handed him the form, and he started to fill it out.

After speaking to his law clerk for almost five minutes, the judge turned his microphone back on and spoke. "I will not Order a continuance in this matter. Deputy District Attorney Blake, the Commonwealth has no weapon, and no victim. Defense counsel is suggesting that you do not have any witnesses who can identify Thomas O'Toole as the alleged gunman and has asked that you provide, on the record, an Offer of Proof suggesting an eyewitness or witnesses who can identify the defendant as the shooter. At this time, can you provide this Court and Defense Counsel with said Offer of Proof?"

Deputy District Attorney Blake shook with anger and he grinded his teeth. He took a moment to speak with Assistant DA Kennedy and Detective Martin before he addressed the Court. "Your Honor, at this time I cannot specifically name a witness who has stated that he or she actually saw the defendant shoot at the victim, Mr. Rossi. However, your Honor, I would suggest that just because it is not in a report does not mean that someone didn't witness the defendant pull the trigger. That is information that can be brought out on direct exam and would most certainly be subject to cross by Attorney Meyer," said Deputy DA Blake.

"That is far short of an Offer of Proof, your Honor," said Ari, "but if you are inclined to find that vague answer of 'well hopefully somebody will testify that they saw it' as acceptable, then I motion for an Evidentiary Hearing, on the record and outside the jury, to go through every single witness for determination, in advance of trial, as to who may or may not have supposedly seen my client pull the trigger. My schedule is clear for the next six months, so I am ready for that."

The judge sat with his hand on his head. He was at a loss. Silence once again filled the courtroom with only the faint sound of a police siren off in the distance. After two minutes, Ari broke the silence.

"Your Honor," said Ari, "we can proceed with an evidentiary hearing. Or, the Commonwealth can withdraw this case from prosecution. Doing so would give them the ability to refile charges when and if they find a gun that matches the crime lab report and/or a victim who may be able to testify as to the identity of the alleged gunman, your Honor."

More than anything else in the known universe, the District Attorney's Office hated to withdraw cases. In fact, Ari never experienced this phenomenon in all his years of practice. The judge looked at the two DAs perched at the prosecutor's table.

"Here," said Ari. He handed the *Nolle Prosequi* form to Assistant District Attorney Kennedy. "Please give this to Attorney Blake. I already filled it out. You look a little shaky. All you have to do is sign," said Ari with a triumphant 'Game Over' expression.

Blake signed the form and handed it back to Ms. Kennedy. She gave it to Ari, and he signed his name. "May I approach the bench, your Honor," asked Ari.

"You may," said the judge. He took the form from Ari and reviewed it. The judge shook his head.

Judge Nelson stated, "And now, this 17th day of November 2019, by consent of Defense Counsel, Ari Meyer, to the Motion of Deputy District Attorney Nathan Blake, on behalf of the Commonwealth of Pennsylvania, in the matter of Commonwealth v. Thomas O'Toole, the Commonwealth of Pennsylvania hereby withdraws all criminal charges against said Defendant and moves to dismiss this instant criminal matter at the case number written above. The Commonwealth is free to refile charges in the future, if warranted. So Granted. Case dismissed." The judge hit his gavel on the bench and rushed back to his chambers.

Chapter Forty-three

The courtroom full of Commonwealth witnesses erupted with noise. Ari took his seat, unsure of what had just happened or exactly how he'd made it happen. Blake blasted open the doors and sprinted out of the courtroom, much to the surprise of the media outside who did not expect anything significant to happen for at least a few hours. Blake navigated the maze of reporters without any of them taking a photo or asking him questions. Kennedy was tasked with staying behind, speaking to the witnesses, and bringing the reports back to the DA's office. The Assistant DA's were off-limits to the media, so there was no chance of her offering a statement.

"Congrats, Mr. O'Toole," said Ari. "The Commonwealth has withdrawn the case against you. They can refile it tomorrow if they want to, but as of now, you are staying out of jail."

"Praise be," said Father O'Toole. "I knew you could do it."

"I'm not sure I did anything. Not sure what happened, but I don't think I really did much."

"Nonsense. You didn't lose your heart, that's what you did. That was all you needed to do. Under the circumstances, quite a heroic effort. Good man!" said Father O'Toole. "What do we do now?"

"We wait for the media to leave the courthouse. We might be here awhile."

"But don't you want to go out there, you know, get your pretty face on camera?" asked Father O'Toole. "Good and free advertising for your private practice, you know."

"I'm okay without it. But I would appreciate if you stayed here with me until I leave."

"Anything you want," said Father O'Toole, brimming with satisfaction.

Ari spun his chair around to face Dr. Flynn. She wrapped her arms around Ari in a big hug. Ari kissed her on the cheek near her mouth and whispered in her ear, "Thank you, Dr. Abby Cat. Thank you for being here today." Dr. Flynn sat back in her chair for a second before she moved behind Ari to congratulate Father O'Toole.

Ari reached into his pocket to turn on his cell phone. He pulled it out along with a business card that read "Jeannette Royale, Esquire - Attorney and Counselor at Law." He flipped it over and found a very small note including a phone number. Dr. Flynn watched from over Ari's shoulder.

She sat back down and said, "Are you going to call her?"

"You better believe I will," said Ari.

"I see," said Dr. Flynn. The joy left her face and she turned away from Ari to gather her things.

"I mean, if you got a note like this, wouldn't you call?" said Ari. He handed her the business card.

Dr. Flynn read the back of the card: "*I knew you would carry the day. Congratulations, big brother.*"

Dr. Flynn was out of breath. "Ari," she asked, "when did you get this card from her?"

"I don't know. I guess when she hugged me, she must have slipped it into my pocket?"

"She wasn't here in the courtroom when the judge dismissed the case, right?"

"No, she wasn't."

"So, how did she know."

"I'll have to ask her. But to tell you the truth, I'm more interested in the latter part of the note."

Epilogue

Dr. Flynn said goodbye and excused herself. The Deputy and the Assistant District Attorney as well as all the witnesses and all the court staff had long since departed. Even the media gathered outside had been gone for some time. Ari had waited them out. The only sound in the entire courthouse came from the squeaky wheels turning under a slop bucket and the mop that slammed back and forth on the tile floor outside the courtroom. A janitor's low whistle and half hum traversed the emptiness of the courthouse to complete the afterhours symphony. Ari sat without speaking next to Father O'Toole, who had long since stopped praying.

At the other table sat Detective Benjamin Martin. He took no notes, paid no attention to his cell phone, did no work of any kind. He just sat there, partially in a state of disbelief over the court proceeding, but more so in a state of complete confusion as to the bigger picture. He was tired of trying to make sense of any of the past two years. He broke the silence of the almost empty courtroom when he turned to address Attorney Meyer and Father O'Toole. "Okay, I need to know now," said Detective Martin, "you have to tell me. I can't live with this whole mess, whatever this is. You got to tell me what the hell is happening here."

"Good choice of words," said Father O'Toole.

"Easy, you don't have to talk to him," said Ari, "in fact, don't. Like I said, they can refile this case tomorrow if they want to."

"Not gonna happen. I promise you that," said Martin, "I, for one, am not spending another minute trying to find Rossi. And I'm not going to spend any time looking for a missing gun. No more talking to witnesses, no more crawling around in the church. None of it. I will not take part in any further work on this case. And it's not likely that the brass'll assign another detective. Plus, I don't think the DA will want to refile. They'll take a beating in the press over this, but the best bet is to let it slowly fade out of the public's view. So please, I am not going to beg you, but please just tell me what this was all about."

Father O'Toole and Ari said nothing. After a minute, the detective removed his badge in the leather holder from his pants pocket. He flipped it over to Ari's table, and it came to rest in front of Father O'Toole. "This is completely off the record," said Martin, "you have my word, Father."

Father O'Toole looked at Ari for a response. Ari wanted to know what happened as much as Detective Martin, but Ari still had a duty to protect his client. "Look, Mr. O'Toole," said Ari, "I can't advise you that this is a good idea. Although the detective is a dick, he does not lie. One of the few honest police still left, I'll give him his due. It's your choice."

Father O'Toole took a few moments to collect himself before he spoke. "I will tell you, detective. Not because I want to, but because it is the right thing to do, and because you absolutely need to know."

Father O'Toole got up from his chair, poured himself a paper cup full of lukewarm water from the pitcher, and took an empty seat between his attorney and the detective. "Remember back to the first shooting, when Dylan Ray tried to kill me?" said Father O'Toole.

"Of course," said the detective.

"What exactly did he say about his unsuccessful attempt?" asked the priest, already knowing the answer.

"He said that the altar boy was not with you when he pulled the trigger. He said he never saw anybody but you. And Jesus Christ. That it was Jesus Christ who put out his hands and stopped the bullets from hitting you," said the detective.

"He did say that. And he was right. Well, he was right about most of it," said the priest in a flat monotone.

"It was a miracle then?" asked the detective, "That's why you weren't killed by Ray?"

"No sir. It was not a miracle. I wish that it had been. That would certainly be easier for me to explain to you, a man of investigation and science, and to you, Attorney Meyer, a non-believer. I have waited my whole life to witness a miracle, and I very well may go to my grave without seeing one firsthand. But what happened that day was no miracle. It was not through God's hand, that is for sure," said the priest.

Detective Martin and Ari Meyer hung on his every word, no less confused than before.

"So, what was it?" asked the detective. "You said Ray was mostly right. What part was right and what was wrong?"

Father O'Toole took a drink from his glass of water. "He was right about Nico not being there when he shot the gun at me." O'Toole's monotone found another level of low as he tried his best to explain the situation. "Dylan Ray caused a commotion getting through the pew so quickly. The ruckus caught my attention. I saw him struggling to get out. I didn't know he had a gun at that point. I looked over at Nico to see if he was paying attention to what was happening. That's when I saw…him," said Father O'Toole. He blessed himself and put his face in his hands.

"I don't get it. Who did you see? Jesus?" asked the detective.

Father O'Toole raised his head to reply. "Nico was no longer standing beside me. And I am certain, with all my heart, on the souls of my family, it was not Jesus Christ. But Ray was correct that hands were outstretched to stop bullets. They just didn't belong to Jesus," Father O'Toole blessed himself again.

Ari spoke up. "Just hold on a minute. Am I to believe that it was a miracle that the bullets were stopped in midair, but it technically wasn't a miracle because of the guy or the entity responsible?"

"You believe what you want to, or don't believe at all, Ari. I am too old and too tired to try to convert non-believers," interrupted Father O'Toole. "But you, sir," O'Toole said directly to Detective Martin, "You do believe. And you believe because you know it's true. It is happening, and it will continue to happen whether anyone believes it or not."

"What is happening?" asked Detective Martin.

"The great battle," said Father O'Toole. "The great battle that happens every day and has been happening since the beginning of time. The battle of good versus evil. It is ever present, and it always has been. The entire existence of mankind is nothing more than one continuation of the same battle, day after day. The battle for people of good character and morals to rise above evil, corruption, greed, and gluttony. Sometimes good people can catch a break, maybe they even get a miracle from time to time to remind them of the fight they engage in every day. But the Devil is cunning and ruthless. And he can take anyone if they drop their guard, even for a second. I don't know if Nico made a deal or gave in at a moment of weakness, or maybe after months and months of insomnia followed by months and months of sleeping pills and wine, he was just too weak to fight him off anymore." Father O'Toole finished his water and put the paper cup down on the table.

"One thing is beyond certain," O'Toole continued, "at some point between when Dylan Ray got up from his spot on the pew and the point where he squeezed the trigger, Nico stopped being Nico. He no longer belonged to us. Jesus, Mary, and Joseph, how I wish that a miracle prevented that shooting. If I thought it was a miracle, I would have praised it. I would have supported and promoted Nico and would have involved him even more in the ministry. The Diocese would have loved that. They would have supported me. To see one of their churches overflowing with people every Sunday, people who wanted to be part of a miracle. My Good Lord, that would have been amazing. Especially when only bad aspects of the Catholic Church make the news these days, that, I tell you, that would have been welcomed. But I just couldn't do that. I saw, with my own eyes, that we were not blessed with a miracle. Rather, we were cursed. One of our own was taken, and right from under my nose."

Father O'Toole leaned back in his seat. He reached around and poured himself another small cup of water. Ari and Martin sat in silence.

"No questions? No response from either of you?" asked Father O'Toole. "I guess to the scientist with a badge and the non-believer, all of what I just said is a bunch of hooey. About as realistic spaceships, aliens, and bigfoot, huh? That would be an error in judgment that you both should be able to avoid at this point. I have nowhere near the intelligence of either of you, but I have something that neither of you will ever have, and you should both thank God that neither of you do: my life experience. I have lived through poverty, filth, sickness, starvation, loss, and heartache of Biblical proportions. I do not relish in the fact that somehow, I have survived when everyone else close to me did not, but I will acknowledge that my experience enables me to see the world differently. My judgment is not clouded by peripheral matters that so easily distract everyone else, you two included. I can focus on the one thing that matters – the battle of good against evil. Because in the end, that is all that ever matters, for our time here on Earth and whatever remains afterwards. I know what I saw when I looked across the altar to where Nico once stood. It was not Nico. Still don't want to listen to an old coot? Crazy old Irish bastard, huh? Look back in your reports. The answers were all there," said Father O'Toole.

"What answers, in what report?" asked Martin.

"C'mon detective, there isn't much time," said Father O'Toole as he pounded his fist on the table and startled both the detective and attorney. "I read the crime lab report about the tests done on the bullets and the gun recovered from Dylan Ray. Various people in the diocese and the Vatican read it, probably even the Pope himself. It was very clear to conclude that there is no scientific or mechanical reason why the bullets traveled only 10 feet before falling to the ground. If science and mechanics can't provide an explanation, then what is the second most likely explanation?"

"Divine intervention?" asked Detective Martin.

"Again, no. Divine intervention suggests that God played a role. But God is good. He played no role in stopping those bullets. So, the answer would be not divine intervention, but rather, something much darker, much angrier, more opportunistic," said Father O'Toole. "And you, Attorney Meyer. Still convinced I'm insane? Still think I struggle to grasp reality, diminished capacity or something whatever? That cute little doctor friend of yours never thought I was insane. She actually got it right. Did you read her conclusions? She said that in her opinion, I shot–"

"The alleged victim in an attempt to help," said Ari to finish his sentence.

"Correct. I guess you did read it. You just didn't believe her. I pulled the trigger, I always said so. And I would do it again if I had to," said Father O'Toole. He pantomimed looking down the barrel of a pistol with both hands in front of him. "But Nico was never in my sights. When I pulled that trigger, Nico was far from with us. So just to remind you once more, I never shot Nico Rossi."

Ari Meyer and Detective Martin both thought they'd heard it all. From their experiences with hallucinogenic drug addicts, with con men of all varieties, with stone cold killers, neither man ever thought they would be listening to such an explanation that made sense on some levels yet remained so unbelievable on many others.

Father O'Toole reached across the table and retrieved Detective Martin's badge in the leather holder. He stared at it for a minute or two before he concluded.

"Gentlemen," he said, "what you choose to do with what I have told you, well, that is on you. It won't involve me. I am too old. I have no more fight in me. I have made my peace with all," said Father O'Toole. He flipped the badge back to Detective Martin. "But I fear that you, Detective Martin, are not yet done with the fight, whether you want to be or not. Nico is here, again, but he still isn't Nico. He is powerful, and dark. I'm sure he won't be hard to find. I don't think he's going anywhere anytime soon. God help you, but you will have to deal with him in one way or another." Father O'Toole pulled the deck of cards out of his shirt pocket. He reached across and placed them in Ari's breast pocket with the bullet hole facing out and the Suicide King closest to his chest. "I think you would be well-served in assisting the detective. Unless of course you're too busy with private practice."

At the same time, under the dim hue of a solitary streetlight, Nico Rossi exited a black SUV with a sign in his hand and a small sledgehammer in the other. There on a seemingly forgotten piece of ground now shadowed between giant state of the art office parks on both sides and the river behind it, on land that once housed an enormous child labor-filled textile mill, on the same land where children once played baseball and dreamt of getting a ticket to The Show, Nico Rossi pounded his sign into the ground. It read, "Future sight of the House of Miracles. Pastor Nicholas Rossi." Nico returned to the SUV, got into the rear passenger side, and drove away.

The End

About The Author: Wil 3 is a father, high school teacher, adjunct professor and retired college assistant basketball coach who graduated from Washington and Jefferson College with a double major in Political Science and Secondary Education. An advocate for the homeless, Wil is a regular volunteer at the Light of Life Mission in the North Side of Pittsburgh, PA. He has authored several one-act plays, including most recently *Gluten-Free Phish*, which was performed by W&J students at the 2020 Winter Tales. *Heartly Law?* is the sequel to his first full-length novel, *Heartly God?* When not writing, Wil can be found trout fishing on a stand-up paddleboard with his son, Rider, coaching little league baseball and occasionally practicing law, if time permits.

https://wil-3.com/

https://www.facebook.com/wilthree/

Made in the USA
Middletown, DE
27 September 2021

49167865R00139